FOG CITY NOCTURNE

*From the Casebook
of Nick Chambers*

EDITED BY
B.J. WEST

the apocryphile press
BERKELEY, CA
www.apocryphile.org

apocryphile press
Berkeley, CA

Apocryphile Press
1700 Shattuck Ave #81
Berkeley, CA 94709
www.apocryphile.org

Printed in the United States of America
ISBN 0-9771461-1-1

CONTENTS

INTRODUCTION

B.J. West

Nick Chambers had a very unusual birth, and a surprisingly large number of mothers and fathers. Our troubled detective hero was conceived in a writing experiment in December, 1999. Looking for a source of motivation and inspiration, a group of Bay Area writers, with experience levels ranging from published professional to purest amateur, got together in the View Lounge high atop San Francisco's Marriott Hotel and let the heady mix of alcohol and altitude work its magic. Together, we created a classic noir-style hard-boiled detective character. We hashed out his biography, outlined his history, his defining flaws, his less-than-optimal situation, and then dropped him into a cold and uncaring post-WWII world. Afterwards, we all went our separate ways to write short stories about Nick, subject only to our shared dossier and two simple rules:

> #1: Thou shalt not kill Nick. But you *can* beat him to within an inch of death. Don't permanently injure or cripple him either, we need him for more stories.
> #2: Likewise, when your story is finished, Nick's situation shouldn't be markedly different in any permanent way than it was when the story began. He can (and *should*)

significantly change the lives of people around him for good or ill, but he can't personally benefit from a "big win" unless you take it away from him again before you are done.

As a motivator, Nick proved less than spectacular. Not all of the writers who participated in his creation actually finished stories, and the few who did submitted them very slowly, one at a time, over the better part of a year. His track record as a source of inspiration was far better; the stories that *were* received made up for their lack of punctuality with a wide range of styles, inventiveness, and the sheer enthusiasm with which we all stuck it to the poor bastard.

Nick's beat is quite familiar to anyone who loves detective fiction. The shabby office that Nick also sleeps in—and the bar below that is his *real* home—is, by a *remarkable* coincidence, very close to the spot where Sam Spade's ill-fated partner Miles Archer met his demise in "The Maltese Falcon."

But this tip o' the hat to the master doesn't mean that our guy is a cheap knock-off. As each story dovetails together with the others, Nick becomes a more complex character, his lot in life more desperate and angst-ridden. While we weren't out to deconstruct and re-forge traditional detective fiction, Nick did indeed develop a unique, fresh voice and a decidedly post-modern nihilistic outlook that borders on misanthropic. His cases take him down back streets that Spade was never unfortunate enough to travel, and pit him against himself as much as any calculating villain. But despite this dismal outlook, Nick still finds some tiny glowing ember still burning in the ashes of his soul, giving him the strength to do the right thing, no matter how much he'd prefer to just forget the whole mess and walk away.

So bundle up in your trench coat, pull your fedora down low, and step out into the cold, dark, fog-shrouded streets of San Francisco. Nick may not be the best, highest-priced or most famous of private detectives, but when he takes a case you can bet that the truth will be revealed, no matter what the cost to all concerned.

A GHOST OF A CHANCE

Bryan D. Tolin

I felt like shit. While other guys were dreaming about Joan Fontaine, I'd been having a series of nightmares about the war for the past two weeks. It seemed to happen with unfortunate regularity every six months or so. As a result, I wasn't sleeping much, if at all, and there didn't seem to be a damn thing I could do about it. I tried for several nights in a row to drink myself into a coma—something I was rather accomplished at—but was having no luck when I'd needed it most of all. Alcohol only exaggerated the nighttime trauma, or aggravated the after-effects the following day. Yet here I was, perched in my corner chair at Gino's for more punishment, staring into the icy abyss of my second gin and tonic.

Gino and I had an arrangement. A while back, when Gino discovered I could pack away the G & T's like water, he started leaving the limes in the glass to remind me how many I'd had. It was more for his protection than mine, serving as a gauge for him to know when to cut me off. To me, the extra limes only represented critical space where gin should have been—but it was his place, his rules. Although if I'd known then what was about to come through the door, I would have asked for a "no lime limit" for the next few days. Moments after I'd finished my second, Gino's door opened, and several lives changed forever.

There was no question the dame was lost or critically in need of something she was ready to sully her reputation for by coming in here.

"Excuse me," she said as she reached into her purse, taking out a small slip of paper as she stopped at the counter. "I wonder if you might know where I can find Nick Chambers?"

I twisted in my seat, then rearranged the hat over my eyes and repositioned myself at the bar, hiding my face in the process. No need to take chances, not yet anyway.

"Nick's office upstairs," was Gino's broken response from behind the bar. The mystery woman smiled, looked down for a moment, and then continued.

"Yes I know, I was just up there, but he didn't answer the door, and well...."

From my darkened vantage point, I gave her the once over twice. It was hard not to stare. Then again, artwork was meant to be admired. I could've sworn I'd seen a photograph of this woman somewhere, but I just couldn't recall the time or place, which, in my condition of late, was more or less to be expected.

"Well, Nick goes out sometimes," Gino responded. Setting down the glass, he gave me the eye. I responded with an ever-so-subtle nod, and Gino continued. "But I think he come back soon." Gino wadded up the towel and put it next to the glass. "Wai!" he shouted toward the open door to the back. From which, Gino's son, a very tall, very muscular young Chinaman appeared, sporting an apron wrapped tightly around his waist. "My son let you in. You can wait," Gino said to the blonde at the counter, then something in Chinese to Wai, who removed his apron, then himself from the bar. The blonde followed close behind. Moments later, when Wai had returned, I crushed out my cigarette, and stood up to leave. From deep within my pocket, I pulled a silver dollar, and placed it on the counter.

"Thanks Gino," were my only words as I made my way toward the door.

Outside, I paused briefly and pulled a pack of Luckies from my left breast pocket. With the exception of the coming mist, the street was unnaturally empty. Only the distant sounds of foghorns and ships' whistles filled the air.

Without realizing I'd done so, I lit another cigarette and inhaled a long, deep breath. My lungs ached from the day's smoke. Exhaling, I turned to face the bruised doorframe which led upstairs to my office. I turned the handle and entered the dim hallway. Slowly, I made my way up the battered staircase. I remembered thinking how, as the cases dwindled to a pitiful few, those stairs were rapidly becoming my one and only source of exercise. Even with a potential case on my doorstep, there was no need to hurry. I'd find out soon enough what would drive a looker like that to a place like this.

I approached the door. I always felt like a doctor when a potential client was waiting in my office. "Hello Mrs. So-an-so. I understand that you're having a problem with your thus-and-such. Take two of these and call me if it gets worse." Funny how playing doctor was the first thing I thought of this night, as an attractive blonde waited in my nearby inner sanctum. Perhaps I wasn't feeling so bad after all.

I entered my lair, startling the blonde and the dust in the process. I had left the radio on with the volume just down to where voices could be heard, my cheap version of a watchdog. Seemed to me someone with a grudge would be less likely to burst in on a room where voices could be heard. At the moment though, Fibber McGee was about to open his closet door, sending mounds of crap down upon him, much to the delight of the studio audience who laughed heartily. Some watch dog.

The mystery woman reacted to my entrance as predicted, with an ever so slight "Oh," and a hand across her heart.

"Sorry, Miss...?"

"Thompson. Darlene Thompson. You served with my husband in the war."

My response was immediate, reflexive, and hopefully invisible. Having emotions was one thing. Showing them could get you killed.

"I'm sorry Mrs. Thompson, of course I knew Mac. I was with him...." Both my voice and tact had faded quickly. I tried for a swift recovery with "on the plane," but the damage had been done. She knew it, and I knew it, and I wasn't going to make it any worse by apologizing for the apology, so I tried to make up for it instead.

"Is there anything I can get you? Would you like a cigarette? Coffee?"

"No thank you, Mr. Chambers. I don't smoke, and please, call me Darlene. "

"Darlene, then," I said motioning to my lit Lucky. "Do you mind?" I asked, hoping she'd say no. Anything to calm the nerves at this point I'd even pay for.

"No, Mr. Chambers, not at all. I'm used to it. Mac used to smoke."

Smoke? He was a goddamn chimney. Thank god she didn't take me up on the coffee either. Not only was it cold, it probably could have killed. I went to the window and opened it so my smoke wouldn't be as irritating as I had become. The cool night air was a welcome relief to the stale atmosphere of the office.

"And call me Nick. We're already closer than most families." Mine anyways.

She dug into her purse and produced a note similar to the one I'd seen from afar downstairs. "I received a rather cryptic telegram from White Star a week or so ago." She unfolded the note and glanced at it briefly before passing it on to me.

"It confirms my husband's passage from San Francisco to South America on the Queen Victoria." She paused for effect. It had one. "Leaving Thursday."

I reviewed the document as the breeze from outside stole the smoke from my fingertips. The confirmation took the form of a telegram, and read simply;

```
CUNARD WHITE STAR LINES QUEEN VICTORIA
CONFIRMS PASSAGE FOR MAXWELL THOMPSON
STOP DEPARTING PIER 23 THURSDAY JULY 31
200PM STOP BOARDING BEGINS AT 1200 NOON
STOP YOURS CUNARD WHITE STAR 23526
EMBARCADERO STREET SAN FRANCISCO
```

On the surface it appeared innocent enough. The only other item of note was that the original address has been scratched out and replaced. Darlene noticed my questioning gaze.

"We moved into a smaller apartment awhile back. They probably couldn't find us."

Aside from this small hitch, if you could call it that, another Maxwell Thompson in the world wasn't so tough to imagine.

"Look," I said sympathetically. "I'm sure it's nothing. Besides, Mac would never use his real name—ever."

She looked down, then at me with imploring eyes. One day I

would probably be offed by a dame who looked at me that way.

"I know, I thought of that. But isn't there anything we can do—to make sure? To...." Again her voice and hope trailed off.

What the hell.

"Tomorrow morning—bright and early, why don't you and I go down to the ticket office, and see who made the reservation? What do you say?" I tried to brighten her spirits, but this sort of conversation was always awkward, and I'm afraid I wasn't very good at hiding the facts.

"Thanks Nick, really—I'll pay you whatever...."

"No look, it's the least I can do. Mac was a good friend." And with that, all pleasantries aside, and with the prospect of a new adventure just around the corner, we said goodnight.

I used to like mornings, I really did. The sights, the sounds, the smells, hell—even the people, whom I liked to call my "cast of usual suspects," were welcomed. One of my favorites was Armando, a loud Italian New Yorker who was one of five people on the planet who could get away with calling me "Nicky" without taking his life in his own hands. Of course, I called him "Mondo," so I guess we were even on that score. Mondo spotted me a paper every morning, knowing it would wind up in Gino's hands eventually, where Mondo would receive his belated payment in the form of a hot cup of coffee. Then there was Gino, of course, whom I made sure to duck in on before heading upstairs to let him know I was in.

As I reflected on these routines, I started to wonder if the attraction of morning wasn't just a byproduct of being back on safe ground. Back home. The illusion of security while surrounded by all things familiar. The fact of the matter was that I was just as likely to get shot in San Francisco as I was in a mission over Germany. Maybe that realization is what was making the gloss fade from the shine of each dawn.

Anyway, morning it was, and Mrs. Thompson and I were on our way to the White Star ticket office on Embarcadero. The hack, like most in San Fran, excelled at everything but speed, with the motorman's mouth leading the way. While he certainly wasn't on my usual suspects list, chances were good he was on someone's "most wanted." Thankfully, the cab pulled up to the curb and we got out. The cabbie gave Darlene an approving glance as I passed him the fare.

"Nice pins!" he said with a wink. I smiled. More from the relief of being out of there than from the accuracy of his remark.

White Star Lines had a pronounced presence on the Embarcadero. Of course it was hard to miss the liner Queen Victoria (or 'The Vic' as she was known to the locals) docked behind the shipping office. During the war the Queen Victoria had, like her royal counterparts, been transformed into a hospital. She had just returned from Long Beach harbor where post-war retrofits had returned her to her regal glory. Thursday, she'd set off at 2:00 p.m. for South America, while her sister ships raced against each other to England. Both the press and White Star had made the most of the event. As a result, both the dock and ticket office were packed. It took awhile to make our way to the head of the horde, where a perky brunette in an even perkier outfit greeted us with seemingly sincere interest.

"Say," I said, "I received this wire," which I produced and passed to her, tipping the brim of my hat back, and placing an elbow on the busy counter where I might sneak a peek at some valuable tidbit, or in lieu thereof, something sheathed in nylon. "It doesn't mention a room assignment."

"No sir. Actual room assignments are made the day of departure. Cancellations, you understand."

Something told me I was in the company of a by-the-book gal. Time to spring the ol' ditsy dame ploy, always a personal favorite. "But it is First Class, right?"

I'd scored. The girl behind the counter responded with caution, knowing there may be a confrontation, which made it my advantage. "No, I'm sorry sir—your reservations were made for Third Class."

"Third Class?" I said feigning annoyance. "Was First Class unavailable?"

She countered quickly, "At the time the reservation was originally made, it was available, yes sir."

"Well who made the reservation? Darcy Lopez right?" Darcy was an old girlfriend, and the first name I could think of. If she had any idea how many times I'd passed her off as my secretary she'd have put a hit out on me. What the hell, she deserved it.

I had a look at the cable. I could feel Darlene give me the eye, but whether it was questioning or condemning I couldn't tell, nor did I have any real desire to find out. The struggling—and no longer perky—girl behind the counter searched a small file box, finally withdrawing a cable.

"Sir, the reservation actually came in from One World Travel on Van Ness two months ago." She offered it to me as an impromptu peace treaty. I had a look and with the assistant's assistance, got the address and phone number.

"Thanks," I said.

"If something opens up, we'll be sure to contact you."

At this, I smiled slyly. If it came to pass, she would no doubt have this exact same conversation again, with the other Max Thompson in reverse.

"That would be great. Thanks." And with that we left.

I bought Darlene breakfast and got the low down on where she was from, how long she'd be in town once this was sorted, etc. Small talk. As we were leaving I stopped at the phone booth and made two calls, the first to One World Travel, where I played the same game. It seemed that Maxwell had come to the office personally to book passage a couple of months back, and paid in cash. But the curious thing was that to make the reservation, he had had to present a photo ID with a home address.

I was afraid there was only one way to find out who the phantom traveler was. We were going to have to go down to the Pier in the morning, and watch several hundred people get on board the Vic. See—that was why I was broke most of the time. Either I took on jobs that had no future or ones that had no resources. Usually all I wound up with in the end was the satisfaction of a good deed done.

The second call I made to my ol' buddy, Detective Brad Ratchet. "You'll never guess who came into my office last night...."

I hated crowds with a passion. As luck would have it, I found myself in the middle of a huge one. From noon to 1:30 p.m. the Vic allowed both passengers and guests to roam the decks freely. To complicate matters, there were two points of entrance where pas-

sengers could check in, via gangplanks fore and aft. Darlene and I
had split up, each of us taking a walkway, and standing by our
respective pursers as they doled out cabin assignments one passenger at a time. I didn't have any illusions about our possible success,
and my enthusiasm for this event wasn't exactly overwhelming. But
I somehow felt obligated to go through the motions—for Mac's sake
anyway.

As 1:30 approached, there was an announcement that all visitors
must begin departing the ship before the 2:00 p.m. departure.
Passengers were still being allowed to board, however, and I was just
contemplating what to do with the rest of my afternoon when
Detective Ratchet appeared at my elbow.

"How's the ghost hunt, Nick?"

I winced, but didn't give him the satisfaction of an annoyed
response.

"Nothing so far," was all I could manage. "What brings you down
here?"

"Thought I'd check in. Curious too, I guess. Where's the damsel
in distress?" He was looking in the right direction, but failed to
notice her until I pointed her out.

The eager throngs of well-wishers were now exiting the Vic in
packs, making it harder to see both Darlene and those still boarding
on her ramp. With less than a half hour to go, it didn't seem like it
would make a dramatic difference. I spied a familiar face closing in
on Darlene's position. For the moment I ignored what was happening on my gangplank, in favor of hers. I figured if the ghost of Mac
past showed up suddenly in front of Ratchet, chances were he'd take
notice.

The stranger I thought I'd recognized either consciously or
unconsciously had his back to me for a minute or two, while talking
with the purser. The purser pointed up the ramp as pursers do, then
Darlene stepped in and greeted the man. Although he did appear to
have a passing resemblance to Mac, the fact that she didn't rush into
his arms—or slap him—told me it wasn't him.

Then she waved at me, and the man turned to face me at last, and
the horrific realization hit me full force.

"Hey Brad!" I excitedly motioned to Darlene. "Isn't that...." My
voice trailed off when I felt the unmistakable cold steel of Brad
Ratchet's revolver pressed between my shoulder blades.

"Easy Nick, easy." He said calmly, twisting me in the direction of the ship. "Let's take a little walk." And as I headed up the gangplank at gunpoint, I remembered, as if it were yesterday, the very first time someone held a gun at my back.

In the tortured skies over Bremen, the bleeding B-17 'Heavenly Body' began to slowly lose altitude. A victim of clear weather and Messerschmitt firepower, the crew was doing their best to stay airborne. Com system failing, they'd lost both the bottom turret and right waist gunner in the last explosion, reducing their crew of nine to three.

Mac Thompson struggled with the controls. "I can't keep her flyin', Brad. Get Nick. Let's get the hell out of here," he said. He reached for the picture of his wife, which had been wedged above the altimeter for inspiration during the past three months. Tucking it into his Mae West, he replaced his hand on the faltering steering column.

"Go on! I'm right behind ya!"

Ratchet reached down, undid his buckle, and rose from his seat. Climbing through the smoke-filled cabin, he paused to look out the nose as he edged his way down the ladder. Although positioned to do so, Ratchet made a conscious effort not to glare at the remains of the gunner just a few feet forward. Continuing on past communications, he was nearing the open waist section when the ship lurched violently to the right. Ratchet was miraculously spared the open window, and the fourteen thousand foot drop which followed.

"NICK!?" Ratchet called, more a plea. Though even if Chambers could reply, his voice would have been drowned out as the war bird's amplified vibrations echoed through the cabin. "NICK!?" He called again. As he approached the tail section, Nick Chambers appeared out of the smoke like a specter in the mist, parachute in tow.

"What?" Came the annoyed answer from the tail gunner as he struggled to extricate himself from his lair.

"Thought you'd bought it...."

"So did I," was Nick's response as he freed himself from the tangle of snapping wires.

"Where's Mac?" Nick asked, now loose from the mesh. Tail gunners were notorious for not wearing their parachutes. It simply wasn't practical or remotely possible to wedge both a human body and any extraneous attachments into a compartment more or less meant for people under four feet tall. Once free from his binds, Nick oriented his chute, and put his left arm through the appropriate strap.

"He's on his way." Ratchet's reply was immediately followed by burst somewhere aft. Chambers and Ratchet shielded themselves against the blast, as the ship began a slow yaw to starboard. With his posterior exposed, it didn't take much for Nick to stumble to the deck, and subsequently slide with the roll of the plane toward the open waist gunner's port. Ratchet slumped to the floor as well, but maintained his footing and grabbed the back of Nick's flight suit. The plane continued to lurch over as Nick clawed at the wires on the floor. Just as he was about to regain his footing, one of the wires sparked to life, sending enough of a shock up Nick's arm to cause him to release his grip, and slide toward the open fuselage. Ratchet bettered his grip, but could not prevent Nick's descent. Nick, choosing electrocution over falling as his sentence of death, tried to regain his grip on the wires when gravity finally won out, and he was literally cast to the wind, with only Ratchet's loosening grip keeping him from plummeting to the ground.

Presented with the choice of releasing his grip and trying to don the chute while falling, or working with Ratchet to return to the plane, he chose the latter. Under the best possible circumstances, the prospect of successfully completing such a maneuver was difficult at best—but with the wind blowing at 80 knots, and in near freezing conditions, Nick's chances of survival were quite literally slipping away. He did his best to work the wind in his favor, and began to swing his dangling arm in an ever increasing arc until at last he put everything he had into one final throw which yielded the desired effect. Ratchet grabbed the bag, and made quick work out of pulling Nick in. Shivering with the fright and blistering cold, Nick quickly donned his chute, as Mac approached. Without ceremony or excess chatter, they jumped.

Nick and Ratchet landed in a cornfield adjacent to a forest. It provided adequate temporary cover in case they had been followed down, but neither believed they had. Just the same, they had both waited until the last possible second before pulling their respective cords. As they undid their harnesses, they stole glances into the field in an effort to find Mac. Nick turned an eye to the woods, where his gaze fell upon their comrade dangling from a tree, seemingly in one piece, but unconscious. They quickly bundled up their parachutes, and headed for him. Before they could get to his position, their worst fear was realized—they had been spotted by ground troops. Nick and Ratchet quickly dropped their bundles and made a mad dash for the woods, while the Germans, closing in from behind, started firing. Nick turned to face his captors.

"Shiessen sie nicht! Shiessen sie nicht! Don't shoot!" he yelled, placing his hands above his head. Ratchet followed suit, and they waited for what seemed like an eternity until the troops were upon them. From somewhere, an order was given and a German dismounted his motorcycle coming to them, and forced them to their knees.

Nick and Ratchet tried to regain control of their breathing as they stared at the ground with fingers interlaced above their heads. A soldier who had moved towards the woods stopped suddenly when he spied Mac. He yelled something in German back to the ranks and several officers approached where he stood. One in particular drew his Luger from his waist and fired in the direction of Mac, hitting a branch near his head. Mac didn't flinch. The German officer stood for a moment then motioned to a group of soldiers and gave an order. The officers stepped forward, brought their rifles to meet their eyes, and fired a barrage of bullets into Mac's body. Nick clenched his eyes shut as the last of the echoes faded into the woods. The officer who had given the order then turned to face the pair on the ground and gave another quiet order. Nick and Ratchet were jerked to their feet, and placed at gunpoint into the back of a truck, which set off almost immediately toward a detention center somewhere in Germany. Although a weird series of events would allow Nick Chambers to regain his freedom some weeks later, Brad Ratchet wasn't as lucky. But at least he was alive....

I accompanied Ratchet through what I could only assume was the third class section of the ship. I put up no resistance, as I was more curious for an explanation than frightened at the prospect of eating a bullet. Come to think of it, looking back now, I was more annoyed than anything else. His explanation for all of this had better be damn good.

After a while we stopped at a door midway through one of the passages and damned if he didn't pull out a key.

"Taking a trip?" I asked, genuinely interested, but making it more a sarcastic remark.

"As a matter of fact, I am," he said while unlocking the cabin door.

There are times when you should definitely keep your mouth shut. Unfortunately, I never seemed to recognize them until after the fact. So naturally I responded with, "Traveling with your friend?"

Fortunately, Brad was pre-occupied with getting himself, his gun, and my back into the cabin as quickly as possible, so the weight of the remark for the most part was lost. Instead, he merely came back with, "Not a friend, exactly. An old acquaintance, you might say."

I couldn't hold back any longer. "*Old acquaintance? Christ, Brad, Werner?*"

He motioned me toward the cabin bulkhead, handing me a pair of handcuffs in the process. "You remembered. I wasn't sure you would, you weren't with us long in our deluxe accommodations at the Luft."

True, but even so, Werner was not someone forgettable. Among other things, Werner had been in charge of the "ferrets" at Luft III. The ferrets were the ones who ducked under the barracks to check for lose dirt or other tidbits deposited by a tunnel crew as they dug their way to freedom. Sometimes, when they were feeling especially sneaky, they'd just crawl in and listen to the goings-on of the prisoners in the hope of thwarting some well laid plan. But it wasn't his management of the ferrets Werner was most known for. It was his creative forms of punishment, no doubt a consequence of his time at Auschwitz.

"I'm sure he'll be touched. He certainly remembers you and your exploits."

I wasn't touched. I was sick.

"Wanna put those on, please? Porthole should do." He nodded toward the couch on the far wall, over which, convenient for all those looking for a place to fasten handcuffs, were two portholes with very secure latches for just such an occasion. As I sat down and began the process of cuffing my left arm skyward, Brad put his revolver in his pocket. When I was done, in pain and pissed off, I popped off another question.

"So how the hell did you meet up with Werner?"

Satisfied I was adequately incarcerated, Brad produced a pack of cigarettes and offered me one. I passed. I needed something with a little more kick.

"I'd rather have a drink."

Being the gentleman he was, Brad made his way to the counter, where a very fine bottle of scotch was patiently waiting. He delicately poured two glasses half full, handed me one, and sat opposite me in one of the armchairs.

"At the end of the war, things got a little confusing. When Nuremberg started up, Werner thought that he might do better in, uh, less formal surroundings?" He took a long drag and exhaled through his nose, blowing smoke into his glass. "Seems they were very interested in his illustrious career as a concentration camp administrator. Anyway, he managed to get into the U.S. eventually, using Mac's ID and uniform. Would you believe the bastard actually just walked right on to a transport? He kinda looks like Mac, so no one questioned him."

"How'd he get the ID?" I knew I wasn't going to like what I heard.

"They were at the camp. They came in with Mac's body. They were supposed to be sent back, but never made it."

"Neither did Mac." If his body had been shipped, like it was supposed to, I wouldn't be sitting here.

"Yeah. Anyway, once he got to the states, things started to heat up. With the trial in full bloom, his picture was plastered in newsstands all over the world. So he went into deep hiding."

"Which brings me back to my original question—how did you two hook up?"

One word said it all. "Legnon."

The Legnon case was the most gruesome crime in the history of San Francisco to date. Shelby Legnon had been a would-be novelist living in San Francisco until a few weeks back, when a pressman from the *Examiner* walked in on his wife with Shelby in a compromising position. Needless to say, the pressman wasn't as awed with Shelby's talents as his wife had been, so to make a point of his own, he cut Shelby into nice little pieces and tossed him into the presses. What made it particularly horrific was that several hundred papers went out that day with little bits of Shelby in them before anyone had figured out what had happened. Shelby had finally made it to print, *the hard way*. The crime itself had been solved without much effort, but the sensational nature of the event had made Brad an instant celebrity.

"He saw me in the paper and figured I might be able to help him with his, uh, 'travel problem.'" Brad took another slug as I followed up on my line of questioning.

"You sold out to the Nazis."

"Sold out? No, I invested in a retirement."

"That's a very convenient spin on facts. He's a war criminal, Brad." I hit a nerve, and the blood rose in Brad's face.

"You know, some day you're gonna have to explain that term to me, cause the line these days is pretty blurry."

"No doubt," I said, fanning the flame.

"No, really Nick—I want to know." Brad was furious, "What is a war criminal? For that matter, what is a crime? How many people did we murder fire bombing Dresden, Nick? A hundred thousand? Two? Was that really any worse than anything the Nazis ever did? Quicker, maybe, but the end result is the same. A lot of innocent people died. The only difference seems to be who won. Hell, if we'd lost, you and I would probably be on trial. Crime? Hell, Nick, war *is* the crime. To me it's all black and white. But when I got back, I found I was living in a gray world, where the only difference between right and wrong seems to be which side of the badge you're on. Well, I just don't have the stomach for it anymore."

He seemed to be calming down, just as I was starting to heat up.

"So now what?" I asked.

"Well, that's partially up to you. In a few hours, we'll be in international waters, and Werner is on his own. He has new identification now, so no more chasing ghosts." He downed the last of his first scotch. I did the same, hoping it would have a numbing effect on the rising pain in my arm.

"We're hoping you and your, uh, companion will stay put for a couple of days until we get to the first port of call in Mexico. Then Werner and I will go our separate ways—and you two can be discovered by the cleaning crew as stowaways."

Once he had mentioned 'companion' I had stopped listening.

"Darlene is on board?"

"In Werner's cabin next door. Insurance that you don't get brave or heroic or something and run to the captain."

"Christ, Brad."

"Don't worry, she's safe. Nothing's gonna happen. Werner's calmed down in exile."

I tried to sort it all out, but it had been too much information, too fast, and my head was swimming with a million questions, a million possibilities. I looked around the cabin as a caged animal might, realizing that it's trapped. Brad noticed my discomfort and offered me another drink, which I readily accepted. With his back to me as he poured, I stared at the friend I thought I knew. I was beginning to realize that the war had claimed another victim. He turned to face me, drink in hand.

"So how much is all this worth? How much is he paying you?"

A frightening look of pride came over Brad's face. "You know, the funny thing is—I was all set to do this anyway. One day I just wasn't going to show up. Hop a plane or train somewhere and never come back. But I didn't have adequate resources. Werner just happened to show up at the right time." And with that, he put his drink on the nightstand, reached under his bed, and pulled out something wrapped in black felt. He laid the seemingly heavy object on the bed, and after a brief pause, unfolded the felt to reveal two very shiny, medium-sized gold bars, each bearing the unmistakable eagle and swastika symbol of the Third Reich.

"My share as travel agent. He has more somewhere. Switzerland, maybe. Who knows."

I'd heard gossip about Hitler's caches of gold, but always thought of them as fanciful rumors until now.

"I was going to have them melted down to more travel-friendly sizes in Chinatown, but now I'll have to wing it." I thought it a curious remark considering the insignia. This time, though, I kept my mouth shut about the observation, and took a healthy slug of the next scotch instead.

As the scotch burned its way home I reflected on whether I should have seen this coming. I'd seen a number of guys lose their lives or minds in the course of the last few years. The fact that Brad was escaping this fate made me start to question my own values. The situation being what it was, it appeared as though I was going to have ample time to consider my own future.

As I went to take another sip, my vision started to blur, then my fingers tingled slightly. It appeared Brad wanted some insurance of his own on my keeping quiet. My glass began to slip from my doped grasp. Brad reached over and took it before it spilled.

"Sorry Nick, but I have business to attend to." And the lights went out.

I awoke some hours later. By now the pain in my arm was excruciating. The only section of the cabin I could not see was the bathroom.

"Brad?" I asked to the dimly lit room. No answer. I stole a glance at my watch. 9:30 p.m. No doubt well at sea by now. I stretched and stood on the couch to have a view out the porthole. I was on the seaward side, no sign of land anywhere, but it could very well have been a hundred yards off the other side for all I knew.

The great thing about getting out of handcuffs without a key is that it has nothing whatsoever to do with picking the lock. All you have to do is insert a flat piece of steel between the teeth of the cuff and the spring-loaded catch. For one who isn't exactly the most coordinated with his hands, this solution was ideal, since it didn't really involve much effort. Problem was, I didn't have a flat piece of steel.

Yet.

On the table in front of me was a fountain pen. When I was a kid, I used to read of Houdini's escapes with great enthusiasm. One of the talents he had perfected over the years was using his feet in tight situations. Brother, *this* was a tight situation. I brought my right foot up to the couch seat and quickly took off my shoe and sock. With some contorted effort, I had the pen in no time, and broke off the pocket clip. While it wasn't ideal, it did have the basic shape and size required. After a few minutes, I was free, replacing my sock and shoe in quick order.

I made my way to the cabin door, where I stood for a moment, listening for anything that might lie in wait in the hall. Nothing. I opened the door slowly and glanced in both directions, making mental note of the cabin number for my return. Brad had said Darlene was being held next door, but there were doors on either side, and she could be in either. For that matter, so could Brad and Werner. No, the only option was to high tail it to the bridge and discuss options with the crew. It didn't take long to find the crew passage-ways. I wasn't sure what I'd say if I met up with a crewman midway through my journey. *Excuse me, but there's an ex-Nazi fugitive in cabin D-24.* It just didn't sound like a winning plan, so I decided to press on, head to the top, and let the captain sort it all out. After climbing several decks, there was no further passageway inside. Hoping I was near the bridge, I opened the door to the night. I was within strik-ing range, but exposed, at the stern, and would have to work my way to the bridge from the outside. I was so worried about how I would explain my predicament to an outsider that I wasn't thinking about being spotted.

"Nick!" From behind came Brad's firm call. I turned, and he was on me. He grabbed me and threw me to the bulkhead.

"I was hoping it wouldn't come to this."

"It doesn't have to."

"Who you gonna tell, Nick?" He partially released his grip.

"You think Werner's just gonna go quietly?" One thing I always gave Brad was his ability to reason at the worst possible moments. Maybe that's why he made the force, and I didn't.

"You think he's just gonna hand over Mac's wife and come out with his hands up?" He had released me completely now, assuming the scope of the situation was clear to me. It was.

"I can't let him walk, Brad."

"You're gonna have to," he said with quiet resolution.

"Sorry," I said, passing him, and starting off once more toward the bridge. He grabbed me as I passed. I was never a very good fighter, but I had a few extra pounds to my advantage and put them to use the best way I could. I was trying for low blows rather than head shots—I figured if I could wear him down, I might actually have a chance to talk some reason into him. I was also hoping some pas-senger strolling along the deck would see us and try to break it up, but neither alternative seemed to be working. Between the after-effects of the drug, and the concentrated effort of throwing my weight around, I'd lost my bearing on position, so that when I went for a cheap wrestling move it had disastrous results. I had thrown Brad onto the rail, and in an effort to regain his balance he'd gone over the side. The only thing separating him from the cold embrace of the sea was my firm grip on his arm.

"OK Brad, reach up with your other arm, and grab the rail." He was in the process of doing so, when someone approached me from behind.

"Let go," came Werner's familiar accent. He didn't need Brad anymore, nor myself or Darlene for that matter. Still, I held firm. He produced an automatic from his coat, and flashed it briefly in front of me. Brad's free hand dropped from beside the rail. I could feel the muscles relaxing in his arm.

"Brad—hang on," I said, but Werner intervened to provide just the effort required, and Brad fell to the ocean, quietly slipping into the wake of the ship. I now had Werner all to myself.

"Can't sit still, eh?" He said, smiling, his automatic pointed squarely at my chest mere inches away.

"Old habits." I said.

"Your friend was very helpful."

"So I hear. How's the girl?" I asked, almost afraid of the answer.

"Oh, she is quite safe—and will remain that way. She could be very useful on such a long journey."

My stomach turned at the possibilities—as it did so, the break I had hoped for came, in the form of an elderly couple strolling towards Werner and I.

"Don't be foolish," Werner said simply as the couple approached. Werner partially hid his gun in his coat. I had him now; the only way to hide the gun had been to point it away from me slightly while the couple passed us. As they did, Werner tightened his grip.

"Nice night," I offered with a smile, throwing Werner into a mild panic betrayed by his cold stare. When the couple was ten or so feet passed, I made my move, pinning Werner against the bulkhead. He had the gun, and I had him. I leveraged my torso in an effort to re-orient the gun barrel. I wasn't sure if I had the advantage yet when the gun went off. Werner's left arm slumped. When it did, I reached in with my free hand and grabbed the gun.

The couple had heard the muffled shot, and stopped to look back. I grabbed Werner with a tight grip and brought him to the rail.

"I'm afraid my friend has had a little too much to drink," I offered, as I coaxed the German's head over the rail. He wasn't in much of a position to argue. When the couple was out of sight, I made sure we were alone. Then, without the least bit of hesitation, I threw the bastard and his gun over the rail.

The following night, we rounded up all the extraneous luggage from the two rooms, weighted them down, and tossed them overboard. After that, Darlene and I remained sequestered in Ratchet's cabin for the remainder of the voyage. We ducked out only occasionally to grab a bite to eat, or for a breath of fresh air when the cozy cabins became slightly stale.

I thought a lot about what Ratchet had said in those final moments. Some of it hit closer to home than I had cared for. The facts were indisputable, but the truth was something we all had to figure out and eventually live with. That bastard had saved my life three times, once after he'd died. For Ratchet and myself, the war, it seemed, was finally over after all.

To pass the time, I filled Darlene in on the heroic exploits of her husband, strategically embellishing and editing where necessary to present a story which could be passed on to their kids when the time came. Daddy was a war hero, and he was going to provide for them even after his death. I would see to that.

The trip back to San Francisco was unremarkable. We hopped a plane in Mexico and made the trip without incident. Once we arrived in the city, we made plans to meet up again for the anniversary of VJ Day at the Presidio.

Since Ratchet was officially on vacation I had all the time in the world to rifle his apartment at my leisure. I'd even found his apartment keys in his cabin, so there wasn't the need to jimmy the lock. Among the bits I took were Rat's list of contacts, and a picture of him and me in happier times. In the end, the whole thing was handed to me on a gold platter.

Even Chinatown was a breeze. There was no reason to have the gold melted down and split up, so I sold it outright for about half of its true value. It was the "Chinese Squeeze" in its truest sense.

I saw Darlene for the last time one misty September morning in the Presidio. She had the young ones in tow, and after all the hoopla was over, I approached, flowers at the ready.

"These are for you," I said motioning them forward. I paused as she accepted my gift. "And this," I remarked, reaching into my jacket, "is for the kids." It was a bank passbook, which I handed over with great pleasure. She accepted it without a fight, and smiled.

That night I finally returned to my routine. I entered Gino's by six, where a folded newspaper was patiently waiting for me on my corner stool. Gino saw me come in and was reaching for the ice as I unfolded the front page. Howard Hughes was being called to testify before Congress regarding cost overruns for his ill-fated "Spruce Goose" project. The Yankees were on their way to another winning season. And down in the lower left hand corner was a small blurb about a city cop who hadn't come back from his vacation in Mexico. I didn't read it.

Instead, I flipped to the funnies to catch up with Dick Tracy and Tess Trueheart. Three limes later, I was knee deep in the crossword when Gino's door opened and a familiar face walked in. Tony Manicelli, Ratchet's "temporary" replacement, although Manicelli made no secret of the fact that he would feel all warm and fuzzy inside if the change was made permanent. He was on the fast track, something that always made me nervous. Cops with something to prove often did so at someone else's expense. I kept my nose to the news and let him come to me.

"Chambers," he said without emotion. I wondered if he had any to begin with.

"Manicelli," I replied with the same enthusiasm. "What brings you into my neck of the woods?"

He looked behind the counter, then put his hands in his trousers and circled my stool like he was trolling for some tidbit.

"Oh, nothin'. I was in the neighborhood, thought I'd see what the attraction was. Brad mentioned this place a couple of times. Still no word?"

He was fishing for facts, but his bait was bullshit, and I wasn't biting. "Nope. You?" God, I hated breaking in the new guy.

"Nah. Word on the street is he may have been into something shifty." He was still dipping that line in the water. "You wouldn't know anything about that would ya?"

"Nope— 'fraid not. Hey, you know a four letter word for...."

"You'll let me know if you hear anything?" Manicelli interrupted with obvious impatience. Well, Ratchet had taught him something after all. I looked up from the paper to meet his gaze.

"You bet," I said simply. He had nothing, and it was going to stay that way. I'd seen to that when I was at Ratchet's place. There were, after all, a couple of bags and several suits missing. The most they could ever possibly get is that Rat had disappeared after a cruise. It had been Mister and Missus Smith who had paid cash and traveled back to San Francisco from there. No connections, no worries.

Manicelli took his hands out of his pockets and headed for the door.

"See you around, Nick."

"Can't wait," I said under my breath.

That night, for the first time in months, I got a good night's sleep.

THE LOW ROAD

B.J. West

I hated the sound of a telephone ringing almost as much as the sound of a gun firing. It was even worse when it was the first sound I heard in the morning, dragging me out of the sweet oblivion of sleep. Each ring was a stab to my brain, and my amazing detective powers of observation were telling me that the empty bottle I kicked as I sat up on the sofa had something to do with it.

When I glanced at the calendar on the wall, Miss February 1954 winked at me from her fireplace vigil, telling me that the first of the month was just around the corner. That meant it might have been Mrs. Lazarino, calling to lean on me about the overdue rent. It could also have been one of the many creditors I was in arrears with, calling to threaten me with legal action. Taking me to court wouldn't have done them much good, as I had no wages to garnish and precious little assets worth seizing.

And getting sued was the least of my worries. I was having to step very lightly whenever my travels carried me anywhere near North Beach. I owed about a grand to Jimmy McNaughton, and he was getting mighty testy about it. Jimmy worked out of a bar on Columbus called *Vesuvio's*, and he measured the lateness of a debt in yards—the more overdue payment was, the farther you had to stay from *Vesuvio's* to avoid having your legs broken. In my case, that sphere of influence was nearly large enough to reach my front door. But Jimmy

McNaughton didn't bother using the phone, he just sent his boys around.

So there was still the slim chance that the person shattering my morning was a potential client. I clung to that thought as I walked over to the desk and picked up the phone. "Chambers," I muttered.

"Mr. Chambers, my name is Jeffrey Sanborn, and I would like to hire you."

His voice was a nasal, irritating whine, but since I already liked what he was saying, I scribbled his name on a notepad. "What can I do for you, Mister Sanborn?"

"Please, call me Jeffrey." I sneered. I had always disliked grown men who insisted on calling themselves Jeffrey instead of Jeff, or Bartholomew instead of Bart. It made me think they might still wear short pants. "I'd rather not discuss this on the phone," he said. "Could you come by my office?"

"When were you thinking?"

"As soon as possible."

"I think I can fit you in. What's the address?"

"I'm at Pier 20, on the Embarcadero. Just ask for the boss."

"I'll be down in about an hour." I could hear his nasal voice thanking me, even as I hung up.

Pier 20 was bustling as I stepped through the enormous doors. Forklifts were darting to and fro like worker ants belching diesel exhaust. I walked over to a dark-skinned guy with huge hands, and shouted over the din. He pointed at a large office about halfway down the pier.

A secretary looked up as I entered, but didn't speak until the heavy door swung shut behind me, blocking out most of the noise "You must be Mr. Chambers." I nodded. "Mr. Sanborn is expecting you." She gestured to the door just beside her desk. I mustered a smile and went in.

When the door to his office closed, it was nearly silent, the roar of commerce held at bay. That explained why I hadn't heard the machinery over the phone. Sanborn sat at his desk talking on the phone in a language that sounded like Greek spoken very quickly.

He held up a finger to say he'd only be a moment, then gestured at the chair in front of his desk. I took a seat and looked around.

The office was fairly posh for a warehouse. Dark wood paneling complemented a huge oak desk. Inoffensive paintings were hung strategically to break up the windowless walls. The only thing that looked out of place was Sanborn himself, leaning back in an over-stuffed leather chair. He was a short, stout man crowned with a puff of kinky black hair. A thick, equally curly moustache eclipsed most of his mouth. The whole office reeked of Mediterranean spices, but I wasn't sure if that was from merchandise or yesterday's lunch. Sanborn finished up his yammering conversation, hung up the phone, and leaned forward to shake hands. Even from across the desk his breath was terrible.

"Mr. Chambers. Thanks for coming." He had no trace of an accent when he spoke English.

"What can I do for you, Mr. Sanborn?"

"Please, call me Jeffrey. I have a very serious problem, and it needs to be handled with great discretion."

He stood up, took a pair of framed photos from the top of the filing cabinet, and handed one of them to me. I nearly laughed out loud when he came out from behind the desk, revealing that Jeffrey was indeed wearing khaki knee-length shorts over some heavy, well-worn work boots and thick wool socks. I hid my smirk behind the photo as I examined it.

It showed a girl, nearly as wide as she was tall, holding a baby that was well under way in following suit. "This is my sister, Angelika, and my nephew, Paul." I handed the picture back, raising my eyebrows for the rest of the story. He handed me the other picture. This one showed another stocky immigrant with dark bushy hair. "This is my brother-in-law, Eleni Patroklos." He spat. "Bastard. He's taken my nephew and ran off."

"Even if he's the father, that's kidnapping. Why didn't you go to the police?"

Sanborn looked down at his boots. "It's not that simple. My sister, well..." He lowered his voice to nearly a whisper, even though there was no one else around. "She's not in this country legally. If the police get involved, she will certainly be deported. Also, it could make me look bad. Eleni worked for me here in the warehouse."

I frowned. "So you want me to get the kid back?"

Sanborn waved his hands wildly. "Oh no! This is *family* business. My brothers and I will take care of Paul. I just need you to find Eleni."

"How long has he been gone?"

"Two days. He and Angelika had a big fight. She'd had enough of his drinking and told him that she wants a divorce. He waited until she was asleep, then grabbed Paul and drove off."

"Any idea where he might have gone?"

He shrugged. It just made him look shorter. "If I did, I wouldn't need to hire you."

I leaned back, pondering the situation. "So you don't want me to apprehend him or anything."

"Oh no! In fact, I'd rather you not let him know that you are looking for him. He might disappear again."

"Hmmm. That makes the job a lot tougher. It's one thing to find somebody with no leads. It's even harder if that person is trying to not be found. But it's close to impossible to look for someone like that without tipping them off that you're looking for him."

"Impossible? But I thought you..."

I cut him off. "*Close* to impossible. It just complicates matters, that's all. Makes the operation more difficult."

He gave me an understanding nod. "How much?"

I quickly tallied up my back rent, tacked on a bit for next month, then padded it for comfort. "Four thousand dollars, half in advance, plus expenses."

"What kind of expenses?"

"Well, for starters, I'll need to rent a car."

"You don't have a car?"

I shook my head. My last jalopy had been repossessed, and I hadn't been able to afford even the cheapest junker since. But I couldn't admit that to a client. "Somebody stole it last week. I can get around the city without it, but I doubt your brother-in-law is stupid enough to still be in the city."

He thought about it. From the look on his face, I'd have guessed he'd been expecting to go higher. "Mr. Chambers, we have a deal."

"One question: what are you gonna do to Patroklos when you find him?"

Sanborn frowned. "Nothing he doesn't have coming." He must have seen from my expression that I didn't want to get mixed up in rough business. "Don't worry, we won't really hurt him. My brothers and I just will just make it clear that he shouldn't ever try something like this again."

I nodded, and we shook hands.

I parked the rental in front of the only lead I had, Eleni's last known address. Apparently he and the rotund princess had separated a while back, and he had taken a place out on Mission. I slid out the passenger door and looked up the façade. It had been a nice building once, but that was some time ago. Now it was a weather-beaten flop house calling itself the Empire Hotel. I opened the skewed front door and stepped inside.

The hand-painted sign over the window said "$3 a day" in about four languages, none of them English. From the look of the stairs, it wasn't a bargain. I could hear a radio yammering in Spanish from beyond the window, but there was no clerk in sight. I headed up the stairs, hoping the radio masked the creaking.

Eleni's apartment was on the third floor. The light was out in the hallway, but enough sunshine leaked in around the edges of the thick drapes over the window down at the end, dust swirling in the resulting beams. I put my ear on the door. I couldn't hear anything going on inside, so I knocked. Still nothing. I knew these old doors, the locks could be picked by an eight-year-old. I slipped a nail file into the keyhole and fidgeted it around until I heard it click. The door opened as if the name on the mailbox was mine.

I closed the door behind me and did a quick sweep. Eleni hadn't left much. The drawers were empty except for some mouse droppings, and his closets were full of nothing but wire hangers. I checked behind the hideous paintings, just in case he was cagier than I expected. Nothing. Likewise, there was nothing under the mattress but stains. There was a loose picture tucked in to the phone book on the bedside table. I opened the book and held it up. It was a pretty girl, certainly not the missus. I checked the back, but there was nothing. Clearly he hadn't felt strongly enough about her to take the picture with him, leaving her as a discarded bookmark.

My eyes shot to the open directory. There, barely visible in the gloom, a phone number was underlined in pencil. I tore the page out, folded it up and put it in my jacket pocket, along with the photo.

Someone passed by in the hall, coughing deeply and wetly. I froze, but the coughing went past the door and down the stairs. I felt pretty sure there was nothing more for me here. Sliding the blinds aside just enough to look down at the street, I watched and waited for the cougher to hit the sidewalk. After a moment he emerged, spat out whatever he'd been working up in the hall, and headed down Mission.

I knew a dive bar on the corner of 16th and Albion that had a pay phone in the back, so I stopped in to work up my first expenses. On weekday afternoons, the place was pretty quiet, the bar populated by a handful of old Portuguese men more interested in playing cards than talking. After buying a scotch and a beer to break a five, I headed back to the phone and pulled out the phone book page I'd lifted at Eleni's place. The underlined listing was for a Helen Dimitrios. I dropped a dime into the phone, dialed and gazed at the photo of the mystery woman as it rang. "Hello?" said the voice at the other end, and if it was the girl in the picture, it was taken a long time ago.

"Hi, is Eleni there?"

The woman was silent for a moment, and when she spoke again, her tone was colder, possibly even frightened. "Who is this?"

I remained amiable. "My name is Enrico Gomez. I used to work with Mr. Patroklos, and I have a job I think he might be interested in."

Again, the woman paused a long time before she spoke, then said only, "You have the wrong number," and hung up.

I didn't learn much, but I'd bet my whole fee that even if he wasn't there, the Dimitrios household knew who Eleni Patroklos was. Without much else in the way of leads, I started falling back to the old standards. I dropped another dime.

"Department of Motor Vehicles."

"May I speak to Dolores Hall?"

"Please hold." The line clicked. Dolores was a girl I had dated once. It hadn't worked out between us, but she was a file clerk with the DMV, which was handy. I sent her flowers on her birthday and took her out to dinner whenever she hit pay dirt for me.

"This is Miss Hall."

"Dolores, it's Nick."

She sighed. "Nick, I'm pretty busy right now."

"Then I'll make it quick. I need whatever you have on a guy named Eleni Patroklos."

"Patroklos? That's a mouth full."

I spelled it for her. "Last known address was 32459 Mission St., Apartment 32."

I could hear her ruffling through the files. "Patroklos, Patroklos, Patroklos. Nope. I don't have anything under that name."

"Nothing at all? You sure?"

"You want to come look for yourself? You can have my job if you like."

"I'd probably get a paper cut and bleed to death. But thanks anyway, you're a doll."

"So I've been told." She hung up.

I drank the last of my beer and considered my options, which was quite a trick considering I didn't have any. The only thing I had resembling a live lead was Helen Dimitrios, and I didn't have an address for her. Since that problem was better handled from the office, I tipped back the shot glass for the last drop of breakfast, then hit the road.

The parking angel was not smiling upon me as I arrived back at the office. I had to cruise Bush St. over and over, searching up and down side streets and through back alleys until someone finally pulled out ahead of me way up on Leavenworth. That left me with a few blocks to walk and ponder my next move. I was still pondering fruitlessly as I climbed the steps, which is probably why I didn't see the woman laying in wait for me on the landing until it was too late.

"Why, Mrs. Lazarino! How are you on this fine morn...."

"Can it, Chambers. You got my money?"

Enid Lazarino was the battleaxe who owned the building, and who, despite her lack of charm, had been quite patient with me these last three long, very dry months. "Actually, I was just coming to see you. I'm working on a job right now..."

"Yeah, yeah, I know this song. 'I'll pay you just as soon as I get paid.' Well you've been singing it too long."

It looked like she meant it this time. As much as I hated to part with some of my new-found wealth, I figured I better do some placating before she locked me out again. "Actually, I have some cash for you right now." I pulled $100 out of my wallet and handed it over. She eyed the money dubiously.

"OK, that covers one month. You owe three more.."

"Like I said, I'm working on a job, even as we speak. My advance was just enough to give you that much, but I'll be able to pay you in full," I held up a finger before she could protest, "and next month's *in advance* when I finish."

She paused, tasting the offer. "How long?"

"Not long. This case should be a cinch."

She crossed her arms. "How long?"

"A couple of days."

She scowled. "It better be. If I don't have it by the end of the week, I'm locking you out and tossing your shit on the sidewalk." With that, she spun on her beslippered heel and stormed back into her apartment, slamming the door.

I took a deep breath. I hadn't seen her that mad in a long time. I was on thin ice and doubtful I'd be getting paid in a month, much less by the end of the week. I fumbled in my jacket pocket for my keys, and hurried into the relative sanctuary of my office.

The place was a shambles. I'd been crashing on the old sofa since I got evicted from my last apartment, and while it was more comfortable than the floor, it was about six inches too short, so I'd been nursing a serious kink in my neck. It took me a while to locate the reverse phone book, which had been last used as a placemat for some take-out Chinese. The search was in vain, however, as Mrs. Dimitrios' phone number wasn't listed. I was considering the viability of driving around the city shouting her name when the phone rang. "Chambers."

"Nick, it's Dolores."

"What a pleasant surprise!" I half meant it. I was getting frustrated with this case already, and she was a welcome distraction.

"You don't know the half of it. I found the file on your Mr. Patroklos."

"Misfiled?"

"Certainly not!" She sounded like I'd called her mother a slut. "The file was out because it was being updated. It seems your Mr. Patroklos has a heavy foot."

"Speeding ticket?" It made sense. Scared people tended to floor it.

"Mmm hmm."

"Please tell me the ticket shows where it was written?"

"Is it good for dinner?

I smiled. "It's good for a *steak*."

"Corner of 5th and Central, in Modesto."

I scribbled furiously in my pad. "Modesto, eh? I guess when he wants to get away from it all he goes all out."

"So when can I collect that steak?"

"I'll call you back in a couple of days. Thanks doll face, you're the best." I set the hand piece into its cradle and leaned back in my chair and wondered where I had filed my map.

The drive to Modesto took six hours if you don't take the scenic route, and that was fine, because there wasn't one. The rental was a Packard sedan with plenty of kick, so I floored it and kept a sharp lookout for the highway patrol. At one point I had to stop for gas at a truck stop, and it was like finding an island paradise in an endless sea of grass. I took a piss, grabbed a cup of coffee to go, and hit the road as soon as the boy working the pumps finished scraping the bug guts off the windshield.

I'd never been to Modesto. It was a bigger burg than I was expecting, with several stoplights and a post office and everything. I stopped in at the first gas station in town and bought a city map, then sat in the car as I located 5th and Central. I figured I'd head over and see what I could see, but that turned out to be *squat*. The intersection was podunk all the way; a closed Dairy Queen sat sleeping on one corner, a hardware store squatted on the other side of Central, a realty office and a dentist held down the remaining points. I drove around, circling block to block, hoping to get a glimmer of something that would have drawn Eleni to the area, but Modesto wasn't giving up its secrets that easy.

I tried to put myself in his shoes. If I were laying low, far from home, what would I be drawn to? There are certain things everyone needs, food, shelter, companionship...*food.*

In the city, Patroklos could get Mediterranean food whenever he felt like it. In Modesto, a good baba ganoush was going to be harder to find than an honest judge. I pulled over at the first pay phone I came across and checked the yellow pages. There was exactly one Mediterranean restaurant in town, a joint called *Sourani.* I jotted down the address and drove away.

I might as well have left the car where it was, as the place was just around the corner. Normally, I'd have waltzed right in, shown Eleni's picture to the good folks who worked there and asked them if he'd been in. But if they were friends, that would tip him off that I was looking for him. Instead, I set up shop in the diner across the street, taking a table next to the window. I was hungry anyway, so I ordered a burger with the works, and got comfortable. I took my time putting it away, lingering over the huge pile of greasy fries that came with it. It was sunset when I finished, and I hadn't seen hide nor hair of Eleni. When the waitress started eyeing me funny, I went ahead and ordered another burger. What the hell, I was gonna expense it anyway.

When I finally couldn't get another fry down, I knew it was time to give up. I shuffled up to the register and paid, and asked about cheap motels. The waitress looked at me like I was propositioning her—unlikely unless she cleaned up better than most—so I headed out to find the pay phone where I'd used the phone book

I was halfway through the doors when I spotted him. Even from across the street, Patroklos stood out from the locals. I ducked back inside, praying that he hadn't seen me. If the waitress had thought there was something hinkey about me before, that cinched it. I checked to make sure Patroklos was out of sight, then left like nothing had happened.

I'd left the car parked across the street so that I'd have a better view when he came out. I slumped down in the shadows and stared at the door. After a bit, he emerged carrying a large bag. He didn't have the kid with him, so it made sense that he was bringing the food home. He piled into his car and drove off. I started up the rental and followed at a respectable distance.

Tailing someone in Modesto was different than follwing a car in the city. In San Francisco, there's always the anonymity of sheer numbers, one car is just like hundreds of others cruising up Van Ness. Following Patroklos, there was no one else to hide behind. I had to lay much farther back than I cared to, and when he turned, I wasn't sure if I really saw where. Luckily, after I guessed and made the turn I spotted his car again. He hadn't gone far, pulling into a threadbare motel close to the highway. I followed him into the parking lot, and watched until I could see which room he went into. I couldn't quite make out the number on the door, so I started the car and drove slowly past until I could.

I headed back to my pay phone. There might have been one closer, but I knew where that one was. I dropped a dime in the slot and dialed.

"Hello?" came the nasal voice at the other end of the line.

"Mr. Sanborn, it's Nick Chambers." I could practically see him squirm at my refusal to call him 'Jeffrey.' It made me smile. "I have what you want."

"Is that so?"

"It is. Eleni Patroklos is in Modesto. He's staying at the Riverside Motel, room 38."

"Thank you, Nick." I wasn't sure how I liked him using my first name. "When would you like to come by my office for the rest of your fee?"

"I'll drive back tonight and drop the rental off. No point in running up more expenses than necessary."

"I appreciate that."

I thought it might be nice to sleep in a bit, but that would mean risking having Mrs. Lazarino hassle me on the way out. "How 'bout I drop by your office at nine o'clock?"

"That should be perfect. I'll see you in the morning."

I'm not generally a sentimental man, but I felt a palpable sense of *rightness* as I crossed the Bay Bridge back into the city. I wouldn't have lasted a week in Modesto without ending up in jail or dead.

After dropping off the car, I decided to skip the bus and strolled home. The night air was brisk but not too cold, not too damp, and I was pleased at the way the case had gone. I'd done a good deed, actually made a difference in someone's life. Plus, it had gone fairly easy. Luck was on my side for a change—God knew it was about time. By tomorrow afternoon, I'd be square with Mrs. Lazarino and have enough to live on until I could set up another gig. I winked at Mrs. Lazarino's door as I passed on my way into the office. Even the mangy sofa seemed more comfortable than usual, and I drifted off to sleep nearly immediately.

In marked contrast to my last visit, Pier 20 was still and quiet. The forklifts were all parked in a row off to the side of the ware-house, and there wasn't a soul in sight. My footsteps echoed hol-lowly off of stacked containers as I approached the office.

There, too, I was in for a surprise. The receptionist wasn't at her desk. I waited a moment, just in case she had merely stepped away from her desk, but before long, it was apparent she wasn't there at all. I rapped twice on the door to Sanborn's office, then went in.

Again, Sanborn was on the phone as I came into his office. This time he was scowling, either angry or frustrated or both. At least until he saw me, then he broke into a big smile. He dismissed whomever he was talking to, hung up, and stood up to shake my hand. His breath hadn't improved overnight. "Nick! I can't thank you enough. You've done a fantastic job."

I looked around. "Sure is quiet around here."

"We work the same schedule you do. If there is a ship to load or unload, we are hard at work, even at three in the morning. No ship, everyone gets a day off. Everyone but me, that is." He smiled broadly. "My work is never done."

I nodded. "Everything go OK last night?"

"Exactly as planned. My brothers drove up and talked some sense into Eleni."

I nodded again. I probably didn't want to know the details. "And the boy?"

"Safe and sound, right where he belongs." He practically glowed with contentment. "Ah! But business never rests." He went back to his desk and reached into the top drawer. He pulled out an envelope and held it out to me. "I hope this will cover the expenses as well. Please tell me if it doesn't."

I took the envelope and counted the bills inside. There was about $100 more than I would have asked for. "Yeah, that covers it." I slipped the envelope into my jacket pocket.

Sanborn was shaking my hand again. "I really can't thank you enough. If I ever need a detective again, you can be sure that you'll be the first one I think of."

"Thanks."

The phone rang. Sanborn smiled. "Excuse me, duty calls. You take care, Nick."

I slid out the door as he resumed yammering into the phone.

Sanborn had said "business never rests," and I had some business that was getting particularly restless. I hiked up Battery Street towards North Beach. I was playing with ideas for making my income more steady when something about the size and weight of a ham hit me in the ribs, just below my right arm. I tumbled to the street and rolled to avoid the kick that I knew would follow. I made a halfway convincing recovery that left me crouching on the sidewalk facing my attacker and holding my side, my right arm on fire.

"You're ten minutes early," I spat.

Jock Refredi, one of Jimmy's most brutal goons, grinned at me like a shark. "You're six weeks late."

"I'm on my way to see Jimmy right now." I was suddenly wishing I'd thought to take my gun.

"Yes." He mumbled around his many huge teeth. "Yes, you are."

He lunged at me, grabbing me by the collar of my coat and dragged me around the corner and into a parked car. He slid in beside me, and the driver, whom I'd never seen before, fired up the engine and pulled away. Jock glowered at me. "You got the money?"

I nodded. "I was on my way to pay up."

"Sure you was. Give it to me."

"I thought you were taking me to see Jimmy."

"I am. I'll give him the money myself."

I shook my head. "Nothin' doin'. I borrowed it from Jimmy, and I'll pay Jimmy."

The lug was reaching back to clock me. I tried to sound calm, but spoke quickly. "How do you think the boss'll feel about you cutting in on his action?"

That stopped him. "What're you talkin' about?"

"You know a guy named Rod Warbick?"

"Never heard of him." His eyes said differently.

"He says he knows you." Warbick was a two-bit hood who mostly relieved young ladies of the burden of their purses. About three months prior, I'd had the opportunity to grill him about a case I'd been working on. He'd let it slip that he'd roughed up someone for Jock, who didn't want to do it himself 'cause he was doing a little business behind Jimmy's back. It had nothing to do with my case, so I just filed that little tidbit away for a rainy day. It seemed to me that it was suddenly pouring.

"What else did he say?"

I managed a smile. "He's a chatty little fellow. But that would only matter to someone he'd been working for. Since you don't know him, it wouldn't concern you."

Jock was livid, but behind the rage I could see the glimmer of fear I was hoping for. "What are you trying to pull?"

"I just want to pay Jimmy what I owe him. At this point, I don't owe him nothin' but money. Whether or not it stays that way is up to *you*."

He gritted his teeth, and it sounded like someone driving on gravel. Still, he got the message. He sat in silence until the car pulled into the alley beside *Vesuvio's*. Then he just said, "Get out." I slid out of the car and strolled into the bar like I owned the place.

Jimmy was holding court at his usual table, surrounded by

business associates and muscle. The former looked up as I approached, the latter might as well have been statues. I knew enough to take off my hat before I got there.

"Nicky, Nicky, Nicky." Jimmy had aspirations of being a made man, so he sounded Italian even though he'd been born in S.F. General. "I'm so glad to see you. I was beginning to worry about you."

I smiled. "I appreciate your concern. And I apologize for how long it's taken me to get back to you."

His accent slipping slightly, Jimmy just said, "Have you got my money?"

I nodded. I opened my coat wider than necessary, allowing the big boys to see all the way in before I started reaching for my wallet. I did it slow and smooth, and my hand came out with nothing but leather. I opened the wallet and sorted out a grand, and put it on the table. One of the older gentlemen at the table picked it up, counted it with the dexterity of a Vegas card dealer, and pocketed it. Jimmy looked up at me. "And the other six hundred?"

"But I only borrowed a grand...."

Jimmy held up a hand. "That was six weeks ago. You've been accruing interest. You know how it works."

I did. I peeled six bills out and put them on the table. I followed it with one more. "An apology for being so late."

Jimmy smiled. "You're a good boy, Nicky. But next time you need a loan, *go to a bank.*" He turned away from me and resumed his conversation with the others. Our business was done.

Jock followed me all the way out onto the sidewalk. Once we were clear of the window he stopped me. "So. What about Rod Warbick?"

I shrugged. "He couldn't talk so good on account of all the busted teeth. I didn't understand a word he said." I held out my hand. Jock stared at it confused for a moment until he figured out what I meant. Then he smiled evilly and shook it. And then *our* business was done.

I decided to celebrate by treating myself to a proper breakfast. There was a nice diner up by Union Square, and I grabbed a newspaper on the way in. The chicken-fried steak and eggs were just the kind of stick-to-your-ribs food that I'd been craving for some time, and the coffee was hot, fresh, and never-ending. The glow I had felt last night was still with me, and the sheer luxury of a full belly only reinforced it. I took my time, reading the paper and enjoying a smoke.

Then I saw a picture that ruined my breakfast. Staring up at me from page four was the smiling mug of Eleni Patroklos, the same photo that Sanborn had shown me. He'd been murdered in his motel room sometime after midnight, three shots from a .45. According to the article, Mr. Patroklos was a recent immigrant from Greece, a model citizen, was single, and had no children.

My stomach churned. Sanborn had lied to me. At the time I had briefly wondered why he had a picture of his sister and nephew—if that was even who they were—and a separate photo of Patroklos, but not one of them together as a family. I'd chalked it up to their being separated. Now it looked like the whole child-snatching story was pure fiction. Sanborn had wanted Eleni dead for some reason, but couldn't find him. My locating him was the signature on his death warrant.

I was so furious I couldn't think straight. I left some money on the table and stormed out onto the street. I don't remember much of the walk, but I made it at a fast pace, and before I really knew it I was storming through the doors of Pier 20, my hands clenched into fists. The place still felt abandoned, and there was no one to object as I flung the office door aside and went in.

Sanborn was at his desk, leaning back in his chair wearing a red shirt. "Listen up, asshole. I don't know who you thought you were..." Sanborn didn't jump to his feet. He didn't pull a gun. He didn't even blink. And he'd been wearing a white shirt when I had been there earlier.

I was suddenly seeing clearly. Sanborn's head was rolled back, staring blankly at the ceiling, his eyes glazed and unfocused. Which probably had something to do with the fact that he'd been shot at close range, right in the throat. His trachea was blown wide open, blood spilled all down the front of him like a crimson bib.

And then I noticed the gun on the desk, arranged as neatly as if it had been a stapler. It was a nickel-plated Smith and Wesson "Chief's Special" snub nose .38 with mother-of-pearl grips. It looked exactly like my gun. In fact, the longer I stared at it, the more familiar it was. I looked even closer. There was a pair of small dings on opposite sides of the barrel. I knew that happened when I'd once used the gun to stop a door from closing before I could get through it.

I looked back up at Sanborn. I had little doubt that this gun—*my* gun—was the one that had opened his neck. If so, it was covered in my fingerprints, and if someone had been careful enough, nobody else's.

I was still reeling when I heard the door open behind me. Reflexively, I grabbed the gun and whirled around. A Mexican cleaning lady stood frozen in the doorway, her face a rictus of terror. Her eyes darted back and forth between Sanborn, the gun, and my face. She screamed, dropped her mop and bucket, and ran, screeching to the blessed virgin for protection.

It didn't take Albert Einstein to know how it looked. I pocketed the gun and got out of there as fast as I could.

I didn't dare grab a cab—I certainly didn't need another witness that could put me on the pier—so I hopped a bus and hoped it moved fast enough. I tried to figure out how much time I'd have before an APB was put out for me. I had to assume that the cleaning lady would go straight to the phone and call the police, but she didn't know me from Adam. The police would need about ten–fifteen minutes to get someone down to Pier 20 and scope out the crime scene. They'd focus on the body first, try to figure where the shooter was standing, try and recover the slug. If Sanborn kept the meticulous records I figured he did, they'd find my name within a couple of hours. If they were clever enough, they'd show my picture to the cleaning lady, and she'd positively identify me. When they figured out what Sanborn had paid me for and put my name together with Eleni Patroklos, I'd be wanted for *two* murders.

The bus huffed to a stop at the corner of Sutter and Stockton. I hurried off and headed toward the stairs on the left side of the tunnel. The usual assortment of bums were piled up in the darkness of the landing halfway up. I saw these guys pretty regularly, and had gotten to know a few of them fairly well. Pete was one of the more consistently lucid of the bunch. He looked up as I climbed towards him.

"Hey, Nick. How's it goin'?"

I reached into my pocket and came out with a handful of change. "You don't want to know." I dropped them into Pete's filthy hand and trotted up the second flight.

I blinked as I came into the light of Bush Street, my home sweet home, such as it was. My mind was already up the stairs and into the office, searching for my next move, when a car door opened across the street. I looked up and froze in my tracks. It was a black and white, and the cop getting out was heading right for me.

I dashed back down the stairs trying not to shout. "Pete! I've got a tail!" Good old Pete leapt to his feet and held a dirty army blanket out like he was a bull fighter. I took the part of the bull and dived into the blanket, wrapping it around me as I tumbled against the wall. Pete started yelling at the top of his lungs and flew down the stairs as I snuggled back into the corner and stashed my hat under what I hoped was a pile of rags.

"You bastard!" Pete stopped just outside the bottom of the stairs. "You stepped on my ankle you goddamned son of a bitch!" He kept ranting non-stop as the cop scrambled down the stairwell, his gun out. He started when he saw all the people huddled in the darkness, stumbled slightly, covering us with the gat.

Down on Stockton, Pete continued his tirade. "Think you're so high and mighty you can just walk on anybody, don't you!" The cop heard him and leapt down the remaining stairs. From the landing I could hear the rest of the performance. "Officer! That bastard stepped on my leg! Just ran over me like I didn't matter. I was a taxpayer once!" The cop didn't even reply, just tore off down Stockton, the way Pete was no doubt pointing. His heavy footsteps quickly receded in the distance.

Pete quit shouting, and after a moment came back up to the landing. He plopped down on the concrete beside me. "How'd I do?"

I slapped him on the back. "You should have been a movie star." I whipped out my wallet and handed him a fiver. He smiled and dug in the piles of refuse for his bottle. He took a drink and handed it to me. Whatever it was tasted like gasoline, but I was his guest and it would have been rude to refuse. I handed the bottle back to him. "Can I get you to check upstairs?" He nodded and trotted up to peek out of the stairwell. I followed a few paces behind. After a moment, he motioned for me to come the rest of the way up.

"His car's still there, but I don't see anyone else."

"Thanks, Pete. I owe you." I scrambled onto the street and into my building, praying that Mrs. Lazarino wasn't home.

I tried to be quiet without slowing down any, already digging in my jacket pocket for my keys. I had them in hand when I arrived at the door and noticed the padlock. Apparently, my payment yesterday hadn't placated her as much as I'd hoped. I looked at the cheap hardware store padlock. It would have been a cinch to pick if I had my tools. Unfortunately, they were on the other side of the door.

I dashed back down stairs and into Gino's. There were often times it was convenient to live over a bar, and this was one of them. Afternoons were usually quiet, and that day was no exception. I skidded to a stop at the bar where Gino sat writing in a ledger.

He looked up, trying to figure out if he should be alarmed or amused. "You in trouble, Nick?"

"I need to go through to the back." I waited for his answer. The old Chinese man sometimes conducted business of his own in the small fenced-off area behind the building where the garbage cans were kept. If he had people back there, it could be very unhealthy to go charging back unannounced. This time, however, he nodded, leading the way.

One of Gino's "sons" was sitting in a chair beside the back door, a baseball bat leaning against the wall beside him. I thought it was Wai, but they were all built like oak trees so it was hard to tell them apart. He stood up as Gino came out, and sat back down when he saw me trailing behind. I made a beeline to where the fire escape came down, but something was wrong.

"Where's my box?"

Gino blinked at me. "Your what?"

"Box. There was a wooden box here." I pointed to the corner of the yard.

"Didn't know it was yours. I threw it away." His eyes darted up to the ladder dangling just beyond reach above me and understood.

"Wai. Help him."

The huge teenager stood and came over. I expected him to lace his fingers and give me a boost up. Instead, he grabbed me around the waist and picked me up like I was a rag doll. He put me on the ladder high enough that I barely had to pull myself up to get a foot on the bottom rung. "Thanks," I grunted. Then I remembered the ledger Gino had been working on. God only knew what it was. "Hey Gino, this place is going to be crawling with cops soon. Might want to tidy up." He thanked me for the warning with a curt nod as I scurried up.

The second floor platform wrapped around into the alley. It was visible from the street, but only if you were standing right there. I hurried and hoped the cop had run a *long* way down Stockton.

I inspected the window. I had taped the top of the sash so I could tell if anyone had gone in or out through it. The tape was intact. I whipped out my pocket knife and jimmied the lock, then raised the window and tumbled through.

Immediately, I was assaulted by the unmistakable smell of insecticide. Mrs. Lazarino must have spent the morning fighting the ongoing war with the roaches. I hadn't noticed a problem, but she declared it a plague whenever she caught site of just one of the little bastards. The office had smelled pretty musty before, so the bug spray was just a change of flavor.

I looked around the office. Two instincts were wrestling with each other. On one hand, I knew my time was short. The cops could be breaking down the door any minute. On the other, someone had gotten into my office and stolen my gun. If I was going to have a chance of figuring out who and how, I had to treat my own office as a crime scene, and tearing up the place might destroy crucial evidence.

First things first. I opened the filing cabinet as quietly as the rusting steel would allow and extricated my gun permit. The serial number listed was the same as the one on the gun, removing any doubt that it was indeed mine. I put the permit back and left the drawer open.

Next, I went to my desk. I normally kept the gun in a locked drawer along with my other semi-valuables, and I had the only key in my pocket. I seldom carried the gun, almost never had a reason to. In my investigations I usually relied on subtlety, deception, and stealth, and nothing was less subtle than a shooting iron. I hadn't taken it out in more than a month, but I did get into that drawer on a daily basis. If it had been missing, I certainly would have noticed. I crouched down to get a closer look at the lock on the drawer. Even in the dim yellow light filtering in from the alley, the lock sparkled with small bright scratches, a clear sign that it had been picked, and recently.

The drawer was still unlocked, and I slid it open. Everything else seemed to be there, including the two full boxes of ammo I kept with the gun. Taking the lid off revealed five rounds were missing. Whoever took the gun loaded it before they left, probably to make sure the ammo used to kill Sanborn matched what I used. I pulled out the gun and flipped the cylinder out. All five bullets were accounted for, only one of them fired. I replaced the spent shell with one from the box and put the gun back in my pocket.

The question of how they'd gotten in remained. I'd already eliminated the window over the fire escape. The painted-over windows on the wall facing the street didn't open, and besides, there was no way anyone but a fly could climb up from the outside. That only left the front door.

About a year ago I had a client who hired me to tail his wife because he suspected she was cheating on him. She *had* been, and I brought him some photos that left nothing to the imagination. Turns out he'd been secretly hoping I'd prove him wrong, and when I didn't, he decided to take it out on the messenger. I had to barricade myself in my office by pushing all the furniture against the door until the police could get there and take the poor sap away to cool down. When it was over, the door was a pile of kindling. Mrs. Lazarino had a fit and demanded that I replace it. Since I had to anyway, I decided to do it right. The next day, I spent most of what I had stashed away on a heavier door and a solid deadbolt that would be nearly impossible to pick. The only person other than myself who had a key was Mrs. L., but I felt sure that she wasn't in cahoots with someone bent on framing me.

A car door slammed shut down on the street, and I nearly jumped out of my skin. I rushed to the windows and peeked through a hole I had scratched in the old black-out paint for just that purpose. The cop had come back. Much to my surprise, he started the engine of his cruiser and drove away. It didn't make any sense if he'd been called out to pick me up. But then, there was no way he could have known about Sanborn and me, not yet. It must have been something unrelated, but I couldn't think of what it could be. But that was beside the point. The cops that were looking for me would be arriving soon. I had to get gone, and fast.

I had no idea how soon I'd be able to come back, so I tried to think of everything I might need. I took what little remained from my advance and added it to what was left in my wallet. That made a couple of bills more than two grand, all the money I had in the world. Another day I might have felt rich, but I had a feeling it wouldn't last long.

I grabbed the briefcase that served as my field kit and opened it on the desk. It already held a flashlight, a box of matches, my lock pick tools, a fingerprinting kit, a magnifying glass, and a few small hand tools. I added in one of the three boxes of ammo from the desk, a half-empty bottle of gin, a thin blanket, a change of underwear and two pairs of socks.

I thought about where I'd be sleeping that night. It seemed a sure bet that the cops would be covering the cheaper hotels in case I didn't leave town. They'd be watching the airport and bus terminal in case I did. It seemed to me the only place I could safely bed down would be the park. I took a moment to wriggle into a thick wool sweater and put a pair of kid leather gloves in my coat pocket.

I looked around. There was plenty else I would like to have taken, but I figured I'd need to travel light and keep a low profile. I sighed deeply, taking in the insecticide-perfumed air one last time, then clambered back out the window and closed it behind me.

The fog swirled eerily in the branches as I crunched down the trail. Golden Gate Park afforded plenty of cover and escape routes, while still being close to all the bus lines and civilized comforts the avenues had to offer. It was getting dark, and the air was already taking on the famous San Francisco chill.

I came out of the trees near 9th Avenue and trotted across Lincoln. I dropped a dime into the payphone on the corner and dialed a number I knew from memory.

"Homicide."

I didn't recognize the voice. "Lieutenant Manicelli, please."

"May I tell him who's calling?"

"Yeah. Tell him it's Archie Goodwin."

He covered the mouthpiece, but I still heard him shout, "Hey Tony, some wise ass wants to talk to you." The line rustled as he handed the phone over.

"This is Detective Manicelli."

"Tony. It's Nick."

He paused for a moment, probably wondering how to handle me. "Hey, buddy. It looks like you're in a bit of trouble."

I had to laugh. "Yeah, you could say that."

"Why don't you come on in so we can talk about it."

"I didn't do it, Tony."

"Yeah, I know. You couldn't have made that shot, even from that close."

"Sure. Kick a guy when he's down."

"But it *was* your gun. We matched the slug to one we had on file from that little incident with Horace Thompson."

"And you've no doubt talked to the cleaning lady."

"Naturally."

"You guys make the connection to Eleni Patroklos yet?"

"His name came up. You have something to do with that mess?"

"Unfortunately, yes, but I didn't kill him either."

"But you *were* in Modesto yesterday night."

"Yup. Sanborn paid me to find him, but that's it."

He whistled. "I don't have to tell you it looks bad, Nick. That's why you should just come on in and..."

"That's exactly why I *can't* come in. You know how badly Kelley wants a piece of me." William Kelley was San Francisco's District Attorney. It seemed I had a tendency to embarrass him and his best men, and each time we butted heads, he liked me even less. "The way things stand, it's an open and shut case. Two stiffs and no one to take the fall for it but me. Kelley must be dancing a jig right about now."

"So what are you going to do, investigate yourself?"

"Something like that. I'm going to find out who's framing me and why."

"You're putting me in a really bad position." He sounded disappointed, maybe even sad.

"I know, Tony. And I'm sorry. But I have to do it this way. You do whatever you have to do."

"OK, Nick. Be careful out there. We'll be seeing you real soon." The line went dead.

I'd hoped Tony might understand, maybe even enough to help. That wasn't going to happen, and I couldn't blame him.

There was nothing more I could do that night. The fog had come in, shrouding the park in a veil of tears. I trotted back across Lincoln and vanished into the murky darkness.

I found a hollow in a grove of juniper bushes and hunkered down as best I could. I cinched my coat up over my chin and covered myself with the blanket. The briefcase made a crappy pillow, but it was better than laying my face in the dirt. I went over what leads I had, and it wasn't much comfort. Sanborn had killed Eleni Patroklos, but I didn't know why. Someone else had stolen my gun out of my office and used it to kill Sanborn. The two had to be connected, and from what I could tell, the only players the two stories had in common were Sanborn and Yours Truly. There had to be at least one more cast member, and I felt certain that finding that person was the key to the whole mess. I took a goodnight kiss from the gin bottle, and forced myself to get some sleep.

A sound brought me to the surface and I opened my eyes. My first thought was that I was dead. I had never been that cold in my life, a brutal cold penetrating clear through to the bone. My face was sopping wet and my eyes refused to focus.

Then I heard the sound again, just a shuffle in the underbrush behind me. It was still dark, though the sky over downtown was beginning to glow. I slowly reached into my coat and drew my gun. It felt like it had been in an icebox. Whoever was behind me shifted again, clearly getting closer. I rolled to face him.

"He" was an enormous raccoon. He wasn't startled by my sudden movement, merely turned and withdrew into the brambles. I tried to laugh but was only able to dredge up a hacking cough.

It was difficult to put the gun back in my coat, my fingers were so stiff with cold that it was hard to release it. The trench coat had gone a long way to keeping most of the dew away from my upper body, but my socks and pants were drenched up to the knee. I forced myself to sit up and fumbled for the chilled gin for some breakfast. It burned going down, but the illusion of warmth in my belly was briefly comforting. Wiping the moisture off my watch revealed that it was just past six. San Francisco would be stirring to begin its day, and it seemed like I might as well follow suit. I dug in my coat pockets for a smoke.

My first order of business was going to have to be survival. I needed to think straight, and being wet and frozen wasn't going to help. The police would be checking the cheaper hotels for me, but my guess was that they'd concentrate their efforts in the evening, expecting me to hunker down for the night. Getting a room in the morning seemed safe enough provided I didn't stay long. I rummaged in the briefcase, swapped some money into my alternate wallet, and tucked it into my pocket.

The avenues were just rubbing sleep from their eyes as I shambled out of the park. I picked a cheap motel on Irving pretty much at random and ducked in. The night clerk had eyes the color of carnations and sat nursing a cup of coffee. He looked up at me wearily as I approached. "Get caught in the rain?"

I pretended to laugh. "This fog is so thick it might as well be rain." He nodded. His shift was nearly over, and that meant he wouldn't be around to answer any questions if the cops dropped in. He pushed the guest book halfway to me and I signed in as Richard Sterling.

"That's five dollars a night. Towels are in the room. You want some coffee? It's a nickel, but it's fresh."

"I'd love some coffee." I put a fiver and a nickel on the counter. The clerk ducked back into the office, then came back with a steaming mug. Apparently cream wasn't even an option. I cradled the mug in my fingers, and it burned feeling back into them. I nodded thanks as I took a sip. "Is there a phone in the room?"

"No, but there's a pay phone around the corner." I nodded and took the key from him, and started up the stairs.

Room 63 was no palace, but it was a far cry from the dump Eleni Patroklos had been staying in. The tub was clean, and the water was plenty hot. I took a very long shower, blasting my body until the chill was gone and my skin was beet red. I left my shoes and socks steaming on the radiator and toweled off as I finished my coffee.

My brain was returning to normal, but my stomach was complaining. I put on dry underwear and did the best I could with the damp suit. My shoes weren't quite dry, but they were better than they had been. It would have to do. I gathered everything back into the briefcase, put on my hat and headed out into the morning.

I headed out a back door so that if the shift change at the desk had already happened, the new guy wouldn't know my face. I located the phone the clerk had mentioned, but it was far too exposed for my liking. I continued down the street until I found a greasy spoon that promised "endless flapjacks," which sounded pretty close to heaven.

Better still, they had a pay phone in a small alcove back by the restrooms. I put away as many pancakes as I could fit around the sausage and eggs, washed it down with two more cups of coffee, paid my tab, and headed back to make my first call.

I wasn't looking forward to talking to Mrs. Lazarino, but I didn't have much else to go on. I dropped a dime in the phone and dialed, then leaned against the wall as it rang. After the fourth ring I was about to give up, but she was there after all.

"Hello?" She sounded froggier than usual. I must have gotten her out of bed.

"Mrs. Lazarino, this is Nick. I...." The line went dead. I scowled. My day was off to a glorious start. I dropped another dime and tried again.

"Listen you bastard. If you think I'm going to bail you out, you have got...."

"I'm not in jail."

"Well you ought to be. I had the cops grilling me here all night. The only reason I haven't tossed your shit on the street is that the cops won't let me."

I shook my head. "Mrs. L, listen to me, please. I'm in big trouble."

"You sure are, buddy. The cops say you killed someone."

"That's not true. Someone is framing me."

She cackled. "That's what they always say. If you think Enid Lazarino was born yesterday..."

"Did you let someone into my office yesterday? In the morning?"

"I'm not telling you anything. This is the last straw, mister."

I had only one card left to play. "I have your money."

"I don't want your blood money."

"It's not blood money! I earned it fair and square. I finished the job I told you about and got paid in full."

She paused, but only for a moment. "All of it?"

I smiled. "All of it. And I can pay you in advance for next month."

"Next month?" I could hear the sardonic grin. "Next month you're gonna be in a room with bars in the window!"

"No, I'm not. I really didn't kill anyone and I can prove it. But I need your help."

"Fine. You get your sorry ass down here and pay up. Then we can talk about me helping you, but I doubt it highly. You've pushed me too far already."

"I can't go there. The cops would pick me up and then you'd never get paid. Can you meet me somewhere?" I scrambled to come up with a place that would do, somewhere with little chance of me being seen, but where I could watch her arrive in case she decided to bring the cops. "There's a bar on Haight St. called The Blue Room. Up near Stanyan."

She feigned offense. "A bar? What kind of woman do you take me for?"

I decided not to answer that. "It's a classy place, and I'm buying."

She mulled it over. "You'll have my money?"

"Every cent."

"Plus next month?"

"Yup."

"OK. I'll be there at one thirty."

"I can't tell you how much I appreciate it."

"If you aren't there, I'll put up a 'For Rent' sign the moment I get back."

"Fair enough." I thanked her again and hung up. I celebrated with another cigarette, and hauled up the yellow pages.

Eleni had been a local boy, and the only connection I had for him was also in town. My bet was Helen Dimitrios was family, and I knew where I could find them—up to a point. I flipped to the mortuary listings, but whistled when I got there. There were pages and pages of funeral homes. Maybe I was in the wrong business. I scanned the names quickly for any that looked like they might be

Greek, but they all had quiet, dignified names like Milford and Baxter or Connolly and Sons. I dug into my pocket for more change and got started. A woman answered where I'd been expecting Boris Karloff.

"Adams Funerary Services, how may I help you?"

I mustered a serious tone. "Hello. I wanted to see what time my uncle's funeral was going to start."

I heard the rustle of pages. "What is the deceased's name?"

"Patroklos. Eleni Patroklos." I spelled it for her.

The pages continued rustling. "I don't see any services under that name. Can you tell me what day they were scheduled for?"

"You know, actually, I'm not positive what parlor was handling the services. Is there somebody who specializes in Greek orthodox funerals?"

"We can handle services of any denomination. May I ask your name, Sir?"

I hung up and moved on to Bellhaven Mortuary Chapel. They didn't have services scheduled for Patroklos either. Neither did Connolly and Sons, Donovan, Evergreen, Fountainhead, Grace, etc. Glancing at my watch told me I was running out of time before I had to get started for my rendezvous with Mrs. L. I'd just about worn out the waitress' supply of dimes—not to mention her patience—and I was down to my last one. I dropped it in the phone.

"O'Malley Funeral Home."

"Hi, what time is the Patroklos service?"

"Nine o'clock tomorrow morning."

I'd developed a rhythm to my calls, and almost hung up before I realized what the gentleman has said.

"Oh! That's great!" I slapped myself on the forehead and became appropriately somber. "I mean, that's very helpful. Can you give me directions to the cemetery?"

He told me that Patroklos was being buried at Elysian Lawns, in Colma, which could have been better news. Colma was down the peninsula, which wouldn't be a big deal if I had a car. It was going to be a long and early bus ride to make it on time. I thanked the mortician and vacated the diner.

I set up in a café across the street from The Blue Room. It was one of those swank places where you couldn't get a proper cup of joe, just hoity-toity cappuccinos and espressos at nearly fifty cents a pop. I hoped Mrs. L wasn't late or the tab might break me. But Enid Lazarino was a punctual woman, and one who got mighty impatient if you weren't just as punctual. She entered The Blue Room at 1:30 on the dot. I tipped back the last of the milky mud they'd served me. Instead of going straight in to the bar, I went around the block once, keeping an eye out for anyone who might be shadowing Mrs. L. I didn't see anyone, so I circled back and strode into the bar.

She'd been smart enough to take a booth in the back of the place, bless her heart, and she was already working on a bloody mary. I paused at the bar long enough to buy a scotch and soda and slid in beside her. "Starting without me?"

She grimaced. "Well I couldn't very well just sit here waiting for you."

"I'll get the next round."

"You're getting *this* one. You got my money?"

Nobody ever accused Mrs. Lazarino of beating around the bush, and I knew that the impatient stare wasn't a cue to talk more. I brought out my wallet and peeled off the back rent plus next month plus enough for the bloody mary and a tip. It didn't leave much. "There. Happy?"

She counted off the bills and put them in her purse. "This better not be stolen." I smiled, since she said it *after* she put the money away and not *before*.

"It's not, I swear."

She nodded, and took another big sip of her drink. "OK, I won't throw your shit out until I hear you're in prison."

I bowed my head in mock gratitude. "That's right kindly of you ma'am."

She narrowed her eyes at me. "Now what did you want to ask me?"

"Yesterday, someone took something from my office. I know it wasn't a break in, I checked. Did you let someone into my office?"

"Just the exterminator. He said you'd called about cockroaches. We don't have 'em anywhere else in the building right now, so I figured you were being such a slob you brought in your own and were putting the bill on me. That's why I locked you out."

I nodded. "I never called an exterminator."

Mrs. Lazarino scowled. It was one of the things she was best at. "Well, he said you did. How am I supposed to know....?"

"I don't suppose you kept the invoice?"

"Of course I kept the invoice!" She dug in her purse. "You can pay me for that, too." She thrust it at me like an accusation.

I scanned the bill. It was from Thompson Pest Control over on Fillmore St. The signature on the invoice read *Ed Hansen.* "Did you see anyone else go in with this guy?"

"No, but I wasn't watching, either." She stared at me expectantly, one palm held out.

I looked at the invoice for the total, took out my wallet again and handed over another ten dollars. "If this means what I think it does, it's a bargain." Then I leaned over and kissed Mrs. Lazarino on the cheek. She actually blushed, then hid her face behind her drink. "You're a life saver, maybe more literally than you know. Hey, you want another one of those?" She nodded, and I trotted up to the bar for another round.

Haight Street was usually fairly busy, so I skulked my way down Page Street instead. It was a quiet grey day, with just enough fog lingering to keep most people indoors. I had to duck into an alley just before Divisidero to avoid being seen by a motorcycle cop, but he kept going, and shortly after, so did I.

Thompson Pest Control was near Japan Town, and I paused outside long enough to dredge up a down-home friendly smile. "Hey there! Is Ed around?"

The guy at the desk looked more like a wrestler than a bug killer. He stood up and came up to the counter. "He's out on a job. What can I do for you?"

"Can you tell me where to find him? I owe him some money and he wanted me to get it to him as soon as possible."

"You can just leave it here for him. I'll see that he gets it."

I laughed. "I bet you would. But he said if I didn't get it to him right away, he wasn't gonna be eating dinner tonight."

He considered me for a moment, decided I seemed OK, then flipped through a ledger on the desk. "He's out in the Sunset right now, but he should be just about done. His next ticket is in Pacific Heights. You could probably catch him there." He scribbled an address on a scrap of paper and handed it to me. "Hey, when you see him, tell him to get his ass in gear. We got four more jobs to get through today."

I saluted and marched out the door.

Going to Pacific Heights meant climbing out of the flatlands, and puffing up California Street to the promised land. The size of the houses went up with the altitude, and by the time I reached the top I was in a place where the average gardener made more than I ever would. The bay was spread out around the area like it's own personal wallpaper, framed by a bridge on either side. Even the air seemed cleaner with just enough breeze to blow any litter off the hill, back down where it belonged.

After a resting a moment at the top of the hill, I pushed on until I found the address the wrestler had given me. An architect might have quibbled with calling the place a mansion, but anything surrounded by columns qualified in my book. Naturally, it perched on top of about a million stairs, so I gathered my stamina and started climbing. I could have driven a car through the front doors without touching either side, and I had to search a fair patch of real estate for the doorbell button. When I pressed it, throaty tones rang inside and hung on the air for several seconds. I waited, and just when I gave up and pressed the button again, the door opened. The bells rang inside like it was a church, and the butler that stood in the doorway eyed me suspiciously. "Yes?"

I held out my hand. "Hi! I'm with Thompson Pest Control. Is our man here?"

His suspicions seemed to be confirmed. "He is."

"Great. Could I see him? I have some instructions I have to give him."

Jeeves didn't say a word, just turned and walked away, but he left the door open, so I assumed I should follow. I wanted to show him that I had, in fact, been born in a barn, so I didn't close it behind me.

He took me upstairs to a bathroom I'd have been perfectly happy to call home. The butler gestured for me to go in, then wandered off impatient to get back to his butling. I stepped inside.

Ed was a short man with a round face and a broad build that looked to be equal parts muscle and fat. He was balancing on tiptoe on the toilet with a sprayer can in one hand, and reaching up with the wand in the other to spray the top of the overhead tank. The air was perfumed with the same chemical fragrance that had graced my office.

"It does my heart good to know that rich folks get roaches too."

Ed looked up, startled that someone else was in the room. "Not roaches. Silverfish." He wiped his comb-over out of his eyes and smiled at me, no doubt wondering who I was. "I'm guessin' you don't live here then."

"Nope. I live downtown. You Ed Hansen?"

He stopped spraying and slowly eased himself down to the floor. He set the tank down and looked me over. "Yeah, that's me. What can I do for you?"

"I'd like to talk to you about a job you did yesterday morning."

"Look, mister. Any complaints need to go through the main office." I handed him the invoice, and he scanned it as he spoke. "I'm sorry if I..." He stopped suddenly and he turned about three shades paler, then looked up at me. "I don't know what you're talking about."

"That's because I haven't said anything yet."

Ed began trembling visibly. "Who are you?"

"Who sent you to that job?"

"The city, that was a city job." He pointed at a box on the paper. "We do a lot of work for the city. What do you want?"

I snatched the invoice out his hands and looked at it. The "originator" box was rubber stamped *SF Dept. of Health*. I folded it and put it back in my pocket. "Who was with you when you went in?"

"Nobody. I work alone."

"So it was *you* who took my gun?"

Panic rose in his voice. "I didn't take nothin', mister."

I took out my gun and showed it to him. "So this doesn't look familiar?"

His eyes were the size of dinner plates, his voice climbing toward the stratosphere. "I've never seen it before in my life! Look, buddy, my brother's a cop and if anything happens to me..."

"Is there a problem here?" The voice came from behind me, so I slipped the gun back into my coat before I turned around. It was the butler, looking stern and annoyed.

"No problem, Jeeves. I was just taking my man to task for some sloppy work he did yesterday." I turned back to Ed. "Now, you finish up here and do a good job. Then get a move on. You've got four more jobs to get to today." I patted him jovially on the shoulder, and he flinched as though I still had the gun in my hand. Jeeves stood aside to let me exit the bathroom and followed me to make sure I found my way to the door.

Just in case Ed hadn't been fibbing about his brother being a cop I decided to get back to safer ground. I cut down Fell Street to the panhandle and back into the cover of the park. I kept my eyes peeled for a pay phone and didn't come across one until I was back to Stanyan. I fished in my pockets for a dime and remembered that I was out of change. I detoured a block to find a liquor store, bought a pack of Luckys and a bottle of Old Farm to break a fin, and backtracked to the phone.

The line rang. "Homicide."

"Detective Manicelli please."

"One moment." The line shuffled, clunked as it hit the counter, then rustled again as someone picked it up. "This is Manicelli."

"Hey Tony. It's your old pal who has run away from home."

"Why, hello Nick. Or should I say *Richard*?"

I grimaced. Tony was letting me know he was on to my alias, so they had found the hotel room. That meant I was out a place to stay for the night, as well as five bucks. On a brighter note, the fact that he'd tipped me off meant that he was still on my side. "Say, Tony, have you got a cop on the force with the last name of Hansen?"

"Uh, yeah, we do. Ray Hansen. Why?"

"You know him? What department is he in?"

"He's a patrolman. Has this got something to do with your, uh, situation?"

"It might. His brother is an exterminator by the name of Ed. Sprayed my office yesterday morning."

"So you got bugs."

"I don't got bugs. But he's the only person other than myself who has been in my office since this whole mess got started."

"You think he stole your gun?"

"Him or someone with him."

"And you think it might have been Hansen?"

"I dunno. Just working a lead."

"Wow. Seems like a long shot to me."

"Maybe. You got any buddies in the Health Department?"

"Not really. How come?"

"He says they were the ones who called the exterminator and sent them to my office."

"I guess I could look into it. Hey! I won't even have to lie when I say it has to do with the Chambers investigation!"

"Nice." I didn't find it as amusing as he did. "Oh, and while you're poking around the old station house, you might want to see who was camped out on my doorstep yesterday morning."

"What do you mean?"

"When I got home after finding Sanborn, there was a cop sitting across the street."

"That's no big surprise. There was an APB out on you."

"That APB went out around, what, noonish?"

I heard him going through paperwork. "Closer to one o'clock."

"I got home around 11:45, and this guy in a uniform was sitting there in a black and white."

"What makes you think he was looking for you?"

"He chased me about a quarter mile down Stockton Street."

Tony was quiet a moment. I'd have bet ten bucks he was rubbing his chin. "It has to be unrelated."

"Maybe. Or maybe someone was already expecting that APB to come down the line."

"You get the car number?"

"Yeah. Car 29."

"Well, if he was sent out there officially..." His tone changed suddenly. My guess was that someone else had entered the room. "Well thank you for your information, sir. Please give me another call if you have anything else." He hung up.

I didn't think Tony would have the call traced, but I faded into the foliage just in case. There was still some daylight left, but I couldn't think of anything constructive to do with it. I walked to the area down the street from the hotel. Sure enough, there was a fairly obvious car sitting across the street, its driver watching the door. I ducked into an alley and retreated back into the park.

I felt frustrated and helpless. There didn't seem to be anything else I could do until the funeral in the morning. I started scouting for a place that might provide a bit more shelter from the wind than I had the night before. I found a spot where a stand of pine trees had woven themselves together, and the ever-present juniper shrubs had nestled up against them, forming a hollow. I dropped to my hands and knees and crawled into it. A scattering of litter told me I wasn't the first to bed down there. I was pretty tired and it felt good to set the briefcase down and get off my feet. The fog was rolling in, shrouding the trees and choking off the sun. I took the bottle of Old Farm out of its sack and cracked the seal. It was going to be another long cold night, and I wrapped the liquid blanket around me as tightly as I could.

Biloxi, Mississippi was as hot and humid as the Devil's breath. Basic training made the place even hotter, and the going joke was that after six weeks under Sergeant Dixon Malone, seeing some action overseas was going to seem like a vacation. The mosquitoes were relentless, apparently trying to suck us dry before we could even finish the fox hole we were digging for grenade practice. Three of us dropped into the hole before the dust had a chance to settle and were straining to hear what Malone was bellowing at us.

"Red platoon, ready grenades!"

We glanced at each other, uneasily. I hated grenades. Guns I understood. You pointed them, pulled the trigger, and the bullet went where you told it to. Grenades were sloppy and dangerous. Once you pulled the pin, you knew roughly how long before they went off, but they varied wildly, some exploding before they landed, others bounced and rolled and appeared to be a dud, but you could never be sure. I had once watched a kid from Montana get tired of counting and peek up over the rim of his hole. *As if that was what the grenade had been waiting for, it went off and a piece of shrapnel had parted his hair all the way down to the skull. He got lucky, and was sent home early with a row of stitches across the top of his head.*

"Red platoon, arm grenades!"

I squeezed the lever on the metal pineapple and pulled the pin. I kept it around my ring finger in case I had to put it back in, just like they told us to. I could feel sweat trickling down the inside of my fist, making the grenade feel slippery. I reminded myself that it was just an illusion, and as long as I held firm, everything was fine. None of us looked at each other, focusing only on the deadly weight we all carried.

"Red platoon, throw your grenades!"

We all stood up, hurled our grenade as far as we could, then dropped back down into the foxhole. The idea was to do it simultaneously, and be well under cover before they blew. Our grouping wasn't too bad, and we grimaced, bracing for the explosion.

Something hit the ground at my feet, hissing. Someone was throwing the grenades back to us! I scooped it up and hurled it overhand out of the foxhole. I didn't think it had traveled very far, so I just prayed it had gone far enough.

It landed in the hole again, followed by two more. My platoon mates started screaming and we all dove to chuck the grenades out. We had barely gotten them aloft when four more came sailing over the rim of the hole. "What the fuck is this?" I screamed. Another grenade struck me square in the chest and the whole world was consumed in fire...

I sat up screaming in darkness. I felt the grenade roll from my chest into my lap. I picked it up and it bit me, so I dropped it. In the feeble moonlight, it looked wrong, like each of the bumps had opened up into a flower petal. It didn't explode, so I picked it up again.

It was a pinecone.

Another one dropped on the ground next to me with a crack. The wind had come up, and the trees were swaying to and fro, the fog blowing through them like an airborne river. I fumbled with the latches on the briefcase and opened it, feeling for the flashlight. I switched it on and looked at my watch. It was four thirty. I briefly wondered if this was really better than being in prison. If I didn't find out who had framed me, I was going to get the chance to find out.

I traded the flashlight for the bottle. My mouth tasted like the raccoon from last night had crawled into it and died. I washed him out with a bit of whisky. A second swallow started working on the cold that had once again seeped into my bones. I wiped my face dry with one of the remaining clean socks and closed up my kit. It was time to hit the road if I was going to catch the morning Greyhound to Colma.

The first few blocks through the park had been agony as my stiff joints complained about being roused from the grave. After a while, I worked most of it loose and was even starting to warm up a bit. I was still soaking wet, and wasn't sure if the sun was going to burn through the fog in time to do anything about it.

As I came down the hill toward Market Street, I must have looked and smelled just like every other drunken bum shambling around aimlessly. The shopkeepers getting their stores ready for the day didn't even look up as I walked past. Being beneath notice was an odd form of cover. I felt almost invisible. I picked up my pace and crossed Market at Van Ness.

The bus station was downtown, near the footing of the Bay Bridge. I fit right in, weaving through the other human wreckage washed up on the city's shore. Nobody bothered me for change or cigarettes. I was one of them.

The girl at the ticket window didn't even look up as I approached. "The bathroom is for customers only."

"In that case, I'd like a ticket for Colma."

Startled, she looked up. Her eyes confirmed her first appraisal, and she waited for the catch. "That's a dollar fifty."

I took out my wallet. It was getting mighty thin, but it wasn't empty yet. I paid her. Still unsure about the transaction, she filled out a ticket and handed to me. "It'll be boarding in five minutes."

"So, I have time to use the restroom?"

I could tell she wanted to refuse me, but I had crossed the line and become a paying customer. She pointed at the door. Once I got inside and saw myself in the mirror, I understood her attitude completely. My overcoat was covered in mud and forest litter. My hair looked like it usually does first thing in the morning, and I needed a shave. My eyes were red and baggy. Hardly fit for a funeral. I washed up as best I could, combed my hair and straightened my tie. There weren't any towels, so I did the best I could on my coat with toilet paper, and quickly discovered it was a lost cause. I took it off and draped it over my arm. I took another look in the mirror. I still looked like hell, but less like I slept off a hangover in someone's trash can.

The bus pulled into the station just as I was coming out. I climbed the steps like I was on my way to a stockholders meeting and went to the back and grabbed a window seat. The bus was mostly empty as it pulled out, and that was just fine with me.

Colma was twenty minutes away by car. By bus it took a bit over two hours. The bus station there was little more than a sheltered bench, and a feeling of isolation broke over me in waves as I got off the bus and it roared away to the south. The sun had come up, and the bus seat had absorbed some of the moisture from my clothes. I stretched a moment, then started walking up the road towards what passed for the town. I stopped in at the first gas station I came to and asked "Where's the cemetery?"

The guy leaning against the pump laughed. "Which one? Colma's nothing *but* cemeteries!" I told him, and he gave me directions.

Elysian Lawns wasn't the Ritz Carlton of graveyards, but poor Eleni wasn't going to suffer much. The mourners were just arriving and were gathering around the coffin propped up over the grave. I scanned the faces, wondering which one was Helen Demitrios. It could have been any of the women. I stood apart from most of the crowd. Feeling my detachment, the priest sidled up to me.

"Did you know the deceased?" He didn't have to ask to know I wasn't family.

"Not well. We used to work together."

He nodded solemnly. "Do you know his family?"

"Just Helen Demitrios. Is she here?"

The padre looked around. "I don't see Helen. I hope she arrives soon, I'd hate to start without her.... Oh, there she is now!" He wandered off to greet her. I didn't follow.

I watched as they embraced, no doubt agreeing what a tragedy it was that Eleni had been taken from the Earth so prematurely. Then the priest gestured in my general direction. Helen glanced toward me, but not *at* me. She shrugged. The priest turned and pointed directly at me. She looked right at me that time, then back to the priest and shook her head. The clergyman merely shrugged, looked at his watch, and after touching her hand, walked over to the small podium set up at the head of the grave. Helen walked a beeline right to me.

"Do I know you?" She was a striking woman, probably around forty-five, maybe less if the sadness shadowing her eyes was more than just the funeral.

"No, Mrs. Demitrios, you don't."

"Were you a friend of Eleni's?"

"Not exactly. We worked together."

Her eyes narrowed to slits. "Do you work for the monster that killed him?"

"Who, you mean Sanborn?"

She spat, and her eyes welled up. "Don't even speak his name, the filthy pig. May he rot in hell." She dabbed at her eyes with a white handkerchief. "Well, do you?"

"I did once, briefly. But don't worry, I probably hated him as much as you do." *Maybe more,* I thought.

"Did you know that he's dead? The police say that someone killed him." I nodded. She stared at the ground. "Whoever did that is my friend."

I was about to answer, but the priest thoughtlessly interrupted by beginning the service. It was the usual schpiel, ashes to ashes, dust to dust. As usual, in death we become saints, all our sins forgiven, all our foibles forgotten, all our weaknesses looked at in a new light until they become charming strengths. Helen stood by my side through the whole thing, which struck me as odd. I had expected her to detach from me and huddle with the rest of the family. In fact, even as they lowered the coffin, as the others all tossed sacred relics and handfuls of dirt into the hole, Helen didn't step forward to join them. When the service was concluded and the family held one another and wailed, she kept her respectful distance.

Once I felt it was kosher to break the silence, I said, "So I take it you aren't family?"

She frowned. "No. Eleni was good friends with my husband. When he was killed in the war, Eleni was kind to me, always watching out for me and helping me whenever I needed him. Eleni's family could never believe that we weren't romantically involved, but we weren't. They probably don't believe it even now."

I smiled. "Does it matter what they think?"

She returned the smile. "No. Not anymore."

She turned to walk toward the cemetery gates. I quickly matched pace with her. "Mrs. Demitrios, by any chance are you driving back to the city?"

She nodded. "How did you know I live in the city?"

"Doesn't everybody?"

She laughed, and it made her look nineteen again.

Helen's white Plymouth sailed up Highway 280, the tires humming on the concrete. She had undone her hair, and it played in the breeze from the open window. "So tell me about you and Eleni," she said.

I hesitated, wondering how much to tell her. I liked her, and decided she could handle it. "I have to be honest with you. I didn't really know him at all."

"What, you just like going to funerals?"

"No, I felt I owed it to him. I think I indirectly got him killed."

She blanched. "What do you mean?"

"I'm a private investigator. Jeff Sanborn hired me to find Eleni."

She slammed her foot on the brakes and car slid wildly to a stop at the side of the highway. "*Get out!*" she screamed.

"Listen, Helen. I didn't know..."

"Don't call me Helen, you murderer!"

"Sanborn lied to me. He told me that Eleni had stolen his nephew."

"And you believed that? Eleni would never do such a thing."

"I didn't know that then. I do now."

Helen started to simmer down a bit. "You didn't kill Eleni?"

"No. But I feel like I did. I led Sanborn to him. But I swear I didn't know that he was going to hurt him."

She stared at me, her eyes rimmed with tears. "Did you kill that bastard Sanborn?"

"No, but I wish I had. Not that it matters. The police think I did."

"So it was you the police were talking about. They think you killed Eleni too."

"I know that. But it's not true. And the only chance I have is to nail the bastards who did."

She wiped her eyes. "I thought Sanborn killed Eleni."

I shook my head. "I doubt he did it himself. He probably paid someone to do it."

"Why should I believe you? How do I know you didn't kill them?"

"Why would I? I still don't know why *either* of them were killed. I can think of plenty of reasons why someone would want to shoot Sanborn, but I have no idea why they were after Eleni."

"Are you going to kill me now?" She waited for my answer. She meant it.

I smiled. "I'm not a killer, no matter what the police say. But you're right. You have no way of knowing that for sure." I opened the door and slid out of the car, then closed the door and leaned in the open window. "I'm sorry if I frightened you. I'm gonna get the bastards that killed Eleni. I have to. I owe it to him. You take care of yourself. Thanks for giving me a lift."

I turned and started walking down the shoulder, my heels crunching on the gravel. I was still a long way from the city, but at least the sun was doing its best to hold the clouds at bay. Helen sat in the car behind me for quite some time, probably crying. Then she pulled out into traffic and drove past me without even glancing my way.

I'd been walking nearly fifteen minutes when I noticed the Plymouth stopped at the side of the road ahead. I maintained my pace until I reached it. I went to the passenger side window again, giving Helen the protection of having the car between us.

Helen's face was striped with mascara. "If I trust you and I'm wrong, Eleni will have died for nothing."

"If you know why they killed Eleni, you have good reason to be scared."

She hesitated a moment, studying my face. Then she motioned for me to get back in the car. I scarcely had the door closed before we were moving again. We sat in silence for a long time. She took the connecting road that carried us over to Highway 101. I left her to her thoughts.

Finally, she took a deep breath, and let it out slow. "Eleni knew what Sanborn was doing."

"Well, he did work at the warehouse."

"It's more than that. There was an accident. A crate fell off of Eleni's truck. It broke open. It was full of guns."

That raised my eyebrows. "Sanborn was running guns?" She nodded. "OK, so Eleni found out. That shouldn't be enough to have him killed."

"He went to the police."

I whistled. "That'll do it."

"I told him not to. I told him to just quit and walk away from it. But he couldn't. Poor Eleni."

My mind was racing. "That still doesn't explain why Sanborn was killed."

"I don't care why he was killed. I'm just glad he was."

"How did Sanborn find out Eleni had called the cops?"

"He believed that the police were in on it. He said he used a pay-phone and a fake name to protect himself, but somehow Sanborn found out anyway. That's why he took the book and ran away."

"What book?"

"Sanborn's book. The one he kept track of the money in."

I shut my eyes. "Stupid, stupid, stupid. Oh, Eleni, you poor bastard." I looked back up at Helen and sighed. "Sanborn would have chased Eleni down to the ends of the Earth to get that book back." I shook my head. "And so would whoever was buying the guns. Empires have crumbled because of such books. It might even explain why Sanborn got popped. If he's selling the guns to the mob, they may have decided he was unreliable. They get the book back and take Sanborn out for good measure."

"They didn't get the book back."

My jaw dropped. "What? How do you know that?"

She hesitated, terrified. She spoke again only in a whisper. "Because I have it."

I was speechless. My mouth worked, but nothing came out. I stared at Helen agape, suddenly understanding her fear, and seeing the depth of her courage. "No wonder you were scared of me."

She nodded, trembling. "If you work for them..."

"You're right. But I *don't*. Helen, if you were to give me that book, I could go after the men who killed Eleni, not to mention save my own skin. But I can't ask you to take that chance if you aren't sure. You can drop me off anywhere you want, and go straight to the airport. Actually, it's not a bad idea anyway. Go back to Greece or anywhere else in the world. They don't know you have the book yet, but if I was able to connect you to Eleni, it's only a matter of time before they do, too." She kept driving. I stared for a moment, then continued. "I'm serious. You need to get out of town."

She was tearing up again. "I told him not to bring it to me. He said he couldn't trust anyone else."

"I'm sorry, but he *did* bring it to you, and now you have it, so you're in trouble, too."

We had entered the city, driving off the highway into the Mission. "Are we close to where you live?"

"Just a few more blocks."

I hunkered down in the seat and took off my hat. "Drive past it. Don't even slow down." I started watching the parked cars.

She didn't even look over at me. After a few moments she said, "This is it on the right."

"OK, go another block or two, then take a right and circle back."

As she made the turn, it was apparent that all the cars parked on her street were empty. She turned again at the next block. About halfway up, an older woman was taking bags of groceries out of the trunk of her car. She didn't seem the assassin type to me. I sat up. "Alright, it's clear."

She pulled up to the curb in front of a new-ish apartment building and set the brake. As we started up the stairs, I said "Let me go in first." She nodded and unlocked her door. I pointed for her to stand behind me, drew my gun, and pushed the door open. When nothing happened, I peeked around. It seemed clear, so I slowly started in.

I did a quick sweep of the apartment. It was small, and decorated sparingly but with taste. After checking the closets and bathroom, I was satisfied that there was no one else there. I nodded.

"Would you like a cup of coffee?" She walked into the kitchen. "I know I would."

"That sounds great." I followed her in.

"Eleni liked his black and very strong. I couldn't stand it so thick at first, but if I put enough milk in it..."

Her composure crumbled like dry cornbread, and she started

sobbing in earnest. I stepped behind her and held her shoulders. She wheeled around into my arms and buried her head in my shoulder. I was suddenly very conscious of how filthy my coat was. "It's going to be OK," was all I could think to say.

She cried until she was done, then stood up and steeled herself again. She wiped her eyes with a dish towel and went back to making the coffee as if it had never happened. "I really do have to go away, don't I?"

"I would, if I were you."

"You think they'll come after me?"

"I'm certain of it."

She set the percolator on the stove and lit the burner with a match. "How did *you* find me?"

I pulled the picture out of my pocket and handed it to her. It was Helen, ten, maybe fifteen years ago. She looked at it and smiled. "Eleni had this?"

"Uh-huh. He was using it to mark your number in the phone book. I think he was sweet on you."

Her eyes grew sad, but her smile remained. She nodded. "I just never thought of him like *that*. He was like a little brother to me. When he went away, he asked me to go with him. I just couldn't."

"Good thing. You'd be dead, too."

She hadn't thought of that before. The smile slid off onto the floor. "Why don't *you* go away?"

I smiled. "Too much unfinished business."

She nodded. "Wait here." She left the kitchen just as the percolator started gurgling. I rummaged in the cupboards for cups and poured the coffee. I sipped at mine, and she was right about making it strong. I splashed a bit of the top of mine into the sink, and made up the difference with water from the tap. I tried it again, and it was drinkable.

I heard her rummaging in the hall closet. From the noise, she moved a lot of stuff, then put it all back. I heard the door close just before she came back into the kitchen holding a large spiral bound ledger book. She offered it to me.

"That's it?"

She nodded. "I hope I never see it again."

"Don't worry, I'll see to that."

I sat down at the kitchen table, and she followed my lead. "Do you think it'll be useful?"

"I won't know 'til I study it. The police never asked you about this?" She shook her head solemnly.

I opened the book. At first glance, it might have been any standard business ledger, shipments in, shipments out, payments in, payments out. The merchandise was detailed as if it had been on sale at Macy's, and the names on the accounts read like a who's who of the underworld.

"We've got to get you out of here."

"What, you mean right now?"

I saw the panic on her face. I smiled. "No, you can finish your coffee first. But then I want you to go pack a bag and go straight to the airport."

"Nick, I...I can't afford a plane ticket."

Somehow I knew that was coming. I checked my wallet. It was a grim sight, but I still had a bit more than two hundred dollars, enough to get her out of the country. I handed all but ten bucks to her.

"I can't take this, I hardly know you!"

"It's worth it not to have *two* deaths on my hands." She continued scowling. "Look, if it makes you feel better, you can pay me back when this is all over."

That seemed to do the trick, but she still looked troubled. "How will I know when it's safe to come home?"

I fished in my wallet for a business card. It had seen better days. I scribbled Mrs. Lazarino's phone number on the back. "Wait two weeks, then start calling this number every weekend. Don't tell her where you are. If she presses you, say you are in Budapest." I handed her the card. "Unless you actually go to Budapest."

She laughed. "No, I'll be in...."

I covered her mouth with my hand. "No! Don't tell me, either." I took my hand away, but her eyes were the size of dinner plates. "First rule of hiding; the fewer people know where you are, the safer you are."

She nodded and mustered a sad smile. "Guess I better get packing, then." She finished the last of her coffee and went back to the bedroom.

While she packed, I continued thumbing through the ledger.

There were several sections delineating the daily machinations of Sanborn's *real* business, and the numbers made the legitimate shipping he did seem like some kid's lemonade stand. Sanborn had kept a fairly large contingent of muscle, but most of the names were men I'd never heard of, which was surprising. Apparently, he'd managed to keep his business completely separate from the mob, maintaining his status as a third-party supplier of firearms, drugs, or anything else you might like brought in or out of the country unnoticed. A few of the entries even looked like passengers traveling in both directions. I imagined shipping containers decked out with posh—if cramped—accommodations. My heart skipped a beat when I came across my own name, and the amount he'd paid me to track down Eleni. I was filed under "miscellaneous expenses."

But that was nothing compared to the surprise coming when I turned the page. The next section was labeled "Kelley." Suddenly, the business didn't look so profitable, huge amounts of cash were being paid out on a regular schedule. *Payoff.* It didn't take Sherlock Holmes to deduce who Kelley was: District Attorney Richard Kelley.

I had always figured Kelley was crooked. I knew several men on the police force, good men like Tony Manicelli. Sure there were a few bad apples, but for the most part, San Francisco was a surprisingly clean town. Still, the D.A.'s office showed funny priorities, going after smaller fish, dropping the ball when taking on the big boys. Kelley was for sale. Give him enough cash, and Lady Justice could be even more blind than usual.

Helen emerged from the hallway, dragging a fairly large, heavy suitcase behind her. I closed the ledger, tucked it into my briefcase and smiled at her. "You about ready?"

"I guess so."

I carried her suitcase out to the car and put it in the trunk while she locked up the house. She met me at the driver's door. "You sure you won't go with me?" She smiled sheepishly, and it seemed to me that she might be offering much more than just travel. It took a lot for me to find the strength to tell her no. She nodded, understanding, and put her arms around me. I held her for a long time, fighting to maintain my resolve. It would have been so easy to run away to some exotic, far-away land with this sweet, lovely woman. I could see what Eleni saw in her, and that was part of why I had to stay.

"Take care of yourself, Nick."

"Heh. It's never been my *forte*."

"I wish I could send you a postcard."

"Go ahead and write 'em, then bring 'em back with you."

She slid into the car and started the engine. I stood back and returned her wave as she pulled out and drove away.

I walked down Mission, looking for a phone and a cheap bite to eat. I picked up a tamale from a cart, and found a graffiti-scrawled payphone near 18th.

"Homicide."

"Detective Manicelli, please."

"I'm sorry ma'am, I'm afraid you've got the wrong department." I was about to protest until I realized that it was Tony that had answered the phone. "You want the Municipal Railroad office, on Powell Street. Anytime after 8:00." He hung up.

So Tony wanted to meet in person. Whatever he'd found must have been weighing on him pretty heavy for him to justify risking his career.

It was coming up on six, so I had time to kill. I continued down Mission, working on the tamale while I walked. Soon, I reached the Empire Hotel, Eleni's last address. The irony of staying there proved too strong for me to ignore. I figured the police would have been finished with Eleni's room, and could hardly expect me to have the *cojones* to berth there. I went in and paid my three dollars to sleep in a bed for a change.

My room was on the floor above Eleni's old dive, but comparable on décor, or rather, the lack thereof. The bed was lumpy and the springs squeaked, but I felt safe from raccoons and falling pinecones. I leaned back to stretch out for a moment. The next thing I knew it was dark outside.

It was 7:30. I threw on my coat and hurried out to the street, taking my briefcase with me, just in case I was wrong about the cops circling back. I knew I couldn't leave Tony hanging out on the street for very long, so I hustled to the bus stop and grabbed the first one heading anywhere near downtown. It got me as far as Market, so I transferred to a trolley to get down to Powell. The Municipal Railway office was halfway to Union Square, getting close to my office. Oddly enough, I felt a bit homesick for my old rat hole.

I stopped in front of the Railway office. Naturally, they were closed, but there were still plenty of people going about their business in the street. None of them looked like Tony. My watch said it was 8:25 and I started to think I'd missed him. Then, a voice behind me said, "Took you long enough."

I turned around. Tony was leaning against the wall, nearly invisible in the shadows except for the dot of red at the end of his cigarette.

"Hey, Tony."

"Hey, Nick."

"You want to go somewhere?"

He emerged into the light and started up the hill. I fell in step beside him. He was the first to break the silence. "Sorry to have pushed you off like that."

"You had company?"

"Oh brother, did I have company. The D.A. himself."

"Let me guess. He's on fire to get his hands on me."

"He's madder than a wet hornet."

He turned left on Sutter and ducked into a bar called the Red Owl. I'd seen it before, but hadn't been in. My usual watering hole was a lot closer to home. We grabbed a table in the back. The place wasn't slammed, but had enough general conversation that someone would have had to sit in our laps to listen in. Tony told me to take a seat, then went up to the bar for drinks. I was relieved, since I was nearly flat. He came back and handed me a scotch and soda. I ignored the soda.

"Looks like you were right about Hansen. He was out in car 29 that morning."

I grunted. "What about the health department?"

"Nobody there has any record of placing that call."

"What a surprise."

"There's more. The exterminator got hit by a truck this morning."

I'd known that slip about his brother being a cop was going to cost him. "Dead?"

"No, just in the hospital."

"Can he talk?"

"Not a peep. His jaw is wired shut. Busted in three places."

"I'm sure that was the idea."

Tony leaned back in his chair. "So how do you think Ray fits in to all this?"

"What would you say if I told you that he was the shooter?"

"Before today, I'd have said you were off your rocker. He's got a reputation as a good cop."

"It gets better. I think he did it on orders directly from William Kelley."

"Oh, man. You have proof?"

I glanced down at the briefcase. "Nothing good enough for court yet, but I'm working on it."

Tony whistled. "Jesus, Nick. You gotta be sure about this."

"Oh, I'm sure, alright. Sanborn was a gun-runner for the mob. He was paying Kelley about six grand a week to look the other way."

"So what happened? Sanborn stop paying?"

"Eleni Patroklos happened. He found out about the guns and went to the cops. Somehow, Kelley got wind of it, probably through Hansen. They let Sanborn know he had a leak, and he had his boys take out Patroklos. But not until after he'd been able to steal the books and stash them."

"So he took out Sanborn to protect himself. How did you figure this out?"

"I've got the books."

He laughed. "I don't know how you do it...." He chuckled again. "So what do we do next?"

Hearing him say we made me feel like there was a chance of getting out of this after all. "The books alone mean squat. I'm gonna need something better than that to take Kelley down. Do you think you can try and pin when Patroklos called the cops and prove that Hansen pulled the call out of the system?"

"I don't know. I can try. What are you going to do?"

"What I've been doing for years. I'm going to make Kelley so nervous that he trips and falls."

Tony reached into his pocket. "Maybe this will help." He pulled out a photo of a cop, and I recognized the face immediately. "This is Ray Hansen. When we canvassed the area around the warehouse and your office, we were looking for you. It never occurred to us to ask if there had been cops around."

I took the picture and stared into Hansen's eyes. His face was clean-cut and friendly, but I knew as well as anyone that you couldn't put any stock in that. "You think I can move around down there without getting nabbed?"

"Depends on how careful you are. You're still wanted, but the crime scene is pretty well buttoned up. I'd take it myself, but Hansen would get wind of it, pronto." He looked me over. "How are you holding up for cash?"

I shrugged. "I won't be staying at the Ritz anytime soon."

"Yeah, I figured." He pulled out his wallet and handed me $200.00. I was far too practical to turn it down.

"Thanks, Tony. I don't know when I can pay you back."

Tony kicked back the last of his drink and set the glass down on the table like an exclamation point. "If you're right about Hansen and Kelley, you already have."

The Empire Hotel hadn't been much better than sleeping in the park. The hookers had a good night, and the creaking of bedsprings was nearly as constant as grasshoppers on a summer evening. Around three some kind of fight broke out in the hall. After what seemed like an hour, the clerk finally came upstairs and broke it up, mostly by out-shouting the combatants. I'd tried to make the most of lying on a bed even though it wasn't much softer than the dirt had been. Overall, the only advantage it had over sleeping outside was that I woke up relatively warm and dry.

I didn't hurry through my morning routine. I didn't have a clearly defined plan of action yet, so I took my time using my three dollars worth of tepid water in the tub. I had the forethought to wash my shirt in the sink before going to bed, and it was waiting for me where I had hung it over the radiator, toasty and dry. Shaving felt pretty good too, but as I was doing my neck I nicked the point of my adam's apple. The blood made me think back on the sight of Sanborn slumped in his chair, his neck blown wide open.

I'd never been in a situation like that. I knew who the killer was. I knew how and why it happened. But I was absolute stymied about how to get proof. I laid back on the bed, listening to the sounds of the street filtering in through the window. Bill Kelley was one of the most powerful men in the city. He was rich, educated, untouchable. He walked the high road, where I walked the low road. On my best days it would have been hard for me to even get him on the phone. As it was, if I got anywhere near him the only road I'd be walking would lead straight to the electric chair.

But Kelley was dealing in low business. He hired people like Ed and Ray Hansen to take care of his dirty work for him, carrying him on their backs so his feet would never touch the filthy ground. It seemed to me that if they fell, so did Kelley. Despite the risk, I headed down the road toward the bay.

I hated canvassing, but it was the kind of work I seemed to do most. Most people are reluctant to answer questions from a stranger, and I couldn't blame them. Still, after pounding the pavement for the whole morning and the better part of the afternoon, I hit pay dirt. It turned out that Ray Hansen had a thing for a good kielbasa, and there was a place on the Embarcadero that claimed to have the best in town. Hansen came in for lunch on the last Tuesday of each month. Marco, the owner, took it as a matter of professional pride that one of San Francisco's finest made his sausage part of his routine. What Marco didn't know was that his shop was two doors down from Pier 20, and that the last Tuesday of each month was when Hansen made his rounds to pick up the money from Sanborn. Then I thought of another place the photo might set people talking. I took the long walk toward home.

Gino looked up at me as I came in and took a stool at the bar. "You not in jail yet?"

I smiled. "Not yet. But they're still trying."

He set a gin and tonic on the bar in front of me. "You think it's safe for you to come back here?"

One sip of the drink told me that Gino wasn't being *too* charitable, he'd used the cheap stuff and was heavy-handed with the tonic. I raised an eyebrow at him and he just shrugged as if to say *what do you want for free?* I took out the picture of Ray Hansen and set it on the bar. "You ever see this guy around here?"

"Sure. He's the cop who chased you down the stairs like a hunting dog." He smiled, his wrinkled face twisting until his eyes nearly vanished. "He's also the cop that was hanging out with the man who came to spray your office for bugs."

I nearly spat out my drink. "You saw them together?"

"I see everything."

"Would you be willing to testify to that in court?"

"No. I don't like court. Smells like desperation. Wai testify. He saw them, too."

"That's great!" It was the first piece of evidence that would put both Hansens in my office. Now I just needed a way to use it. "Gino, let's say you want to talk to somebody. Somebody who probably wants to do you a lot of harm. Where could you meet so that you'd be safe from them, but that didn't give them such a disadvantage that they wouldn't go there?"

He looked at me very carefully for what seemed like ages, clearly weighing something, probably my trustworthiness. "You don't want to hurt him?"

"No, just talk."

"But you don't want him to arrest you."

"For starters. This man is a killer."

He nodded solemnly. "You want Li Po."

"What, the bar in Chinatown?"

He nodded again, and something about his expression made it abundantly clear that he wasn't joking. "You know of the Tong, yes?"

"Yeah, the Chinese Mafia, right?"

"Hmph. Such a vulgar way to put it. They are far more ancient than the Italians, their ways are much more complex. However, though they would lead outsiders to believe they act as a single unit, as with many such organizations, there are often disputes between internal factions."

"Yeah, like when the guy who controls the Eastside starts movin' in on the Westside's territory. Just like the Mafia." I smiled, and Gino scowled at me. I realized I shouldn't push him too far if I wanted him to continue. I bowed elaborately. He merely waved it away and went on.

"When such conflicts get so heated that they must be resolved or blood will be spilled, the warring parties go to Li Po."

"You gotta be kidding. They just belly up to the bar and hash it out over drinks? What if they aren't able to reach an agreement and decide that spilling blood is just fine?"

Gino shook his head. "There is a room in back. There is only one door in. There are no windows. All who enter must be completely unarmed."

I raised my fists. "Nobody is ever completely unarmed."

"There are men like my son Wai. *Big* men. They are not unarmed. One stands behind every man at the table. No one is even allowed to raise their voice."

I thought it over for a minute. "So the guys at Li Po act as referees for Tong fights?"

"They facilitate peaceful resolution of conflicts."

I smiled. "They should branch out! I bet there are a lot of married couples who could use an arrangement like that!"

Gino smiled. "It would make the world a better place." The smile faded, and he was deadly serious again. "But as you can imagine, this room is not used for such trivial battles. To be allowed to enter requires a referral." He ducked behind the bar and came up with a sheet of rough, cream colored paper with ragged edges. He set it on the bar and started writing on it with a bamboo brush which he occasionally dipped in a small pot of foul-smelling ink. He flicked at the paper, making elaborate Chinese characters with well practiced strokes. I watched, fascinated with the surety with which he placed each line, rolling the tip of the brush to bring the end of each stroke into a razor sharp point. When he stopped, he blew on the ink until it was dry, and rolled the parchment into a scroll and tied it with a length of twine. He handed it to me. "You must tell them that Qin Huo sends his respect and admiration." He said it, "*Sheen Hwo.*" It was the first time I'd ever heard his proper Chinese name.

I took the scroll and bowed my head slightly. "Thanks, Gino—I mean, *Sheen Hwo.*" He smiled, pleased with my pronunciation, and I felt closer to the old man than I had in all the years I'd been living over him.

By the time I left Gino's it had started to drizzle, just enough to get me damp again, not enough to wash the mud off my coat. I knew a bar on Sutter that had a phone booth inside, but someone had beaten me to it. From watching her eyes I could see she was with the guy currently being dragged all over the pool table by a wiry guy with deep set eyes and a beak like an eagle's. I sat at the bar and nursed a beer until the eight ball went down. It didn't take long. The sore loser dragged his date out of the bar, scowling the whole way. The guy who held the table looked up at me as I approached, thinking I might be a challenger, but I fell out of his universe completely when I slid into the phone booth.

The phone rang several times, and I was just about to hang up figuring that Tony wasn't home yet when he finally picked it up.

"Hello?" He sounded out of breath.

"It's Nick. I hope I'm not interrupting anything."

"I just walked in the door."

"Well, I've had a banner day. Officer Hansen wasn't too concerned about keeping a low profile."

"Yeah, well he's a cop. Who's gonna question a cop?"

"I am. You got anything more for me?"

"Do I? I went over the phone logs with a fine-toothed comb. There was one anonymous tip that something illegal was going on at Pier 20, just about a week before Sanborn got snuffed."

I glanced over at the pool table. The guy had found another sucker and was already cleaning the table like he could do it in his sleep. "That's it?"

"Yeah. But I can guess why. The very next day, Officer Hansen twisted his ankle playing softball. They put him on the front desk until he could walk again."

"Which was when?"

"His first day back in a car was the day your office was sprayed."

The eight ball slammed into a corner pocket. The pool player shook his victim's hand, which had never held a cue. Money was exchanged, and the loser walked away. The winner scanned the bar hungrily for another taker, trying hard to mask how pleased he was. I knew exactly how he felt.

Chinatown dances to a different rhythm at night. She works hard during the day, shouting and jostling, hurrying through the frantic pace demanded by commerce. By sunset, she's weary but still restless, and changes into her party clothes. Decked out in neon and candles, she lowers her voice and speaks in seductive whispers.

Don't be fooled, commerce is still her partner, but it's an entirely different sort of dance.

The entrance to Li Po looks like a cave, or maybe a wine cellar. I opened the heavy wooden door and descended the red painted steps. Even though it was night, my eyes had to adjust to the darkness inside. Once they did, it was as though that door had somehow magically opened into Shanghai. As with any bar, the shelves were crowded with bottles, but these were mostly ceramic jugs hand-painted in gold, red, and black with characters that were probably simple brand names, but refused to divulge even such mundane secrets to me.

The clientele were exclusively Chinese, and they all looked up at me as I came in, wondering what I was doing there. The chatter didn't stop, but it slowed and quieted. The bartender extracted himself from a conversation at the far end of the bar and met me at the near end. "What can I get you?" He was already preparing a place for me at the bar, keeping me as close to the door as possible. I took the stool offered.

"Ng Ka Py." Gino had told me what to order when I arrived. I had no idea what I was in for. It surprised the bartender, and apparently most of the other customers as well, as the bar fell mostly silent. With an odd smile, the bartender selected what looked like a brown vase from the shelf and wiped the dust off of the top with a rag. He poured a shot's worth into a small teacup and sat it in front of me. It was dark red and cloudy, like oxidized blood.

All eyes were on me, and I silently wished Gino had warned me that it was going to be such a big deal. I raised my glass to my audience, and tipped it back.

Ng Ka Py was half mustard gas, half turpentine, and half sugar. They didn't combine into one flavor, but washed over me in waves. First came the aroma, like the most noxious medicine in the nightmares of children. If I hadn't already been committed, I'd have called the whole thing off before it even crossed my lips. The smell was obliterated in the wave of burning that followed as it hit my mouth. One time I'd eaten a whole habanero pepper on a dare from a supposed friend. This was worse. Then the turpentine kicked in, washing the burn away along with most of the skin in my mouth. Then angels descended from heaven and were moved to put me out of my

misery by drowning me in honey. The pain was gone, taking with it
the front half of my brain.

I realized I was still holding the empty cup in front of me, so I
delicately sat it on the bar. All eyes were still on me, so I did the only
thing I could do. I croaked, "Another, please."

The whole bar erupted in laughter, and everyone went back to
their conversations. The bartender refilled my cup, this time even
closer to the rim than before. "You like that, eh?"

I attempted a smile. "I've never had anything like it in my life."
He capped the bottle, confident that I wouldn't be going for thirds,
and returned it to its hallowed place on the shelf. While his back was
turned I said, "Qin Huo sends his respect and admiration."

He turned around, his eyebrows trying to climb up into his hair.
"You are a friend of Qin Huo?"

I nodded. "I've known him for years." I reached into my coat and
retrieved the scroll. "He said to give this to you."

He unrolled the paper and scanned it. He looked back up at me,
scowling, then read the paper again. He shouted over his shoulder
in Chinese, and one of the men at the bar stood and walked over.
The bartender handed him the parchment, and they both shouted at
each other while he read it. He scowled at me too, and said "This is
for *you*?"

"It is."

They argued some more, then apparently came to some agreement. The bartender continued muttering, but went back to his conversation. The other man said "Come with me" and started walking
toward the back of the bar. I slammed the rest of my *Ng Ka Py* and
followed him.

The negotiations lasted long into the night. The main sticking
point had been that Hansen was a cop. They didn't like the idea of
doing business with the police, they felt it might make others less
confident in using their service. I managed to convince them that
despite the badge, Ray Hansen was no cop, and that if everything
went the way it should, he wouldn't be in a position to tell anyone
about the meeting room for very long.

In the end, I sold them, and then we spent the next hour haggling about the fee. Usually, when disagreeing parties go to Li Po to settle their differences, huge sums of money are involved. The price for using the room is negotiated based on the value of the conflict. In my case, there was no money involved at all, merely the avenging of an unjust death and the removal of corrupt city officials. It wouldn't be the first time that a matter of settling a score over a killing had been brought to Li Po, but there was no way around the fact that neither party involved had the ability to cough up much dough. In the end, as a favor to Qin Huo (and because it was all I had), they agreed to settle for $200 up front. It cleaned me out, and I wouldn't have even been able to pay that much if Tony hadn't fortified my wallet.

When I finally laid my head on what passed for a pillow at the Empire Hotel, my mind was boiling like a tea kettle. I had to convince Ray Hansen to meet me at Li Po tomorrow at midnight. If I failed, or even if he said he'd be there and didn't show, I lost my appointment, the $200, and the chance to talk to Hansen safely. Some part of my brain kept rehearsing all night long, and I finally drifted off around 6:30. Which wouldn't have been so bad if checkout time hadn't been at eleven.

Hunger doesn't just affect the stomach. When I haven't eaten in a long time, my mind gets fuzzy. I needed to think more clearly than ever, but there wasn't anything I could do about it. I thought of all the people I could borrow a bit of cash from, but it doesn't take long to compose an empty list. I was just going to have to tough it out. It wasn't the first time, but that offered little comfort.

What I did have plenty of was time. Ray Hansen was on shift until six. It was looking like I had nothing to do until I could try calling him at home after that. That left me with a long gray day to kill, with little to take my mind off the horrific sounds my stomach was making.

The thought of food stayed with me as I walked aimlessly through the Mission. For lack of anything better, I was heading towards Twin Peaks. If I had to kill time, it seemed to me that I might as well do it somewhere with a view. At Valencia the smell of hot chorizo sizzling on a grill slapped me square in the chops, setting me drooling. If there was one thing I shared with Officer Hansen, it was love of a good sausage....

Like I said, I wasn't thinking clearly, otherwise I'd have realized sooner that it was the last Tuesday of the month. Jeffrey Sanborn might have been dead, but that was only one of the reasons that Hansen went to Pier 20 on a regular basis. I was betting that he was the kind of man who held on to well-worn habits.

I changed course and headed down Dolores, trying to throw together a plan while I walked. An idea hit me when I came across a small cemetery near the church. I walked through, and when I thought no one was looking, I lifted a fairly impressive spray of flowers off of a recent grave and skedaddled.

Time was against me. I had no idea when Hansen ate lunch, and I didn't even have a dime for a bus. I walked as fast as I could, trying to keep the briefcase from battering the flowers too much. I took every alley and cut every vacant lot I could to straighten my path, stopping only at an isolated pay phone to check it for dial tone and make a note of the number. By the time I got to Marko's Cable Car Diner, my calves were burning and my feet felt like I was standing on a griddle.

I dug out a business card and wrote on the back of it: *Sorry about Ed. Call me. PA7-2600.* I swapped it for the note previously stuck in the flowers and carried it up to the front counter. Marko remembered me from before. "Hey! It's the detective! How's it goin'?" He eyed the flowers. "Those aren't for me, are they?"

"I'm afraid not. Hey, you remember that cop I asked you about? The one who likes your kielbasa so much?"

"Yeah, what about him?"

"His brother got hit by a truck. Could you give these to him when he comes in?"

He glanced up at the clock. "You can give them to him yourself when he comes in. He should be here any minute."

"I wish I could, but I have to go. Thanks a lot!"

I dashed away, leaving the flowers on the counter, ignoring Marko's protestations until the door closed them off behind me.

The phone booth I'd chosen was just a few blocks away, far enough off the beaten path that I was safe from being spotted. I sat down on the curb and waited. A few minutes later, a guy that looked like he could have pulled a plow stepped up, digging in his pocket for change. I lept to my feet. "Sorry, buddy, I'm waiting for a call."

He towered over me and knew it. "I'll just be a second."

I shook my head. "My call's *important*."

He opened his mouth, no doubt to explain to me how few tears he'd shed if I missed my call. But then he noticed why I was holding my jacket pocket open. One glance at my gat and he hurried off to find another phone.

As the minutes ticked by, I began realizing what a shot in the dark the flowers were. Hansen might have quit eating at Marko's the moment his reason to go down there kicked. He might have decided to go on a diet and give up sausage altogether. I reminded myself that I didn't have anything better to do, and if he didn't call, I still had his home number to try that evening. It was a chilly day, with just enough breeze to force the cold into your clothes. I clung to the fact that it wasn't raining and continued to wait.

Ray either ate late or really slow, but the phone rang at 1:15. I leapt to my feet and answered it. "Hello, Officer Hansen."

"Who is this?"

"You've got my card." Apparently he hadn't thought to flip it over and read the other side.

"What do you want?"

"We need to talk, Ray."

"We got nothin' to talk about."

I kept my voice soothing, like I was talking to an upset child. "I think we do. You're mixed up in some nasty business, Ray. Killing Sanborn, for starters."

He chuckled. "The way I hear it, *you* killed Sanborn."

"You tried to set it up so people would think that. Unfortunately, you're a messy boy. I've been very busy cleaning up after you."

He breathed into the phone for a moment, then finally mustered, "I got no idea what you're talkin' about."

"I believe you, Ray. That's why I'd like to explain it all to you."

"Why?"

"Because I think you're headed for a bum rap. The way I figure it, taking out Sanborn counts as community service. Especially when you were only doing it for your boss. And what an ungrateful bastard *he* turned out to be! Poor, poor Ed."

"What do you mean? You leave my brother out of this!"

I knew I had him. "I'd like to, Ray. Too bad Kelley didn't see it that way. I don't think he deserved to get busted up like that."

He was seething, his breath fast and heavy into the mouthpiece. "You don't know what you're talkin' about."

"There's only one way to find out. You know of a bar in Chinatown called Li Po?"

"I've heard of it."

"Yeah? What have you heard?"

"Enough to know that a round-eye like you can't get anything but a drink there."

"You're wrong. I have a reservation for a quiet, safe place for you and I to have a little chat."

"When?"

"Tonight at midnight."

I could practically hear his mental clockwork grinding away. "How do I know it ain't a trap?"

"If you know about Li Po, you know it *can't* be a trap. For either of us."

He chewed on it a bit more. "OK, I'll be there. But I swear, Chambers, if you try anything, I'll..."

I hung up. It was hard not to do a somersault right there on the sidewalk. It had gone better than I'd hoped, and I'd even gotten Hansen to pay for the call.

I arrived at Li Po at 11:25, wanting to be sure that I was well ahead of Hansen. The bartender—a different guy than the last time—noticed me the moment I came in, and immediately called out in Chinese. Mr. Lao, the manager I'd made the arrangements with, came out from the back room, wiping his mouth with a napkin. "Ah, Mr. Chambers. You're early."

"I can come back if that's a problem."

"No problem at all. Right this way."

He led me into the back, only this time we didn't go up the narrow stairs to the office. He knocked twice on a door nearly invisible in shadow. When it opened, Lao gestured for me to go first. I did, and found myself in a mud room of sorts. It was dimly lit, and a young Chinese girl helped me with my coat and hat.

Mr. Lao tapped twice on the inner door. It opened and a man built like a Sherman tank stepped into the room. "This is Mr. Jang. If you have anything forbidden, he will hold them for you until your meeting is over."

I handed over my gun, then held out my arms as Jang started patting me down. He was very thorough, no touch too intimate to risk missing a hidden knife or zip gun. Despite his size and attention to detail, he was surprisingly gentle, and somehow respectful. He was used to patting down people that probably counted as royalty around here. Once he finished, he went through my briefcase with the same attention. He wasn't interested in anything that couldn't be used like a weapon. In the end, he confiscated my flashlight, penknife, and handcuffs, closed the briefcase, and handed it back to me. He then stood back and nodded at Lao, who smiled. "You may now enter."

Jang opened the door for me and stood aside like a sentry. I stepped through the door into splendor. The meeting room was decorated like a Chinese palace. Rich tapestries and elegant watercolors adorned the walls. A huge teak table with inlays of dragons dominated the center of the room, with no less than sixteen silk uphol stered chairs around it. Gino had been right about there being no windows or doors other than the one I had come in through. The girl directed me to a seat at the center of the table, and Mr. Jang took up his station standing motionless behind me.

The girl smiled demurely at me and said, "Would you care for refreshments? Something to eat or drink while you wait?"

I shrugged. "I'd love something, but I'm afraid I gave your boss my last cent." She nodded and left the room.

After a moment, she returned with an elaborate silver tea service, set it on the table, and poured me a cup. I thanked her with a nod and she left. She returned a moment later with a small plate of meatballs covered in a vivid red sauce. The plate was standard kitchenware, not up to the grandeur of the rest of the setting. I figured it wasn't part of the package that came with the room, but purely a gesture of hospitality. She smiled as she set it in front of me, then hurried away. I couldn't tell what kind of meat the balls were made of, and I didn't much care. The sauce was spicy and sour, and I devoured them quickly. It wasn't a large meal, but it felt like a feast.

I was still sucking the last drops of sauce off my fingers when the girl appeared to take the plate away. I was beginning to feel that her timing was always too perfect to be accidental. There might have been no visible windows in the room, but I'd have bet my teeth that one of the tapestries concealed a way to watch or listen to the proceedings in it.

No one needed a secret listening post to hear the commotion coming in from the antechamber. Even through the closed door I could clearly hear several men shouting at the top of their lungs. Eventually the shouting stopped, and the door opened. Ray Hansen stormed angrily into the room, his face flushed and his clothes disheveled. The girl reappeared to lead Hansen to the seat opposite mine on the far side of the table. Jang's counterpart, every bit as large and imposing, followed Ray in and came to a stop standing behind him.

Hansen spat, "You didn't tell me they were perverts." The human mountain standing behind him showed no sign of hearing or caring.

I smiled. "Was there anything for them to find?" I may have been mistaken, but I thought I saw the corner of the mountain's mouth twitch slightly upward. Hansen, on the other hand, just turned a darker red.

"This was your idea, Chambers. Don't waste my time."

"Time is the one thing you have plenty of, Ray. You're looking at a lot of it. Assuming you don't get the chair."

"You brought me here to threaten me? You're stupider than I thought."

"Not to threaten. To deal."

He barked. "What could you possibly have that I want?"

"Right now, I'm the only person in the world who can prove beyond reasonable doubt that you killed Jeff Sanborn."

"Bullshit."

"Like I said on the phone, you're sloppy. A bright eight-year-old could have followed your trail."

Hansen leapt to his feet, and the mountain put him back in his chair with a single hand on his shoulder. He struggled a moment, eventually realized how futile it was, then relaxed, holding his hands up in a gesture of compliance. The mountain released him and resumed his eternal, silent stance.

I continued. "The biggest mistake you made was in trying to pick me up before the APB went out. A lot of people saw you and will be happy to say so in court."

"So I had a hunch."

"The same people saw you go into my building with your brother. That gives you access to my gun."

"Bullshit. There was nobody there."

"Nobody *you* saw. There's also people who can put you at Pier 20 when Sanborn was killed."

"You're making this shit up."

"And I've got Sanborn's secret ledger." Hansen's mouth dropped open, but nothing came out, so I kept talking. "He kept very detailed notes about how much he paid Kelley, and when you stopped by to pick it up."

He finally got his mouth working again. "I don't believe you."

I put the briefcase on the table and opened it, then glanced over my shoulder. "Mr. Jang, I'm going to show Mr. Hansen something he's going to want to take from me. Your pal there will see that he doesn't, yes?" Jang merely looked up at his partner, who nodded firmly, without moving otherwise. That done, I took the book out, opened it to the appropriate page, and held it up for Hansen to see.

He glanced over his shoulder. The mountain hadn't moved, but somehow we could both feel that he was a tightly coiled spring. Hansen then leaned forward—gently—and squinted at it. "Son of a bitch. I heard that Patrakula guy took it."

"*Patroklos*. And he *did* take it. He buried it in a field, and I found his map."

Hansen's bluster was gone. "Well, fuck me running." He ran his fingers through his hair. "So what do you want?"

"I want you to go ahead with your plan." He stared at me like I'd been speaking Chinese myself. "Look, you guys wanted to kill Sanborn and pin it on some schmuck. Trouble is, you picked the wrong schmuck."

"I don't get it."

"It's simple. You guys say someone killed Sanborn with my gun. Well, that's true. I say someone stole my gun from my office. That's also true. You and I know that both people were *you*. You want to say it's somebody else? That's no skin off my nose as long as that somebody isn't me."

A smile slowly broke across Hansen's face. "You just wanna get off?"

I nodded. "Well, that and I want fifteen thousand dollars for the inconvenience you two have caused me."

The smile collapsed. "You think you can blackmail Bill Kelley?" I shrugged. He just shook his head. "Mister, you are in *way* over your head."

"Maybe, but I'm not alone. If I get picked up for killing Sanborn, I play all my cards." I tapped the ledger. "*All* my cards. If you and Bill would rather take the heat yourself, that's fine with me. If you want to make it worth my while, I could leave it up to you to arrange your own substitute. Either way, I walk."

"Bill's not gonna like it."

I shrugged again. "You tell Bill that if he wants to play ball, I'll turn over my gun in exchange for the cash."

"What do we need the gun for?"

I slapped my forehead. "Come on, Ray, you're a cop."

The light came on. *Murder weapon.* I nodded like a proud parent, and he scowled. "What about the book?"

"You get the book once the charges against me have been dropped and somebody else is convicted."

He chewed on it. "OK, let's say he goes for it. You and I meet somewhere and make the swap?"

"No. I make the swap with Kelley, face to face."

"He won't do that. What's to stop you from popping him?"

"If I kill Kelley, there's no way I get out of the Sanborn charges. And if you kill me, my safe full of juicy tidbits gets put into key hands. Either of us flinches, we both lose. If we keep cool heads, everybody wins."

He nodded. "How do we get ahold of you?"

"You don't. I'll call you tomorrow. Where're you gonna be at noon?"

"I'm off. I'll be at home."

"Oh, one other thing. How much cash have you got on you?"

His face started turning red again. "What?"

"Hey, you got me into this. I've been sleeping on the ground." He took out his wallet, pulled out about sixty bucks and pushed it across the table to me. I smiled. "Thanks. Well, I'll talk to you tomorrow, then."

Any doubts of eavesdropping were erased when Mr. Lao chose that moment to enter the room. "Gentlemen, is your business concluded? I hope an agreement was reached?"

I nodded. "We have reached an understanding."

"Excellent. Since Mr. Chambers is the paying client for this meeting, he shall be the first to leave. Mr. Hansen, we will ask you to remain here for twenty minutes." Hansen started to protest, but Lao stopped him with a single finger. "For your inconvenience, refreshments will be provided at no charge."

We shook hands. "Thanks for everything. May I recommend that Mr. Hansen try the *Ng Ka Py?*" Lao smiled the most subtle yet undeniably wicked smile I have ever seen.

The infusion of cash was like manna from heaven, buying me the first solid dinner I'd had in ages, and a room at a flophouse in the tenderloin. I slept like the dead, hauling myself out into daylight just in time to look for a payphone. I stopped at one after another, finding each dead, the handset missing, or surrounded by low-lifes using it as their private office. I walked most of the way to Van Ness before I found one I could use, and it made me a bit nervous being close to such a high-traffic area. I dialed the number ten minutes late.

"Yes?" Hansen sounded nervous, even in his own home.

"Are we on?"

"Yeah. You know where Alamo Square Park is?"

I had to think about it a moment, but I placed it, just off of Fulton. It was on top of a hill, with clear visibility of the blocks around it, yet one would be able to scope it out fairly well from a distance without being seen until you wanted to approach. It was a good choice, too good for Hansen to have come up with it. "Yeah, that works for me. When?"

"You made me meet you at midnight last night. Now it's your turn to stay up late."

I smiled. I was nearly always up 'til at least midnight. "I guess that's fair. Remember; just you and Kelley. No one else."

"Right."

"And if anything happens to me, and I mean *anything,* everything I have comes out into the light of day."

The line went dead. I hung up to get a dial tone and dialed another number.

"*Chronicle.*"

"Can I speak to Chet Lawson please?"

"You got him. Who's this?"

"It's Nick Chambers. How'd you like to be in on the ground floor of the biggest story of the year?"

"Hot damn! You're already hot news. Is it true that you killed Jeffrey Sanborn?"

I chuckled. "Always the reporter. You don't get anything *that* easy."

"It never is with you, Chambers. What do you want?"

"I want you to hold something for me. If I don't call you back tomorrow morning, it's yours. If I do, you don't touch it until I come and get it. Got it?"

He hesitated. "What is it?"

"Nope. That's against the rules. You don't peek. But either way, there's a scoop in it for you. Think you can trust me on this?"

He'd trusted me before, and my leads had paid off about half the time. "You say this one's big?"

"Bigger than your dreams."

"When can you drop it off?"

"That's the catch. I can't go anywhere near you without getting picked up. I need you to come get it."

He grumbled, but I could hear him wriggling into his coat. "Where and when?"

I had Chet meet me at the payphone I'd called him from. He pulled up about fifteen minutes later, just after I hung up from talking to Tony. I slid into his car before he came to a full stop. "You know where Alamo Square Park is?"

"Uh, not really."

I scowled at him. "I thought reporters were supposed to know the city. Just drive and I'll direct you...."

I still had hours to wait, but a park was as good a place to spend them as anywhere else, and it would allow me to make sure Kelley didn't sneak anyone in before I got there. I made small talk with Chet to fend off his unending questions, locked my briefcase and set it on the seat as I got out of the car.

"Hey! It's locked! How do I get into it?"

"If you don't hear from me by noon tomorrow, just pry it open with a screwdriver." I closed the door and he drove off. I figured that if he was worth his salt as a reporter, he'd have the locks jimmied open within ten minutes of getting the case back to the office.

The day had been warm enough, but once the sun went down the temperature plummeted, par for the course in San Francisco. Some of the locals began to notice me hanging around, but they figured me for a bum and ignored me.

By 10:00 the park had lost its charm. I'd spent hours contemplating the elaborately painted Victorians surrounding the square, enjoyed the sliver of downtown you could see from the crest of the hill, and explored every bush and blade of grass the park had to offer. By eleven, I was almost as bored as I was cold. I kept wishing I'd thought to pick up a bottle of something to keep me warm.

Even as the bells of a nearby church were tolling midnight, I spotted two figures walking up the grassy hill from Steiner Street, one of them carrying a briefcase. I recognized them both from their silhouettes. I did one last scan around the perimeter as they climbed towards me, and couldn't see anyone lurking nearby. Kelley and Hansen reached the top and stopped a yard in front of me. Hansen was out of breath, Kelley looked as clean and pressed as if he'd just started his day.

"You've got some balls on you, Chambers." Kelley seemed amused. "This is better than I would have expected of you."

I grinned right back at him. "If you were worth impressing, it wouldn't have gone this far."

He ignored the barb. "I'm also surprised at you. Somehow I got the idea that you had principles."

"What would you know about principles?"

"Principles are my stock and trade, Nick. I buy and sell them wholesale. I didn't know you were in the market."

"I'm not. This is a one-time thing."

He smiled, knowingly. "So you're willing to let someone else take the rap for you—just this one time?"

"It's not *my* rap!" I snapped at him. "You set me up."

His smile got wider, pleased that he'd rattled me. "But you're still willing to let someone else go to jail for something they didn't do."

"Yeah, well, better him than me. We gonna talk ethics all night or have you got my money?"

Kelley nodded to Hansen, who held the briefcase out to me. I took it, laid it on the ground and flipped the latches open. It was packed full of cash, and I flipped the ends of a couple of bundles to make sure they were all real. They were.

"Satisfied?" Kelley smirked, even in defeat.

I closed the briefcase and stood back up. "Yeah. I'll count it later, but it looks about right." I reached into my coat and drew my gun. His eyes suddenly wild, Hansen's hand darted into his jacket and came out with his.

"Relax, Ray, you'll blow a gasket." I scowled at him like he was a misbehaving child and handed the gun to him butt first. It broke my heart to part with it, partially because it was one of the only valuable things I owned, but also because if there was a double cross coming, I'd just opened the door. Ray flipped the cylinder open to see if it was loaded and five brass eyes winked back at him. He put his piece back and covered me with my own gun instead.

Kelley nodded approval. "That's a pretty gun, Nick. Very elegant."

"It gets people's attention."

Hansen scowled. "It shoots for shit, though."

I glared at him pointedly. "*You* did well enough with it." He squirmed. Apparently he wasn't comfortable hearing it said out loud.

"Isn't that right, Bill? Ol' Ray here's a crack shot, even with a snub nose."

Kelley was silent. Hansen fidgeted. "What are you getting at?"

"Oh, come on, Ray, think about it. There's a mountain of evidence already on the table. Once I'm ruled out as a suspect, your buddies in Homicide are going to go over it all again. And it all points to one person."

Kelley kept his voice level and soothing. "Don't listen to him, Ray. He's just trying to get your goat."

"Yeah, Ray, don't pay any attention to me. I'm sure ol' Bill here has got your best interests in mind. Just like he did with your brother."

Kelley cut me off. "*That* was unfortunate." He turned to Hansen. "But you know as well as I do that he brought it on himself. If he hadn't opened his mouth, Mr. Chambers here would already be in prison."

"Maybe," I said, "but that still doesn't change the facts. The evidence can only point to one of two people, him or me."

Hansen thought about it a moment, then nodded. "Yeah, and I don't see you handing *me* a suitcase full of cash."

Kelley's façade of cool was showing cracks. "Come on, Ray. Do you really think I'd let you take the fall for this?"

"Rather than take it yourself? Yeah, I do."

"What are you trying to do, Chambers?" Kelley was getting angry.

"I'm just trying to give Officer Hansen here a clue about what's coming his way."

"You think I'm stupid. Both of you do." He turned the gun on Kelley. "I'm nobody's patsy, Bill."

Kelly tried not to look at the gun, but failed. "Ray, think about it. With me on your side, you're *untouchable*. But if you shoot me, you're buying a one-way ticket to the chair."

"I'm not going to shoot you, Bill." He gestured towards me with my gun. "*He is*." He took aim at Kelley's breastbone and fired. Kelley cried out and crumpled backwards. Even before he hit the ground, Hansen had whipped his own gun out of his coat and was pointing it at my chest. Shots came ringing out of the darkness behind me. Several rounds hit Hansen square in the chest, spinning him around in a spray of blood. He hit the ground hard, shuddered once, and then was still.

Tony and two other men came pounding from their hiding places in the shrubs. They covered Hansen until one of them kneeled down and checked his pulse at the neck. He shook his head. They then rushed to Kelley, who was moaning and clutching his chest.

"Rob, get an ambulance." Rob ran down the hill to the car to radio for help.

Stating the obvious, the other cop said, "He's alive."

"Of course he's alive." I said. "I had target rounds in my gun."

Tony's mouth dropped open. "You what?"

"Real cartridge, real slug, no powder. They look like normal bullets, but they've only got the force of the primer."

The guy holding Kelley's head said, "Yeah? Then how come he's bleeding?"

"That was damned near point blank. I bet he's feeling it, but he'll live." I leaned over Kelley. "I figured they'd probably be digging them out of *me*. If I had known your lap dog was going to turn on you, I'd have used the real thing."

Tony glared at me. "You could have told me."

"I didn't want you to think I wasn't in danger."

"I told you this was a stupid idea."

"You didn't have a better one."

Tony looked up at the moon. High clouds drifted past it like a veil. Then he reached into his coat and came out with handcuffs.

"That really necessary?"

He nodded. I turned around and put my arms behind me. He ratcheted the cuffs on, put a hand on my shoulder, and led me down the hill.

I sat in my cell, trying to ignore the aroma of sweat and urine coming from the mattress. The wino in the next cell was muttering to himself under his breath, occasionally breaking into shouts whenever the demons in his head got too close. All in all, it reminded me a lot of the Empire Hotel. The difference was you could leave the Empire, where I'd been sitting here for three days.

I heard the locks on the main door clatter open, and Tony came in looking like the poster boy for clean cops. He stuck his hand between the bars. "Hey, Nick."

"Tony." I got up to shake, then dropped back to the cot.

"How you doin'?"

"Been better. How's Kelley?"

"Those target rounds of yours have more kick than you thought. Chipped his sternum and came within a quarter inch of his heart."

"You mean there's scientific proof he has one?"

A grin flashed across Tony's face, but it didn't stick. "He had to drop the murder charges against you, but he's pushing ahead with an obstruction of justice rap. It's practically a done deal."

"How long am I looking at?"

"Somewhere around six weeks."

I shrugged. "He's always been a sore loser."

Tony nodded. "Speaking of which, he's not going to be making your life any easier once you get out. Or mine."

"What else is new?"

"Your reporter friend published the entire contents of your brief-case. Apparently he transcribed everything before he handed it over to us."

I smiled. "Imagine that."

"The governor has launched an investigation into Kelly's deal-ings."

"It won't stick. Everything I found that pointed to him could be explained just as easily by Hansen working alone."

Tony scowled. "Yeah, that's the case Kelley's building. He says that Hansen was lying to Sanborn about collecting for him."

"Has he come up with a reason why Hansen would do that?"

"Naturally. If he said the D.A. was involved, Sanborn would be more intimidated than if he was just a rogue cop shaking him down."

I had to laugh. "How convenient for him that they're both dead."

"You're not."

"Yeah, but if there's any doubt about the ledger, there's no proof he's connected. My testimony won't mean a thing. He'll just have to clean up his act until the investigation is over, then it'll be back to business as usual."

"Maybe. I'd like to think that because of all this, people are going to be watching him more closely."

I stood up and came closer to the bars. "Hey, I never got a chance to thank you for that night at the park. If you guys hadn't been there, I'd be dead."

"I still say it was a stupid idea. I don't know how you made me believe that Kelley would just make the deal and walk away. I really wanted to bring them both in. Instead, they got away."

I laughed. "I don't know that I'd call three slugs in the chest get-ting away."

Tony shook his head. "It's not what I wanted." He stepped over to the door and rapped on it twice with a knuckle. Cliffie the guard peeked in through the small window, then unlocked it. Tony hesitated on the threshold and looked back at me. "Hey, Nick. Do you think we ever really make a difference?"

I thought about it a second. "I dunno. Most times, I don't think so."

"Think we should quit trying?"

I chuckled. "You got something better to do?"

He shook his head, smiling sadly, and pulled the door closed behind him.

THE SMILING MAN

Keoni Chavez

Your name is Nick Chambers. You're a private eye. You sit in your office, choking down the remains of your lunch: something red on something white that the guy at the deli across the street called pastrami on rye. It isn't very good, but it's food of a sort, and you've long ago stopped promising yourself never to eat there again. It isn't very good, but it's familiar; it's something you can count on.

Someone knocks at the door, startling you so badly that you spill your bottle of warm beer into your lap. You shove the chair back and yell out, "Come in, Goddammit! Door's open!" You sop up the foam with some important papers as the office door opens and a man walks in.

The man is dark-haired and slender, and appears tall in the office, though his eyes are level with yours without his having to stoop. His clothes are somewhat severely cut, with plenty of sharp creases in all the right places. He seems to bring in an air of importance, of some kind of presence. He seems new somehow. He looks vibrant and alive. You decide that he must be from out of town.

"Had an accident, Mr. Chambers?" The man's voice is languid and smooth, like a radio actor's. Somehow, you had known that it would be.

"Yeah, you could say that," you mutter. "I'm not used to getting visitors up here." You finish wiping off your front and sit back down, trying to muster up some kind of professionalism. "What can I do for you, Mister..." you trail off, indicating 'fill in the blank' to the man across the desk.

"My name is Derek Halcyon, Mr. Chambers. I'd prefer you to call me Derek, if you would. I'm looking for someone who seems to be missing. I think you're the right man for the job. You are a missing persons man, aren't you, Mr. Chambers?"

"I'm a lot of things, Mr. Halcyon. That's an unusual name, by the way. Halcyon. Where's it from?"

"It's Greek," he says, pleased. "From the mythical Halcyon bird. Stories say that the Halcyon was a gigantic creature which would only lay its eggs upon the surface of the ocean. To keep the surface smooth, it would beat its tremendous wings to calm the turbulence, thus ensuring a successful lay. Hence the word comes to us today, halcyon, meaning placid and tranquil. I'm rather fond of the name. I like to think that it fits me well." He smiles, an odd bending of his lips that seems to require no muscular movement.

You know the name must be a cover. The way the man presented his little story was well rehearsed, and doubtless told a hundred times. Living in San Francisco, you meet many people who've changed their names, as though ashamed of their given ones. Not that you cast judgment; you let no one know what your real first name is. But you never take pride in your name either; you dislike calling attention to yourself.

"Well, if you want someone found, I can do it for you, no problem. Been missing long?" You indicate the chair opposite him.

"Years, Mr. Chambers. It's been so long that I don't know whether we'd recognize each other anymore." Halcyon sits down, removes several photographs from an inner pocket of his jacket, and hands them to you. "We may both be two completely different people now. And please, call me Derek."

You look the photos over. Each one is shot with exquisite focus, every object as sharp as its neighbor. Like Halcyon, there seems a vibrancy to each shot, almost as if you're looking through a tiny window, even though the pictures are black and white. Here is the inside of a well-appointed study, walls lined with shelves of books and the furniture of a dark wood. Dominating the shot, a white male, presumably the missing party. You search the face, attempting to memorize significant details. A broad forehead, somewhat thin eyebrows above dark eyes crinkled in a smile. A nose of no particular feature. And a smiling mouth, merely two lips opened over white teeth. All in all, a face that might belong in any crowd, with a possible exception: this man looked happy. That in itself is remarkable to you. You can't remember when you'd seen happiness on any face in this city. Pleasure, yes. Delighted avarice, usually. Once, even sadistic gloating. But never true happiness.

"When were these taken?" You look up and watch a wistful expression pass over Halcyon's face as you ask.

"Different times, Mr. Chambers. Different times." Halcyon banished the expression with another of his effortless smiles.

You glance at the other photographs. An outdoor scene, the smiling man talking with a pair of children in a park. Another indoor picture, of the man wrestling with a large Golden Retriever on the floor of what might have been the same room as the first shot. And finally, a tight focus of the smiling man with his arm around the shoulders of Derek Halcyon, the both of them grinning broadly, as though sharing a private joke.

"Well, I've never seen this guy before, Mr. Halcyon, but I'll run down some of my local contacts anyway. Somebody might know something. I'll get started right away." You start to return the photos, but Halcyon waves them back.

"You hold on to them, Mr. Chambers. I trust you will keep them safe. You may need them later." He rises from his seat and hands you a slip of paper with a phone number written upon it in a grand, flowing script. "You may reach me there if you have a need to call. Ask for Derek; all my friends call me that." He reaches forward to shake your hand.

"There's still the matter of the fee and expenses," you say, ignoring the hand, still sitting behind your desk. Halcyon appears almost surprised for a second, then reaches again inside his jacket. He hands you a plain white envelope. Upon examining the contents, you give an impressed whistle. It looks like you'll be able to pay the rent for this month. And last month. And the next.

"That ought to do for a while, Mr. Chambers. If you have need of anything more, please feel free to give me a call. Don't worry, I trust you. You simply have that sort of face, I suppose," he chuckles.

"Instantly trustworthy. I look forward to hearing from you. Good hunting." Halcyon gives a sharp little half-salute then leaves the office, closing the door silently behind him.

It isn't until much later that you realize that you hadn't asked for the missing man's name. You decide that it isn't important. A happy face in a city like this would shine out like a beacon.

As you hit the street, you regard the sky. It's a leaden color, which suggests that when it rains, it'll rain nails. There were skies like that in Europe, but those rained something else, and it wasn't flowers.

You speculate upon Derek Halcyon as you walk, running him through your mind. His insistence on your using his first name was irritating. It was as though he'd expected nothing less from a total stranger. Definitely new to the city, you think. This is not a place where you regularly meet someone's eye; people go about their business here. You like that. It makes you the one asking the questions, and you like that even more. Things here are dependable. When you walk down the street, there are no surprises hiding around the next corner. No one lying in ambush. It's all familiar and controllable. And you like that the best of all.

You begin your search at Gino's, hitting up your usual informants and shooting the breeze with the old Chinese barman. None of the regulars recognize the man in the photos, though Gino himself has an unusual reaction to the shot of Halcyon.

"Look sneaky," he says. "Got big secrets. Don't trust this guy," he asserts, tapping the photo with a yellowed fingernail.

You shrug. "I don't trust anyone, including you. But the ones with the secrets pay the best, Gino. Don't worry 'bout me."

The barman grins. "Not worried about you. Worried about the other guy. You bad company," he barks a laugh, his eyes disappearing into his seamed face. He looks again at the photo. "Not good to be friends with big sneak. His secrets become your secrets, then maybe you go missing." Gino walks off to attend another customer, cackling. You don't see the humor. It's obvious to you that Halcyon has secrets, but who doesn't? You're not getting paid to look into

Halcyon's life anyway. You spill some change onto the bar top and leave.

The rest of the day finds you trawling along the regular avenues of inquiry: the Wharf; the low-rent housing south of Market Street; other watering holes, but to no avail. No one's seen the guy in the pictures, nor recognized his beaming face. In a bit of a snit, you take the photos to Father Connolly at St. Mary's Cathedral. The elder priest had helped you before, during your short-lived stint as janitor for the church a few years back.

"No, Nicholas, I can't rightly say that I've ever seen this man before," he says in his thick Irish brogue. "Though...there is something slightly familiar about his face...." Father Connolly sits down on the front pew before the nave.

You sit across from him on the steps, feeling a little interest come back into you for the first time today. "If you can ID this mook, padre, I'd be obliged."

The priest furrows his brow, trying to remember. "You know, I'd have to say that this lad's got a definite Slavic cast to his features, wouldn't you, Nick? Reminds me of a fellow I went to seminary with years ago....it's the forehead which puts me in mind, 'tis. And the shape of his eyes." He turns the photo he's been studying around to face you. You lean forward to look again.

Father Connolly begins to ramble a story, reminiscing aloud about the good old days, as usual, and you supply encouraging noises at the right spots, but you're not really listening. When you hear Slavic, you think Russian. And that brings up all manner of unpleasant associations. But damn it, Connolly was right; there is something there that you find familiar as well, now that it's been mentioned. The shape of the head, perhaps? The set of the jaw? The eyes say nothing. It's a poetic fantasy that you can read a man's soul through his eyes. You learned that in World War II. Emotions come from everywhere else: the drawn-down mouth, as it weeps or screams; the flared nostrils, smelling death creep closer; the curdled brow as the mind tries to understand why it's being forced to experience all of this. And other signs: the sharp relief of knuckles strangling the stock of a rifle. The waxy sheen to a sweating neck. The jumping throat.

A touch, and you nearly jump out of your skin. Father Connolly's hand is on yours, his face concerned. "My word, lad! Are you all right, now? I'd swear you were a million miles away!" You look back down to the photo in your hand and it's just a picture again. It has stopped being a window to the past. You nod, and stand.

"I'll see if I can connect some dots," you say, shaking the priest's hand. "Thanks for the tip." The older man smiles and blesses you as you leave. You accept it with the same nonchalance that you do when someone blesses your sneeze.

You make your way back to the office, thinking disconnected thoughts about God and happiness. Once inside, you give Halcyon's number a call. A sweet female voice answers. You ask for Mr. Halcyon and the voice says, "Oh, Derek? Hold on, please." There's a click, a pause, and the radio actor's voice comes through the line. "Mr. Chambers! May I assume that this is good news?"

"Not yet. I need to ask you about your friend's ethnicity. Did he, excuse me, does he have any Russian blood in him, maybe?"

"Well, you know, he's never mentioned it before, though I suppose one could draw that conclusion. Why, yes, it seems rather obvious now you mention it." Again comes the warm chuckle. "It's funny the things you don't know about a person, though you may have known them for most of your life. Isn't that so, Mr. Chambers? I imagine you associate with a rather interesting assortment of characters in your line of work, hmm? Perhaps you don't know them as well as you ought?" Halcyon seems amused at the thought that you may not be as on top of everything as you like to put out.

"I know what I need to, when I need to," you reply, a little stung. "And what is it that you do for a living, Mr. Halcyon?"

"I wish you would call me Derek. We needn't be so adversarial." You can sense that he's dying to call you Nick, but he's too polite to ask for the familiarity, and you won't allow it. "Well, I'm in travel, Mr. Chambers, continental and abroad."

"Really? Business lately can't be good, what with the recent unpleasantness overseas, Mr. Halcyon." You try to match his socialite purr, but can't quite keep the sarcasm from leaking through. "Good enough for a hefty advance on my fee, though. With a promise for more, as I recall. Something I should know?"

A slight pause from the other end. "I have had plenty of time to set up my affairs with an eye toward the future, Mr. Chambers." A slight note of irritation has seeped into his resonant voice. "You may drop your suspicions. And if your retainer displeases you, I'm sure we can work something out."

"No, it's enough, Mr. Halcyon," you say, a bit too hurriedly. "I can live on this. I'll let you get back to whatever it was you were doing. I'll call again when I have more for you." You hang up before he can answer.

A little hint of something untoward there, regarding money. You wonder what it is Derek Halcyon really does for a living. If he does anything.

A lifetime of hiding your given name has left you without contacts among the Russian section of San Francisco. In fact, you can only think of one person who may be able to help you, though it fills you with apprehension to think of asking her. It's a long shot, but with no other leads, perhaps it's time you visited your mother.

Things have been strained between the two of you since you returned from the War. The horrors you saw there made you unable to completely get along with the woman who raised you, who'd never known such things. Once you'd gotten back to the United States, you'd worked your way across a stunned and cringing country, trying desperately to return to some kind of normalcy. Some reliable pattern of working, eating, and sleeping without the constant fear of losing your life in a moment of inattention. But when you ended up in California, with no more country left, you decided that it was far enough from Europe to attempt a life.

In a moment of feeling dutiful, you called your parents in Maine to tell them you were alive after all, and doing well. Then you'd learned that your father had passed away. Your mother never said that it was from worry over you, but she hinted at it enough for you to know that at least in her mind, it was. And so, feeling guilty, you convinced her to come to San Francisco and stay with you.

And now you make the journey up to Greenwich Street, to the apartment you left to your mother, after it became clear that your father had left an absence too big for the two of you to fill. You knock, even though after all this time you still have the keys to the front door.

The door opens and your mother stands there, surprised to see you on the step. "Nikolai! Hello, I didn't expect you! You didn't call. Come, come inside." She tries to be warm, but even her awkwardly-accented English doesn't hide the fact that she's somewhat shaken by your sudden appearance. You don't take it personally, though once you might have.

The door closes behind you, you embrace stiffly, then move into the living room. Nothing of what you'd originally brought to the apartment remains, replaced by lace and bright rugs, ornate furniture and dried flower arrangements. The room smells like aged linen. You mother sits in an overstuffed orange chair and you sit on the couch to her right. It sighs as you settle into it. There is a table in front of you that you feel like resting your feet upon.

After a small silence, she offers you tea, which you refuse. You pretend to look at the decorations as you try to think of a way to broach the subject. "The place looks nice, Ma," you offer, but she shakes her head and says, "Tell me why you've come, Nikolai. Something bad has happened, yes? You want money." And that's how bad things have become between the two of you.

You strangle the first words that come to mind, and merely reply, "No, Ma, I just need your help with this thing I'm working on, OK? I want you to look at some pictures." You reach into your pocket for the photos and pretend not to notice the look of relief which passes over your mother's face. Sometimes you still wonder if there's any way to reconcile your differences, but mostly you don't care anymore. Whatever life there was died with your father.

You hand the photos to her. "Tell me if you recognize anyone in these."

She takes the photos from you and puts on a pair of reading glasses she's taken from a pocket of her blouse. You don't expect that she will be able to identify any of the faces; Russian Hill is not so small that she could know everyone. You start to think about what your next move will be as she leafs through the pictures. You think about going to Gino's to play a little pool for a while. You think about asking help from the cops. You think about snooping around Halcyon's place.

"I don't know who this is in the picture with you, Nikolai."

You stop thinking. "What?"

She lays the picture down on the table so you can see. "Who is your friend here? He is very handsome." She points her finger at Derek Halcyon, with his arm around the smiling man. And with a jolt you realize who the smiling man is.

"His name is Derek," you say to her. Your mother is exclaiming over the other photos, but you're thinking of the things Halcyon had said. You are a missing persons man, aren't you, Mr. Chambers? And everything that followed. You're thinking of Gino's advice. You're trying to remember the last time you were truly happy.

Somehow, you're outside, wandering around Russian Hill and trying to make sense of what's happened. You still don't recognize the smiling man in the photos, but you know unquestionably who it is. He had a face only a mother could once have loved. But a face unmarked by fear. Unscarred by self-loathing and survivor's guilt. A face that could not be a part of this gray and tired world. But where else? From what world had the photos come? Could it ever have been your face?

And you are suddenly filled with rage: at Halcyon, for bringing something unexpected and unwanted and new to your world; at your mother, for recognizing in the photos the son she wishes you were; at your life, for not allowing you to become that smiling man. And as suddenly, the anger subsides, and you're in control again, and you know what you will tell Halcyon.

Once back at your office, you call Halcyon's number and this time he answers himself. "Mr. Chambers," he purrs in his smug, self-satisfied voice. "Have you anything new to tell me?"

"Yeah. I found the guy you're looking for. But he's dead."

Silence on the line without even the hiss of static. This was a good connection.

"Did you get that, Mr. Halcyon? He's dead now, and has been for a long time. I'm sorry if that's not what you were expecting, but sometimes life's just full of little surprises."

You hear his long, indrawn breath, then he speaks while he sighs. "Well, then, there's no need for me to trouble you any longer, is there? You may, of course, keep your retainer. I don't begrudge you that. I suppose I'll have to look for help elsewhere."

"You don't listen so good, Derek. I said the guy's not around any-more, OK? He's deceased! Pushin' up daisies! What don't you get about this?" The anger is back and it feels good, like a warm bath after being out in the cold.

"Mister Chambers, when one has been in the travel business long enough, as I have, one eventually comes to realize a few important things: everything takes longer than you expect, anything lost can be found, and most importantly, there is always another road. Thank you for your assistance." He hangs up, and you're left with a dead line.

Your name is Nick Chambers. You're a private eye. You sit in your office, watching night fall on your city, thinking about your life. It isn't very good, but it's familiar; it's something you can count on.

ABRAMELIN'S DAUGHTER

John R. Mabry

I was getting my ass solidly kicked by a marsupial from Tonga when she walked in the door. She moved like a cat through the smoky haze of Gino's gin joint, hesitant, with an arch in her back that promised a quick retreat at the first sign of trouble. In contrast to the sea of seedy patrons numbing themselves to blind inevitability, she had grace, style, youth, and, more dangerously in a place like this, money. She wore the kind of hat only rich dames can get away with, swept up in the back, with feathers stuck in it. She looked as out of place as a nun in a whorehouse, and she swept up to the bar like a drowning man riding a wave to a lifeboat.

I felt a sharp blow across my shoulders. "Your turn, goose-man," the marsupial barked, threatening me with his pool cue, but I noticed that he, too, was unable to remove his gaze from the young woman at the bar. The Tongan was not to be put off, all the same. His face was beet-red from drink and his belly distended like he had something to hide. I expected a baby or a kangaroo to rip through his shirt at any moment.

Normally I'm not stupid enough to play for money, but the unfortunate combination of gin and debt to the Tongan had persuaded me to take up his offer of double-or-nothing. I was facing five balls on the table, and he only the eight-ball. I was weighing the benefits of arsenic over the pummeling that would be dished out by the marsupial's pack. Despair was just settling in when the beatific vision floated into hell, and all my thoughts of suicide flew out the window.

"Screw the game," I hissed, lining up a shot out of the corner of my eye while I studied her. She hadn't come here to drink, that was for sure. She waited for Gino to finish up with another customer, and looked around the room with a disapproving scowl. Fear had given way to disgust, and I watched her test the bar with her white gloved finger before setting her purse on it.

I unconsciously lined up my next shot, watching as Gino leaned over the bar to hear her over the din of the juke box. Gino nodded and pointed through the spider-web wisps that formed the bar's atmosphere—directly at me. She shot him a questioning glance and her lips formed the unmistakable words, "Are you sure?" Gino nodded and pointed at me again, then he turned his back on her to tend to his bar.

I fired off another shot and stood up straight to meet her as she wound her way through the grimy tables to where the Tongan and I were locked in billiardal combat. The marsupial looked down at the pool table for the first time since he laid his evil eyes on her and in an enraged bellow shouted "Fuck me!"

This stopped the dame up short, unsure whether this was an expletive or a command. Unsure myself, I surveyed the table. "Holy shit, wombat-ass, I think I just settled our score." I shot him a grin that in lesser company might have landed me in a ward at SF General. Thank God for distractions, I thought to myself, as the object of my inattention drew near enough to be heard.

"Are you Inspector Chambers?" she asked hesitantly.

"No, lady, inspectors are real cops. I'm a private dick. That's a lot lower on the totem pole and higher on the pay scale. And the name's Nick, but you got the right guy. You in trouble?"

"You could say that," she said, looking down. "Um...is there a place where we could talk...." She shot a glance at the marsupial. "...in private?"

The Tongan slapped his cue to the slate and sneered at me, "You got off easy this time, white-demon-dog." He then toppled tables, chairs, and patrons in a beeline to the bar until Gino's mammoth son Wai blocked his path. He then ambled more amiably to the bar for a refill.

I motioned the dame to follow, and headed for the stairs at the back of the bar. A shrill whistle caught my attention, and I whirled to see Gino holding up a bottle of gin. I waved him off, as I still had half a bottle to get through on my desk, and continued up the stairs with the dame in tow.

I turned on the valve to the radiator as we entered my office and closed the door behind my client. It was a bone-cold San Francisco night, and the radiator banged like a pair of newlyweds as I swept the pile of papers and flakes from the ceiling to one side on my desk. The dame hovered in the middle of the room, unable to find a chair suitable for her ladyship. I dusted off one in the corner that had more of its original fabric than the others and motioned her to sit. I then selected two of the cleaner coffee cups and poured a couple of fingers of gin in each.

"Well, Miss...." I handed her one of the cups. "This would probably be easier if I knew what to call you."

"Liecester. Rachel Liecester." She looked disapprovingly into the cup and set it to one side, flaring her nostrils.

"What can I do for you, Miss Lester?"

In the space of a second, all of her stuffiness sank to her feet. In its place was genuine, heart-felt grief. "Mr. Chambers, I'm so...I'm so angry. And embarrassed. I don't know where to start."

"Start anywhere you want. I've got all night." I sniffed at my gin and gave her my best concerned look. Encouraged, she screwed up her face, fought back a tear, and started in.

"My father is...was Richard Liecester. I always loved my father, until...until he died, and I found out the kind of monster he really is...I mean, was."

"Did your father die recently?"

"Yes. A month ago." She looked up at me and then away to the window. "It was an accident."

"Tell me about it. What happened?"

"I was on my way back home from Stanford, where I go to school. I keep a small apartment on Columbus, but I thought I would stop at Daddy's house to say hi on the way."

"Are your parents divorced?"

"No, Momma's been dead for several years. I'm an orphan now." This brought a flood of tears. She couldn't have been more than eighteen or nineteen, tops; an orphan, indeed. I drank half of my gin and waited for her to get a grip on herself. The radiator had stopped banging, but there were still ice crystals on the leftover roast beef sandwich on the bookshelf. Or maybe that was mold. It was halfway across the room, and my eyesight isn't what it used to be.

She removed a handkerchief from her purse and I kicked myself for not offering her a tissue. Then I kicked myself for not having tissues to offer in the first place. Kicking myself is one of my primary skills.

"I stopped by his house. The door was open, so I just walked in. I wanted to surprise him, so I didn't call for him. Instead I snuck around, and that's when I saw it."

"Saw what?"

"The room." If voices had colors, hers would have been black as midnight. "His 'workshop.' Momma and I were forbidden to enter it, for as long as I can remember. I was always a good girl, Mr. Chambers. I never did. Besides, it was always locked. He told me...." Tears of rage were forcing their way out of her eyes now. "He always told me he was working for the government. Some secret project for the war effort. I always believed him. That room stole half of my father's life away from me. He was always holed up in there, from the time I was a teenager. And I thought he was some kind of hero. Bastard!"

This revelation brought on a new bout of crying. I poured myself another couple of fingers and waited it out.

"It was the first time I had ever seen the door to that room open. I guess he thought it was safe with no prying females around. I was still planning on surprising him, when I stepped in, and, and...." She struggled to master her anger. "Do you know what was in that room, Mr. Chambers, besides his corpse?"

I sat up straight and leaned over my desk toward her.

"It was some kind of temple, w-with black drapes and weird symbols all over the floor. There was a cage of rats in a corner, that he—god knows what he did with them, sacrificed them, maybe. He was a Satanist, God damn him—God damn his evil black soul to hell!" There was no stopping the tears or anger now, they flooded out with every syllable. "All during my growing up, I lost my father to the Devil, and now—I've lost him for good!" A floor lamp cast her shadow long over the wall and ceiling, turning her rocking and sobbing into a puppet show featuring the tentative advance of a dark and looming spider.

"And he was dead when you found him?"

She looked down and nodded. "Do you know what that is like, Mr. Chambers? To find out that the man you most love in the whole world has been lying to you all along? Do you have any idea of the magnitude of betrayal that I feel?"

I had to admit I didn't. I've seen some pretty fucked up things in my day, but her story was indeed remarkable. "I don't see where I come in, yet," I mentioned.

She nodded again and blew her nose. Then she spoke as if in a trance. "I just stood there in that evil place, feeling a spirit of oppressiveness descend upon me. I stared at his corpse for what seemed like an eternity, pouring into it all of my rage and disappointment. Pouring from my eyes. His cold, black heart...." She must have realized that she'd stopped making sense. She shook her head like a dog after a bath and continued. "The first thing I did was call the police. Then I went back for a better look at the place that stole my father from me. I found a cabinet full of diaries in my father's hand. I put them in a cardboard box and carried them to my car. That's when the cops arrived. I gave them my statement, and then...and then, Mr. Chambers, I'm ashamed to say, I went home and got drunk."

"Good girl," I said.

"Excuse me?" She looked up at me curtly.

"I mean, it was a good thing you called the cops right away. They don't like to be left out of anybody's reindeer games." I steepled my hands and thought for a moment. "Why did you remove the books?"

"I'm not exactly sure. It was instinctual. I guess some part of me figured that all the time he didn't spend with me was recorded in them. At the time, I wanted to take them home and burn them. But I couldn't do it. I put the box under my bed instead. I haven't touched them since."

"Did you tell the police about them?"

"No. No, I didn't." She looked at me, uncertain. "Did I do something wrong?"

"Well, they would say you did. But if you had, you might never have seen those books again. They'd be evidence, in case it turned into a criminal case. I'd say you did the right thing."

"That's comforting. Thank you."

"Miss Lester, I sympathize with you, but I still don't see where I fit into the picture."

"I'm getting to that." She stood and walked to the window, unconsciously pulling her fur coat tighter around her neck. She stared at the city lights as she spoke. "My father apparently had a number of cronies. They called themselves the Lodge of the Hawk and Serpent. They're all ghastly men."

"You've met them?"

She whirled in response, "No, of course not!"

I leaned back and gave her a quizzical look that begged her to explain. She opened her purse and withdrew several pieces of notepaper. "I've been getting these." She threw them on my desk.

I picked up the first of the short stack and smoothed it out.

> *Dear Miss Leicester,*
>
> *We, the members of the fraternal Lodge of the Hawk and Serpent, wish you every condolence on the occasion of your father's untimely death. Please know that he was a beloved and esteemed member of the occult community, and we shall miss him dearly. Unfortunately, when he died, your father was engaged in some very important magickal workings, which, for the good of all mortal souls, should not remain incomplete. If you would be so kind as to bequeath to us his magickal diaries we shall see to it that his work, which was of great importance to him, is finished in due and proper order. We know you would want to honor your father's legacy, and we patiently await your answer. Please also know that if there is anything that the fraternity can do for you, we are at your disposal. Your father was a wise lodge-master, and the debt we owe him we now owe to you.*
>
> *Sincerely, the undersigned members of the Lodge of the Hawk and Serpent.*

There were several signatures, some of which contained numbers, and none of which seemed a proper name. There was, however, an address.

"Very cordial," I said. "They seem to have held a higher opinion of your father than you do."

"Go on," she said darkly.

The next scrap of paper was written in the same hand, but was much more brief.

Dear Miss Leicester,

We are very disturbed to have not had a reply from you, and the time is growing short. It is of utmost import that certain rituals be performed and that right quick. We need your father's diaries, and are willing to pay. Please contact us ASAP.

Frater Heronimous

I turned to the next note, which was scrawled in a much different hand, with many ink stains.

Rachel,

We need the diaries now. We are not to be dallied with nor ignored. Do not underestimate our power. You will be very sorry if you do not cooperate.

HONOR THY FATHER

Lucis 42

"Now we're getting somewhere," I said with satisfaction, beaming up at her.

Anger flashed on her face. "Do you think this is some kind of game, Mr. Chambers? I'm being threatened by Satanists, and you think it's amusing?"

"No." The smile left my face like the feigned and fleeting innocence of a whore. "No, it's a terrible situation. What I mean is, I finally understand what it is you want me to do. You want me to find these creeps and make them leave you alone. And you couldn't go to the police because of the little matter of removing evidence from an accident scene."

"Yes," she said, and turned again to the window.

"Have they done anything besides sending you threatening notes?"

"I'm...I'm afraid to say."

"What do you mean?"

"I've been having nightmares, Mr. Chambers. Terrible nightmares. I wake up screaming and then can't remember a thing. I'm afraid to go to sleep at night. I'm just not myself these days."

"And you think these dreams, that they're some kind of attack?"

"I do."

I poured myself another gin and bit at my lower lip. Anyone who found a parent dead, and in such macabre surroundings, would have nightmares, but I didn't want to argue with her about it. The poor broad had been through enough already.

"I get fifty bucks a day, plus expenses."

"Then you'll take it?"

I nodded, "Yeah. I'll pay these jokers a visit and get them off of your back. No sweat. I'll start tomorrow. Can I keep these?" I raised the stack of notes.

She nodded. "I'm very grateful, Mr. Chambers. I can't tell you how upsetting this has been."

"Just write down your address and phone number, and I'll be in touch." She quickly wrote down her contact info and straightened her hat. "Good night," she said, and walked out, her high heels echoing in the hallway as she retreated.

I walked to the window and lit a cigarette. The night roiled like inky, poisonous tendrils, threatening to extinguish every last tiny, vulnerable dot of light.

Morning broke, but you could hardly tell. The fog was thicker than cream cheese. And not that fancy, whipped cream cheese, but the real, thick thing. My head felt equally mired in the dregs of last night's gin. Nothing a stiff cup of coffee and a pack of butts couldn't correct. I started on my fourth cigarette of the morning as I climbed another hill.

God, did I need this case. Gig for a rich dame like Rachel Leicester would pay my rent for many moons. The first thing to do was to meet these Satanists, to see who I was up against. I followed Haight Street to the address at the top of the Lodge stationary the first of the letters was written on. A grim Victorian imposed over the sidewalk, obscured by an overgrowth of weeds in the tiny yard. I mounted the stairs two at a time and rapped sharply at the front door.

After what seemed like an eternity, a hinge squeaked as a small viewing door the size of my fist swung open and an eye like I've never seen—on human or animal—blazed through. It was an eye that saw all, the eye of a predator, the eye of God.

"State your business," said the eye in an aspirated rasp.

"My name is Nick Chambers. I'm here on behalf of Rachel Leicester."

The eye of God blinked and tried to look around me. "Come in, but be quick about it."

The door swung inward, and I stepped out of one fog into another. The air was warm, but heavy with the smoke of incense and cheap cigars. The room was obviously an antechamber, a waiting room of sorts. Overstuffed couches sat at right angles to each other in half of the room, and every conceivable inch of wall space was fitted with bookshelves, which were themselves overflowing with books. Old books, too. The musk of decaying leather almost overpowered the incense, but not quite. Against the far wall was a desk, stacked high with papers. The place had needed a good cleaning for a couple of decades, by the look of it. The remaining wall was taken up by a scarlet curtain, obscuring the next room from casual observance. Above the doorway was a statue of a goat-headed man, one hand raised in a gesture at once comforting and forbidding.

This all took less than a second to take in, and when my host had closed the door behind me, I turned to observe him. He was a wizened old man with a long, flowing beard. Ringlets of hair dangled from his ears, and as he turned to face me, I noted a beanie on his head, the kind that Jewish menfolk wear.

I was feeling pretty confident until he turned the eye upon me again. His right eye was normal, a dark brown pupil bouncing up and down, raking itself over my clothes, my shoes, my face. But the other eye did not move. It was slit from top to bottom, like a cat's, a sliver of silver shining out from a corona of blood red.

"The trilobites," he gasped. His shoulders heaved, and he thrust a bony finger at me that seemed to point in three different directions. "They know."

Before I could reply, he shuffled to the curtain. He shrugged off his slippers and went inside. I waited patiently and in a moment found myself eyeing papers on the desk. There were other documents on the Lodge's stationary scattered across it. Mostly, though, there appeared to be receipts and bits of powder and bark. A large leather-bound book sat open on a brass bookstand, its pages yellowed and ancient.

My attention was commanded by sounds from the next room.

The old man seemed to be arguing with someone, although his was the only voice I heard. He did not seem happy, but as he seemed to be conversing in another language—German? Yiddish?—it was difficult to glean any context. Just as the "conversation" was reaching a fevered pitch, I caught a glimpse of a list on the desk. Again, it was printed on the Lodge's stationary and appeared to be a carbon copy, maybe three carbons deep, from the sketchiness of the print. Without pausing to consider it more closely, I stuffed the list into the pocket of my trenchcoat, and turned my attention to a shelf of books.

Many of them were in other languages, some I could not even identify. Those that were in English were almost as indecipherable, however. *Divine Union* read one of them. Another was titled *Magic in Theory and Practice*. These were more recent books. Some of the older ones did not have titles on the spines. I turned my attention to the book on the stand. Careful not to lose the place, I flipped the heavy leaves to the title page. *The Book of the Sacred Magick of Abra-Melin the Mage. Being a compilation of learned speculation and explication of that most revered and mystical tradition.*

The curtain opened sharply, with a flourish. My host stood between the billowing waves of scarlet and nailed me through the heart with his eye. He stood motionless as a statue, resolute as a general entering a battle. "I know who you are," he rasped.

A shudder wound its way from the top of my head to the tender globes of my nuts, breaking the momentary spell. "Yeah, old man, I know. I *told* you who I was when I knocked on the door."

"No..." He shuffled towards me until he could have pierced my heart with his beaked nose. "I mean to say...I know who you *are*." I tried looking him in the eyes, but couldn't really manage it. I kept shifting from one to the other. In his normal eye I caught sight of him, his own little, wizened soul. In the other I saw...someone else.

"And who *am* I?" I asked him.

"A living and grateful being." He turned and made his way behind the desk. His eye cast around for something, and not finding it, looked up again at me sharply. But he didn't accuse me of anything. If he had hackles, they would have been raised. As it was, he cocked an eyebrow at me and bid me sit.

"What do you require from me?" He asked.

"You don't know?" I asked. His doddering head indicated that he did, but felt it necessary to dance with me a little more.

"You work for Ra—Miss Leicester."

"I do."

"Perhaps you can help us."

"I work for *her*, old man. It seems to me that she's the one who needs assistance, not you."

"You do not see clearly." He cocked his head so that his other eye—his eye that was *other*—looked straight into my soul, as if to say, "But I see clearly...very very clear..."

"There are no enemies *here*, Mr. Chambers." He let that sink in before he spoke again. "But there *are* enemies, as you well know."

"And what assurance do I have that you are my friend?"

"Oh, Mr. Chambers, you misunderstand. I am not your friend." He ran his withered fingers over the pages of the book on the stand, lost for a moment in his own thoughts. Then, with all the abruptness of a puppeteer's jerk on the strings, he straightened. "But neither am I your enemy."

"And Miss Leicester? Are you her friend?" I asked.

"Miss Leicester is afraid. She has every reason to be. If she does not cooperate with us, every living being on this planet has reason to fear, including you, Mr. Chambers. Miss Leicester clings to her father's notebooks out of sentimentality, when in fact the secrets she guards govern the fate of the world."

"Whose world, old man?" I asked. "This world?" I swept my hand over the collection of musty books and arcane parchments.

"You are a fool, Chambers. I mean the only world we know. I mean the world of trees and oceans and rocks and rivers and sunshine on the hills; I mean the world of laughing children and the reverend memory of the old, of laboring men and the embrace of wives and mothers. The world of business and industry and prayer and holy mitzvahs. Do you understand what I am telling you, Mr. Chambers? It is your world which is in danger, not just mine." It was the eye of the other which held me in its gaze as he spoke. Then the old man shuddered violently, and reached out to collect his balance.

When he had gained it, the other, normal eye found me. "Have you ever held a trilobite, Monsieur?" He found a stone underneath a shock of papers and held it out to me in his quivering fist. "They *know*."

I gave him my card and excused myself. I could feel the eye of the other burning its way into the back of my head all the way to Gough.

The old man with the eye shook me more than I immediately realized. I stopped to wolf down a cheeseburger at Tony's Grill and go over my notes before I realized that I hadn't even gotten the old man's name. I kicked myself for being such an ignorant sucker and drowned my sorrows in a cold Coke. As soon as I wiped the grease off of my hands I pulled out the list I'd snagged from the Eye's desk. It appeared to be a membership roster, complete with addresses and phone numbers of all the lodge members—all four of them. My sins were soon absolved when I found the one address that matched the lodge. "Jacob Luria," I breathed aloud.

It was obviously a recently updated list, as Richard Leicester was nowhere to be found. I decided to visit as many as I could get to before nightfall. Since it was winter, that didn't give me more than five hours. "Good enough," I said to myself. "This case is giving me the creeps."

The first two addresses left me knocking. I resolved to try again later, and set my teeth in pursuit of the third. It was all the way in Pacific Heights, so I hailed a cab and played with a toothpick until he found the address. The house was in the style of a Spanish Villa, built in an incongruously vertical fashion, as is the way of things in San Francisco. The doorbell was loud and resonant. Actual bells were sounding somewhere within. The whole building exuded wealth. My observations were affirmed when I saw the inside. A butler met me with the typical air of professional indifference. "Is this David Lazaris' place?" I asked.

The butler nodded, and swung the door wide, "Would you be content to wait in the foyer for a moment while I see whether the master is receiving visitors?" he asked flatly.

"Of course," I said, and took a deep breath.

Surroundings that pricey made me nervous. I was certain I would permanently indenture myself by breaking something priceless. I watched the tails of my coat like a hawk and gave anything ceramic a wide berth. The Spanish motif was carried on inside, with exquisite taste. No black and red color schemes for this place; it was all earth tones: tans, terra cotta, and greens. I had no sooner sit than I was bid stand again and follow. I was led up a short staircase to a study that was the very antithesis of Luria's antechamber. Though bookshelves were built into every wall here as well, no particle of dust was permitted quarter. No musty smell permeated the perfumed air, and the light entering from the French doors on the far side of the room was almost blinding.

When my eyes adjusted I took in my host. A younger man than myself, perhaps in his early thirties, he strode towards me briskly and pumped my hand vigorously. He was dressed smartly in a cream-colored vest and trousers. A tasteful tie added color and accentuated a warm and inviting face. "Welcome, Mr. Chambers. I am David Lazaris. Please make yourself at home. May I offer you a cigarette?" The case on his desk gaped invitingly. I snagged two and lit one of them. If Lazaris noticed my intentional boorishness he made no sign. "Tea?" he asked, but then, before I could answer, turned to his butler. "Tea for two, please, Charley," he said. "Oh, and do close the door after yourself."

"Of course, sir." The door latched and the echo hung momentarily in the ice-white air.

"Mr. Chambers, how can I be of service to you?"

"I'm here on behalf of my client, Rachel Leicester. She's suffered a terrible loss, as you know, and now on top of that trauma she's being threatened by your little gaggle of thugs."

David turned his head sideways the way a dog does when it is confused. "I'm afraid I don't follow you."

I placed the first letter from the Lodge in front of him on his desk—the polite one. "Do you recognize this?" I asked.

He held it up where he could see it better. He then thought better of it and pulled on a pair of spectacles. "Oh, yes," he said. "I drafted this. Is there a problem?"

"Not with that one, no. But how about this?" I placed the rest of the stack in front of him. His face clouded as he made his way to the bottom.

"Oh, dear. Oh, I am so sorry...." He stood up and paced behind his desk, removing his glasses with one hand and rubbing his eyes and nose with the other. "My most heartfelt apologies to Miss Leicester. She has every right to be upset. I had no idea...."

"You didn't know about this?"

"I assure you, Mr. Chambers, I did not." He fitted his spectacles back onto his nose. "But I know who did."

"Luria?"

"No. Jacob can be a trifle unsettling at times, but he is not capable of this. He was very fond of Alan Leicester and would not threaten his daughter. I am sure of it. Besides..." he studied the last of the letters again, "I know this handwriting."

"One of your members?"

"Well, not anymore. This is the work of Balzaar, our former member, I'm sure of it. You must think we are all the most abominable sort of men."

"Well, you *are* Satanists."

A chuckle caught in his throat as he looked up at me in surprise. When our eyes met and he saw that I was serious, the full laugh broke past his teeth and spilled out like a fountain. "Oh, Mr. Chambers! Is that what you think? How in the world...?" He shook his head and looked at me incredulously.

"You're...*not*...a Satanist?" I ventured.

Just then the butler arrived with a tray of tea. Lazaris came out from behind his desk and sat in one of the delicate armchairs near mine. A small table separated us, and was soon adorned with cups, saucers, and a gleaming silver teapot that probably could have paid my rent for a year. When we were alone again, Lazaris answered.

"Rest assured, Mr. Chambers, you are not dealing with evil men. No, we are *not* Satanists—well, maybe Balzaar, but no legitimate Lodge member could be accused of such a thing."

I filed the Balzaar bit for future reference. "So if you're not Satanists, why all the hocus-pocus stuff?"

"Are you familiar with the Kabbalah?"

My eye twitched. I decided that this was probably not an evasive non-sequitur and waited patiently for him to make sense of it for me. He stood and went to a large painting on the wall. It showed nine or ten brightly colored globes connected by straight lines.

"This is the Tree of Life. Have you ever seen it?"

I shook my head.

"Nobody knows how old it is. Tradition says that the ancient Hebrew patriarchs taught its mysteries secretly, from father to son. In any case, it is a map of the universe of great antiquity."

"I thought the planets traveled around the sun." I said, studying its strange arrangement of spheres. "And aren't there too damn many of them?"

"Oh, I see..." Lazaris smiled. "This is a map of the *universe*, not the solar system. The only part of this map that is visible to us is the lowest sphere, Melkuth. This is the realm of the sensible world of matter, where we live. All of the rest of it is...speculative. There may be inaccuracies, but the truth is, it works. By understanding this model, it is possible to understand the order inherent in the universe, however chaotic it may seem to us down here in Melkuth. All of these paths describe how the various sephiroth—globes representing aspects or emanations of God—relate to one another, connect each with the whole." He stood back and studied the picture with satisfaction.

"This is what we are about, Mr. Chambers. It is the aim of the Western Mystery Tradition to find these connections, to understand them, to discern the order in the universe, to work *with* it, instead of against it." He turned to face me and replaced himself in his chair. "Now the question I'm sure you're asking yourself is whether this order we discern is innate or imposed by our imaginations? Who knows? Perhaps if there is to be any real order in the world, we have to make it. Perhaps any model will do. But this is the best we have found to date."

"And this was what Leicester was into, huh?" I stood up and went closer to the picture to get a better look. Actually, I was nervous and way out of my league. I didn't know whether to believe Lazaris or not. Trouble is, I liked him, and I'm usually a decent judge of character. "So exactly what was he doing? What was so important that you folks can't leave a woman to her grief?"

"Well, Mr. Chambers, I hesitate to say, since I'm fairly certain you will not believe me, no matter how delicately I put the matter. It is, even to me, incredible. It is, however, very much the truth."

"I'm ready to stop beating around the bush whenever you are."

"Yes, well...Mr. Chambers, can I trust you to keep my confidence?"

"Not from Miss Leicester. But from anyone else, you got it...so long as it isn't criminal."

"That's good enough, then," he said, and rose to remove an old leather-bound book from the shelf. "Alan Leicester was engaged in what is probably the most important magickal working in human history. The fate of the world hung upon the success of his work, and he succeeded. Unfortunately, the work was left unfinished, and if the threads are not tied up, the entire work may...unravel." He smiled. "To use a metaphor."

"I'm listening. Are you going to start making sense soon?"

He placed the book in my hands. It was identical to the one on the brass bookstand in Luria's antechamber. "*The Book of the Sacred Magick of Abra-Melin the Mage*," he announced. "Its source is the renaissance magkical workings of Abramelin, who devised a very....strenuous system of magick. Essentially, the magician must sequester himself from all cares of the world for a period of no less than six months. It calls for a rigid regimen of prayers and rituals over an extended period. Eventually, if it has been successful, the magician can maintain the level of magickal power and efficacy with less attention, but it still requires enormous time and effort."

"Well, that would account for Leicester's being such an inattentive father for six months, but Rachel says that he's been holed up for...."

"Since she was twelve? As I said, six months is the minimum amount of time to see results. For something as complex as Alan was attempting—as Alan accomplished—it would take much longer. Alan had been doing the working for six years, Mr. Chambers. Six years...." his voice drifted off, apparently in awe of his departed colleague.

"And there's nothing Satanic about this?"

An impatient look crossed Lazaris' face, but he masked it quickly. "I understand that Miss Sarah thinks we're Satanists. We're not Satanists. Far from it. I beg you to take a look at the ritual of Abramelin the mage." He opened the book to a well-worn section. "See? Enough God-talk and prayers to make a priest beg for mercy. No, there's nothing even remotely Satanic about it. But it is powerful, and if performed incorrectly, very dangerous."

"OK, I'll play along. So exactly what does this...system...do?"

"It facilitates the magician's communication with his Holy Guardian Angel."

"Somehow I suspect that the Sunday School portrait of the angel escorting the two little children over a bridge does not apply here."

"You are correct. The Tree of Life and many of our tools are derived from various systems of Jewish mysticism, such as the Kabbalah I mentioned earlier. The Jewish mystics saw the human person as being comprised of several parts. They called the body 'the Fool,' or even 'the Goof,' and the lower, or animal, soul is called the *Nephesh*, which even animals possess. Ghosts are *Nephesh*, looking for a body to inhabit again. Unfortunately, they aren't very bright. The higher soul is called *Ruach*, which is the intelligent spirit we most often think of as the 'real' us. But beyond that is the part of God that is in us all. That is the Holy Guardian Angel, the *Neshamah*."

"Look, I'm grateful for the history lesson. But how does this help us?"

"Why, Mr. Chambers, can you not guess? If the connection between you and your Holy Guardian Angel is active, then your will and God's are one. And when your will is synonymous with the will of God, can you not then command the hosts of heaven?"

It was starting to make sense, much as I hate to admit it, but while my wheels were spinning, it must have looked like I spaced out, because Lazaris continued with an arrogant huff. "Look, you don't need to believe me, Mr. Chambers. The important thing is, *we* believe it. We believe that the world is in danger, and we're the ones who have to do something about it. Ever feel like that, Mr. Chambers?"

Had to admit I did. But I still had questions. "What about the rats?"

"Rats?" Again, he exhibited the cocked head of a dog.

"Yeah, there was a cage full of rats in his...temple. What are the rats for?"

A smile broke out across Lazaris' face so broad I thought the corners of his mouth would meet and his chin would fall off. "Rats! Of course!" Animatedly, he jumped up and paced the floor, rubbing his hands. His eyes were darting back and forth like alibis in a room full of johns.

"Care to let me in on the secret?" I ventured.

"In Abramelin's system, the magician examines his yard for trails left by foxes every morning. He is able to read these trails, and to augur the efficacy and direction of his work."

I wasn't sure I'd ever augured anybody in my life, but it didn't sound pretty, and I was sure there'd be trouble with the cops if I ever tried it. "You lost me."

"It's a way of getting feedback from the universe on how well your work is going. The magician reads the tracks of the foxes...like you might read tarot cards or tea leaves. It is an ancient form of divination that most magicians have abandoned. But it's still there in the book, of course." He stopped pacing and poured us another cup of tea. "We don't get many foxes in San Francisco, but it sounds to me like Alan had found a substitute that none of us had thought of. And a very appropriate one for a city—or for an age of cities."

"Rats?"

Lazaris burst out laughing, spewing a bit of tea in the process. "Ratomancy!" he declared gleefully. Creepy. "I'll wager, Mr. Chambers, that if you examine the scene of the cr—accident, you'll find a sandbox of some sort for the rats to run in. Alan read the sand, see....." He stopped and looked at me with concern. "Miss Leicester didn't mention any sandbox, did she?"

"No."

"I think there's a lot that Miss Leicester isn't telling you."

"Oh?"

He went to his desk and withdrew a carbon copy of another letter. Again, it was on lodge stationary and was definitely in Lazaris' style.

Dear Miss Leicester,

We are very disappointed you have elected to ignore our entreaties. We are very concerned about your safety, and indeed, the safety of the free world. We have investigated the police reports and believe that you have been less than forthcoming in your statements to the authorities. The fact that no journals were reported found at the scene seems suspicious to us, and we believe that foul play may not be entirely out of the question. How far you are involved is yet to be determined. Please reconsider your lack of cooperation with us. You may find cooperating with the district attorney more difficult.

Sincerely, the undersigned members of the Lodge of the Hawk and Serpent.

"This is preposterous," I barked. "She secured those journals for sentimental reasons."

"Perhaps. But if there was no foul play involved, what reason should she have to believe that any of her father's property would have been impounded?" Lazaris forced a smile. "We might be guilty of extortion in this very unusual case, Mr. Chambers, but we're not thugs. I suggest you have a talk with Miss Leicester again."

"Yeah, maybe I will. I think my work is done here. Here's my card, Mr. Lazaris. May I call you if I have any further questions?"

"Of course." He called for the butler, who quickly found my coat and hat. "We are on the same side, Mr. Chambers. I'd like to help in any way I can. But I warn you: Rachel Leicester is not telling you the whole story."

I grabbed a quick bite at a diner and dialed the two remaining Lodge members, but without any luck. I let both phones ring about twenty times, and then went back to my coffee. I didn't like Lazaris' implication of Rachel, but I couldn't automatically dismiss it either. The fact that it made me angry on some level wasn't helping. I wasn't sure if I was angry at Lazaris for besmirching the honor of an unimpeachable woman or if I was mad at myself for not seeing that the peach was rotten.

I had the better part of an evening before me and no immediate leads to follow up, so I thought I would examine the scene. I phoned Rachel to ask her to meet me at her father's estate to let me in, but was met by the same endless ringing. Well, I thought, who needs a key?

I hailed a cab and within ten minutes I was handing the driver his fare and surveying the landscape. The house was enormous by San Francisco standards, almost a mansion. It wasn't any good checking the front door, so I set out to circle the house and see what avenues of entry I could find. I hopped a fence without any trouble, and found a window on the second story that was open a crack. I didn't go into this business for safety, or because I'm any kind of intelligent: I climbed a tree and hopped to the outjutting of a first-floor roof. I walked at an angle until it met the beginning of the second story, and edged my way to the open window. I was relieved when it slid noiselessly into its track. I climbed in and caught my bearings.

I was in a bedroom, and an unremarkable one at that. A guest room, no doubt, since there was a lack of sentimental paraphernalia around. I slid into the hallway and made my way downstairs. The "temple" was not hard to find, even in the near-dusk light seeping in through the windows. It was the only door on the floor with the exterior hardware necessary to affix a padlock. Dead giveaway. I threw the light switch and stepped inside.

I don't know what I expected. A stone pagoda out of a Tarzan movie, perhaps. I was momentarily stunned by the mundanity of the place. It was a sizable room, and so as not to miss anything, I began a systematic visual surveillance beginning to the immediate right of the door, taking mental inventory as I made my way around the 360 degrees of the room.

The first thing I came across was a bookshelf—big surprise. More musty, leather-bound books interspersed with more recent fare. In front of the books were various arcane objects: ornate daggers and even a crystal ball. I wondered if that was a humorous addition, or whether he actually used the damn thing. Following the bookcase was a wardrobe. It wasn't locked, so I looked inside. There were black robes that were obviously intended for ritual use. I couldn't see anyone wearing something like that to a ball game, or even the opera. I realized that I had no experience with what people actually *do* wear to the opera, but I put it out of my mind and turned my attention back to my inventory.

The wardrobe was fitted with a couple of drawers, but when I opened them they were empty, or almost empty. A single newspaper clipping was crinkled and pushed to the back, no doubt by the former contents of the drawer. It was from the *San Francisco Chronicle*, detailing one of the battles of the Russian army against the Germans in Poland. I didn't quite understand its relevance, but I flattened the tattered paper as best I could, folded it, and put it in my breast pocket.

After the wardrobe came the north wall of the room, which contained a large metal cage. "The rats!" I breathed aloud in triumph. It was big enough to hold about twenty of them comfortably, and I wondered if he used them all at once or in shifts. Directly to the right of the cage, just as Lazaris had predicted, was a large sand box, framed with high wooden sides and standing on wooden legs about waist-high. A metal run connected the cage to the sandbox, where, theoretically, one could leave the door open all night, the rats being free to come and go between the cage and the box. There were no rats there now, and I wondered what had happened to them. Had they escaped? Had they been released into the wild? I decided I didn't need to be worrying about the fate of a dead man's pet rats and continued working my way to the right.

A chest was centered along the remainder of the wall, and when opened, it shone gold. There was an enormous chalice and several other metal implements, each arranged impeccably in little compartments built especially for them, and lined with black velvet. "Ritual hoo-haws," I mumbled.

It was the East wall that was amazing. Black curtains hung about two feet out from the wall. Two stone pillars stood on either side of a huge stone altar, one black, one white, each fitted with an equally massive stone artichoke or pine cone or some such thing at the top. The altar was elevated on a three-inch riser, all of it carpeted and fully-finished. A black blemish on the stone caught my eye, and I ascended the riser for a closer look. There, on the edge of the stone table, was the stomach-churning red-black smear of dried blood.

Could the old man have had a heart attack, stumbled forward, perhaps tripped on the riser and hit his head? Rachel had been awfully sketchy when it came to the details. It was time to get some facts.

I had just begun my survey of the south wall when a loud bang intruded itself upon my concentration. Footsteps echoed in the hall, several of them. I slid behind one of the black curtains hanging on either side of the altar and willed my breathing to its shallowest. I was too cautious to sneak a peek around the corner and hoped I could wait the intruders out. Burglars are usually not this noisy, so that left....

Cops. I waited until I was sure there was no one in the room, and then wandered out into the hall, feigning non-chalance.

"Hold it right there, buddy, or we'll shoot!"

Three coppers surrounded me with their pieces drawn and trained on my torso. I acted surprised. "Officer, what are you doing here? You almost gave me a heart attack!" I fumbled for my pack of butts.

"Don't move, asshole! Keep your hands where I can see them!" I already had the pack in my paw, so I held it up. "Smoke?"

"What are you doing, trespassing on private property?"

"I'm not trespassing, Officer."

"Then what are you doing here?"

"The owner of this house, Rachel Leicester, is a client of mine. If you'll call off your dogs, I'll show you my creds."

The one who was obviously in charge looked at his companions and then back to me. He nodded. I snagged my wallet from the inside of my coat and handed it to him. "Miss Leicester is concerned about some underworld connections her father might have had. I'm trying to ascertain what those connections were and determine if there were any unsettled scores. Miss Leicester is an honest woman who doesn't want any surprises biting her in the ass in a month or so."

The officer-in-charge handed my billfold back to me and nodded again. "Smart woman. Your I.D. checks out. So you're Chambers, eh? I've heard of you. Manicelli even sings your praises now and then. I guess you're OK. I'm Hart, this here's my partner, Gretzky. We got a call from some neighbors about someone jumping the fence. You seen any intruders while you were here?"

"Yeah, just a kid cutting through the yard. Long gone by now. Something I would have done at his age, too. I didn't pay it any mind."

"That sounds about right. Sorry to disturb you, Mr. Chambers. Best of luck with your investigation."

"Thanks, officers. Always good to know you're out there."

He gave me another all-purpose nod and corralled his posse out the door. The deadbolt was shot, but I linked up the chain and let myself out the back way. Questions shot through my head like popping corn. What was in the empty drawers? The journals? That made sense. Why had Rachel not mentioned the violent way her father had died? I'd assumed it was a heart attack when she described it, and it seemed odd that she hadn't mentioned the blood, or the fact that her father had obviously hurt himself when he had fallen. I had some phone calls to make, some more questions to ask. And I was afraid I wasn't going to like the answers.

Night was punishing. My dreams were more brutal than an interrogation session by the most hardboiled plainclothesman on the force. Helpless to yank myself into waking, I relived the night my bomber went down behind German lines. I was forced to watch my comrades die all over again. Saw again my commander, Ratchet, pass himself off as a German to save himself; saw my brutalized, terror-filled self alone in a hostile land. I watched as if in flight from above, as if it were happening to someone else; saw how I had inexplicably passed by an entire platoon of German troops in one city unseen; relived the miracle of my unlikely salvation. Then the bird whose eyes I was using circled around, gliding effortlessly, like a hawk—and then flew into the sun.

When I woke I felt the full force of that native, hydrogen-busting celestial body burning behind my eyes. I pried myself from the couch in my office and staggered to the washroom I shared with the other offices on the floor. I dropped a couple of bromo into a half glass of gin—breakfast of champions. I ran a washcloth over my torso, and plunged my head beneath the spigot, baptizing my brain with cold clarity. Painful ablutions complete, I went back into my office and threw on a shirt and my least-stained tie. I grabbed my coat and keys and headed down to Gino's for some coffee.

Wai met me at the bar and poured two cups without being asked. He knew the routine, of course. "Rough night, Mr. Nick?"

"Depends on what you call rough. If fighting World War II all over again counts, then yeah, it was a tough one."

"Did we whup the Jerries again?" I gave him my best glare, but he wasn't intimidated. Not a whit.

"Special ingredient?" he asked with a wink.

"Already had the secret sauce. Straight caffeine, please. Easy on the water, heavy on the beans, if you don't mind."

"I ain't makin' another pot just for you, pops." Wai grinned at me. "You'll have to take your beans the way you found them."

Words to live by, I thought. I downed half of a cup and then looked around expectantly.

"Calls to make, Mr. Nick?"

"Oh, yeah. I guess I was looking around for the phone. I'm not all here yet."

"Don't feel bad, Nick. I don't think you've been all here for years." He pulled the telephone from the shelf below the bar and set it in front of me. I dialed Gottlieb at the morgue without bothering to check my address book. When I'm tired enough, I am able to somehow directly access my unconscious. I wouldn't remember my own number when I was fully awake.

Karl Gottlieb answered on the third ring. "Hey, Karl. Nick here. Listen, I got a question for you. You got a minute?" He did. "Do you remember a stiff brought in about a month ago, name of Alan Leicester. Weird spelling: L-E-I-C-E-S-T-E-R. Yeah, I know, you see a million of them. Would you mind pulling the file for me?"

I listened as he set the handset down and rustled through his files. When he picked up the phone again, he sounded as tired as I felt. "Yeah, yeah. Now I remember. Old guy. Very neat. Must have been married."

"He was a widower. Why do you think he was married?"

"Meticulously groomed ear hair. No bachelor could do a job on himself like that."

"Look, Karl, I know you haven't had hair for a while, but there are still barber shops, you know."

"Yeah, yeah, save it for someone..." he tried to think of something clever, but I beat him to it.

"...with hair?"

"Yeah," he said, mock-seething, "Save it for someone with hair. Now what do you want to know about John Cadaver here?"

"There was blood at the scene where he was found, but my client didn't mention any injury. I assumed it was heart attack, but I think I'm being kept in the dark about something. Any help?"

"Oh, yeah. Cause of death was a sharp blow to the back of the head, probably a table, or something else with a well-defined horizontal edge. The force of the injury was commensurate with the weight of the man's falling body. This guy was formidable, but this is one case where his size worked against him."

"One more thing. Was he wearing any unusual clothing when you found him?"

"No. Black trousers, white shirt. No tie. Paisley smoking jacket. Nothing unusual for a rich guy."

"Thanks a million, Karl. I'll let you know if I need any more detail, but I think you've hit the nail..."

"...on the head?" he finished.

"Yeah. Right on the back of the head. Seeya." I cradled the phone and felt my stomach twist into a pastry. There's nothing I hated more than being lied to, unless it's being lied to by a client. I had one more nagging question to answer, though, before I could make any confrontations.

I dialed David Lazaris, and once again was fortunate enough to catch him in. "Mr. Chambers, how pleasant to hear from you again. Is there anything I can do for you?"

"As a matter of fact there is. Would Mr. Leicester always be wearing....I don't know what you call them....ceremonial robes or something in his temple?"

"No. Only for certain prayers and workings."

"Would he ever be working or praying in his street clothes?"

"Yes, probably. I rarely vest for my daily practice."

"OK. One more thing. Are there any rituals that would require Leicester to walk backwards?"

"Hm....some Goetic workings, but I know for certain that Alan eschewed such practices. So no, never."

"OK, I'm going to pretend that we both know what you just said and take that for a no. Thanks....David." I placed the phone back in its cradle and tasted the weird feeling of the man's familiar name on my tongue. The next call I made was to Rachel, and this one was not going to be so friendly.

As if some little bird had beat me to the punch, Rachel was already crying when she picked up the phone. She appeared to be in terrible shock and insisted that I come over immediately. I slapped enough change on the counter and nodded at Wai. He raised his hand to stop me and in a matter of seconds was handing me a large paper cup filled with steaming java. "For the road, Nick. On the house."

I nodded my thanks and passed the scorching cup from hand to hand as I walked. Within a couple of minutes I had secured a cab, and found myself at Rachel Leicester's apartment before I'd finished half of my coffee.

When she answered the door, I could see that the faucets were still running. "Oh, Nick!" she said, throwing her arms around me and starting a new round of tears. The flat was a wreck. Rachel looked like she hadn't slept in days. If she hadn't been hugging me and repeating my name over and over, I might not have known it was her.

I pried her from my chest and handed her a handkerchief. "Oh, Nick, Oh...I mean, Mr. Chambers. I'm so...so...sorry....." Her grief was so great that she sank to the floor right there in the doorway and was lost in another wave of tears. I heard the sound of feet coming up the stairs and went into action without thinking. Nobody should see a lady in this much distress. My instinct to protect her privacy overriding my anger at her, I scooped Rachel into my arms, and removed her from the doorway. I kicked the door shut, and I carried her to the bedroom, laying her gently amongst the mussed bed-clothes.

"I'm sorry....I killed him. I killed him. I killed him."

I went into the kitchen and found a bottle of brandy. I poured a double into a juice glass and returned to the bedroom. I sat next to her on the bed, and handed her the glass.

"Drink," I said. "Then talk."

She gulped at the brandy and made that face that any real lady does.

"Who did you kill?"

"Oh, Daddy. I killed my Daddy...." her whole body was wracked with sobs, and I found myself reaching out to hold her in spite of my better judgement. In a few moments I felt the sobs subside and her breathing return to normal. Soon, her body went limp, and her breath deepened into petite snores.

I laid her out so that she would be comfortable and pulled the blankets up around her. This wasn't a show. Something had happened that had converted her rage into genuine grief. I returned to the kitchen and found a near empty bottle of gin. I poured what was left of it into a coffee cup and wandered into the living room to wait for Rachel to wake up.

Her apartment was elegant, but not ostentatiously rich. This could have been the flat of any single secretary with good taste—or any kept woman. Comfortable, classy, with the touch of someone who knows the real value of a buck. The curtains were closed, so I drew them back, flooding the room with midmorning sun.

The coffee table was covered in books a couple deep. I sat on the couch and picked one of them up. It was handwritten, and a quick glance assured me that the others were as well. I lit a butt and tried to read the tight scrawl that filled so many pages. It was legible, but I didn't understand a word of what was written there.

One of the volumes was opened, lying face down. I turned it around and noted that Rachel had apparently underlined several passages.

...the war effort. Finding it hard to maintain my practice now that Lucy is gone. Too sad. Can't concentrate. But if I don't, I'm afraid there's no way I can help the English. The bombs are coming, there's no question. If I cannot remain diligent, then the isles are surely lost.

I remembered both Lazaris and Luria saying something about Leicester's work being important to the fate of the world, but up until now, I hadn't connected it to the war. But if he had been doing this for over six years, he certainly would have been active during the thick of it all. But doing what? I didn't quite see the connection between Leicester's ability to concentrate and the Luftwaffe's attack on Great Britain.

On the end table were a couple of larger books, scrap books, from the look of them. I put down the diary and opened the first of the large albums. It was filled with magazine and newspaper clippings, nearly all of them devoted to the war. The battle at Midway, the storming of Normandy; it was all there.

About halfway through the second volume, I felt my blood freeze. My own ugly mug, grinning like an idiot, beamed forth from the pages. It was a two column story from *Stars and Stripes*. I scanned the story, allowing the rush of memories to flood through me. I read more carefully when I came to where Rachel had underlined my own words.

"I can't explain it," I read. *"I thought I'd be able to hide out in this village for a couple of days, but the place was thick with Jerries. I had to get out of there, but the only way open to me was to cross a busy street. I could see the treeline only a few hundred feet away, but there were more soldiers in the street than civilians. I was still in my uniform, so there was no way I would be able to make it out of there alive. For some reason, I felt a strange peace come over me, and I just walked right out into the open. It was as if I were watching myself from a distance. I walked right across the street, right past about fifty enemy soldiers. Not one of them noticed me. It was unreal. It was a miracle."*

At the bottom, the same hand that wrote the diaries had scrawled a date and some kind of numerical notation. I set the binder aside and felt my own arms, my chest, my face. I had to see if I was still here. I was afraid that somehow, now that the secret of my salvation was being made known, it might somehow unravel, that I might suddenly find myself dead, buried in some mass grave near the Black Sea.

But reality held, and I downed the rest of the gin to steel my nerves. I instinctively lit a cigarette as well. Once I had regained my composure, it occurred to me that the numerical scribbling in the scrapbook might be some kind of cross-referencing. I arranged the diaries in more or less chronological order and searched out the date at the bottom of the page. It didn't take long to find the accompanying text in the diaries, and the numerical code led me to one specific page in general.

It was obvious that many of the words were shorthand for things I could not divine. "LBR" and other abbreviations mocked my comprehension. But finally, some observations were scratched in beneath the shorthand. "Was drawn on the Astral to a solitary soldier. High stress/terror, picked him out of thousands. Wrapped my arms around him, surrounded with energy. Led him to safety. Too tired now. Sick. Threw up twice. Invisibility spells and cordon bleu do not mix."

The bastard had saved my life. The only reason I'm sitting here reading this is that this guy picked me out of a hundred thousand scared kids and possessed the magnanimity to do something about it. My chest hurt, and I felt like I couldn't breathe. I dragged long on the butt in my hand and looked around. No one in sight. No one to notice if I have a good cry. My face crumpled up between my fingers, and a trail of smoke from the cigarette wafted up as if from the bullet hole in my skull that might have been.

I must have fallen asleep. A blanket had been pulled up around my shoulders, and the sun was halfway through its descending arc in the West. "Hey, sleepy-head," said a soft voice. Rachel was walking out of the kitchen with a cup of coffee in her hand. "Cream or sugar, Nick?" she asked. I shook my head and accepted the cup gratefully.

No sooner had I sat up than the waterworks started in again. Rachel's, not mine. Only this time, they were sad, slow tears, not hysterical like before. "I was wrong, Nick. I was so wrong. And I killed him...."

I gave her an encouraging, grim smile, and waited for her to continue. She didn't, so I plowed ahead. "He wasn't a Satanist, was he?"

"No, I don't think he was. I don't really understand exactly *what* he was, but I don't think he was a Satanist."

She wiped her nose and looked out the window. "You know, other kids, their fathers went off to war. They were out of their lives completely. Some of them never came back. My daddy was too old to go, but at the time I just thought...I thought he was a coward." Her face fell into her hands again and tiny whimpering noises escaped her. In a moment she threw her head back and from then on, allowed the tears and the snot to run freely as she talked.

"But he wasn't a coward, was he, Nick? He didn't go away to fight the war, he came home to me every morning. I saw my Daddy every day, even if I didn't see him much. And...he...won...the war. He did it, didn't he? He saved all those people...." she glanced around at the scrapbooks. "Midway, Iwo Jima.... He even saved you. Somehow he was there, he was able to help. He...turned the tide. He was a...*good man.*"

"Yeah," I said. I cradled her in my arm, and she folded into me like an egg into batter. "He was a good man."

"I just didn't know what to think...when I found him...when I found his...his room. At first he was angry. He told me to get out, that I knew I wasn't supposed to be in there. He seemed hurt. I figured I was a big girl and I could handle it. I guess...I was wrong. I didn't understand. I thought...well, you know. I started yelling at him. I blamed him for abandoning me as a teenager, for selling his soul to Satan. I thought I had lost my Daddy to the Devil. I don't remember all the things I said. I just knew I was screaming at him, hitting him in the chest with my fists, pushing him back...back...until he tripped...and *hit his head....*" She opened her mouth in a howl of grief like I have never heard before or since. It was long and horrible. A sound that could suck the marrow out of a man's bones and stuff it back in with a spatula. It was a sound I hope never to hear again in all my days. The howl subsided into sobs. "I killed him...killed him...I...."

I squeezed her shoulder against mine and kissed her forehead. "It's OK, Rachel. You didn't murder him. It was an accident. It could have happened to anybody. You aren't responsible. If he hadn't tripped, you two would have talked it out. It would have been tough, but you would have got through it. I'm sure that, wherever your father is, he doesn't blame you. I'm sure he's just sorry that he didn't get to explain himself. It's OK. It's OK...." I kept repeating those words until her sobbing quieted.

Finally, she turned on the couch to face me. "I'm not evil, am I, Nick?"

"No. You're not evil."

"He wasn't evil either, was he?"

"No, honey. He wasn't. It's OK...."

"Nick?"

"Yes."

"Make love to me. Will you?"

At any other time, I might have found her request enticing, if professionally compromising. But I knew she didn't want me, she wanted all the things I represented for her since her father died: security, safety, and simple kindness. I didn't have the luxury for moral dilemmas, however, since no sooner had I opened my mouth to decline when the plate glass window shattered inward and a hatchet spun through the flying shards and buried itself in the wall above the couch with a gut-churning "thuk!"

I leaped up and ran to the window. There was no sign of the attacker in the street. I could see no one in the building across the way. I looked back at Rachel to find her untying a note fixed to the handle of the hatchet. I grabbed her and spun her through the door into the bedroom. She didn't seem to mind the roughness. She understood that she was an idiot to stand up in the line of fire.

We read the note together. It didn't take long.

The journals or your life. Your choice.

"Lock the doors," I said. "I have to see an asshole about an attempted murder. Ours."

"Don't leave me, Nick." She was right. I shouldn't leave her. But it was blind rage driving me now.

It was time to pay a visit to the one person I had been avoiding: the real Satanist, Balzaar. I phoned Lazaris to obtain the address. David wasn't in, but his butler answered. I threatened him until he acquiesced and gave me the information I needed. I thanked him shortly, banged the phone into its cradle and set off South of Market at the pace of a man hoping to outrun the Devil.

I was a couple of blocks past Market when a sharp blow between my shoulders caught me off guard. My knees buckled, and I went down. I don't remember hitting the pavement, because I suddenly found myself elsewhere, staring out at the cityscape in my first ever goddamn mystical experience. As if in a dream the shining tendrils of city light that separate the fragile strands of blackness faded, and the strands melted into one another like the fraying of a great tapestry. In horror I watched the Fourth Reich build its weapons out of atoms, and I hid my face as the fabric of the universe unravelled like the yarn of the Fates at my imagined feet.

When I opened my eyes I was on my ass, sweating like a pig and vomiting on the pavement, a circle of black shoes closed around me. The dusk was settling into dark and I was having a lot of trouble getting a good gander at my surroundings. The only streetlight was a block and a half away, almost entirely obscured by the silhouettes of my attackers.

There were a lot of them, nine or ten at least. As I stared up at them from the street, they looked like black globes hovering a couple of feet from my face. They swayed back and forth menacingly. Then they started chanting. I sat up and scrambled backwards until I was sitting with my back against a wall. The globes followed me without hesitation. "Mr. Chambers, is it?"

"I'm Chambers," I said, arching my back against the pain emanating from it. "Who the hell are you?"

A match was struck, and one of the looming globes lit a lantern. Suddenly my perspective shifted and I found myself looking at what appeared to be a merry band of rabbis, from what I could tell. They were dressed all in black, with large black hats with wide brims— the globes. Ringlets of hair hung in front of their ears and bobbed up and down like springs as they moved. I had to suppress the urge to laugh; the pain in my back aided me in my effort.

"Look, guys, forgive me for being nosy, but I'm a little unclear on why a band of rabbis would want to mug me."

"We're not rabbis. Well, Levi is." A wizened man near the back of the gaggle smiled, bobbed his head up and down and waved at me as at a child. "But the rest of us are not."

"Fine. Why are a bunch of Jews—and one rabbi—mugging me?"

"Oh, we're not mugging you." The one who seemed to be their leader looked at me with what appeared to be, oddly, kindness. "It seems you have been bumping your nose into other people's business."

"And who are you, the Jewish Mafia?" I was joking, but amazingly, they nodded their heads.

"I suppose you could say that, yes," the leader admitted. "But we prefer to think of ourselves as God's little helpers."

The pain was ebbing, and I was feeling a little bolder. These guys hit me pretty good, but I was getting a grip on what was real and what was left over from the vision.

"So what are you going to do, rough me up?"

They looked at one another questioningly.

"Wait a minute," I said. "You guys don't have a plan?"

"Of course we have a plan. It simply isn't necessary for everyone to know it."

"I'm unclear on exactly what you guys want."

"We want to warn you, Mr. Chambers. You are dealing with forces beyond your understanding. I suggest you stop trying to fight fate, for in doing so you are unwittingly aiding the forces of darkness and contributing to the unmaking of the world."

Unmaking of the world. That was a new one. "OK, look, fellas, I'd love to hang out all day and shoot the shit with you and all, but I have work to do."

"It is your work that we intend to put an end to."

"And just how do you intend to stop me?"

"We could put your eyes out." They all smiled and nodded. One of them drew a sharpened stake from the folds of his coat.

OK, this had been simply bizarre, maybe annoying, but now we were firmly in creepy territory. "Oh...now...wait a minute, guys. This isn't necessary." Four of them moved forward to hold me down. I was starting to panic. These guys might seem harmless, but they did have me outnumbered. I didn't have my revolver with me, either, damn it all. They were good talkers, so I tried to stall until a beat cop came by.

"Isn't there some kind of Jewish law against this sort of thing? You know, thou shalt not put thy neighbors' eyes out, or something like that?"

The others looked at the leader. "He's just stalling," he told them.

"Show a little mercy, please," I pleaded, beginning to actually feel desperate. "Anybody got any gin for the pain?"

One of them handed me a bottle. My left arm was released, and I screwed off the top and took a long pull—and spat it out. It was the sweetest, most revolting wine I'd ever tasted. "This is terrible!" I said.

"Ingrate," one of them spat back.

"Well, the wine might not be the best, but you *are* in excellent company." The leader smiled.

"Yeah, well I was cut on the eighth day, too, you know."

The smile vanished. "You're bluffing."

I narrowed my eyes, "I'm not."

The leader called over his shoulder. "Levi, you tell me if he's bluffing."

I'd long since stopped struggling against the goons who were pinning me, but they continued to hold me tight. Their grip gained new conviction when the wizened old Hasid emerged from the fringes and approached, his bony finger held out in front of him like a divining rod. It wavered uncertainly just above my nose. It was making my eyes cross, and I hate that, 'cause it gives me vertigo.

Levi's eyes were spooky, like Jacob Luria's, but his face was kinder. He wasn't a mob goon, he was a sweet old man who was palling around with the young guys. "Yes, he is bluffing." He wagged his head and shot their leader a grin, "But!..." he shot his finger in the air, and turned back to me with what seemed to be true compassion. "What he doesn't know is, he's telling the truth." The old man leaned down to me, and touched my cheek with his hand. It didn't feel weird, either. There wasn't anything erotic in the gesture. Instead, it was maternal, nurturing, and (I realized with a mild shock) vaguely messianic.

"Nikolai, my son," he said, looking straight into my soulguts, "Don't be ashamed of your mother. She wasn't a communist, you know. She was a Jew."

I shuddered. I didn't want to hear this. "You're full of shit." I spat.

"Yes!" he straightened up and threw back his gray head, laughing. "All of us. We are all full of shit. Look, Isaac, already he is quoting the Talmud!" He nodded furiously, his nose just inches from my own. "Beautiful, blessed shit," he grinned at me.

The old man looked deep into my eyes, as if trying to read something long buried there. His smile turned bittersweet, and he pushed his sleeve back on his arm, revealing the tattooed numbers on his forearm. "You must help us. You see, I don't want to go back...." his voice trailed off, and I could see tears beginning to well up in his eyes.

"Look, I understand why this is so important to you. I fought the Jerries, too. In fact, I wouldn't be here today if it weren't for the work that old man Leicester was doing. I'm trying to help. Really."

The leader waved his hands and the goons let me go. "I am relieved to hear it. You are one of us, Nikolai. The Lord bless you and keep you...."

"But, Isaac, we can't let him go yet, they haven't had time...."

Isaac spun around and caught the speaker in the mouth with the back of his hand. "Shut up, idiot. You can go, Nikolai. My soul is satisfied. It is well."

My head was spinning as I got to my feet and stumbled out of the black circle of Semites. Old Levi pressed something in my hand. A silver star of David. He smiled and patted my head. I shoved the star in my coat and double timed it back the way I came. So it was a diversion. I had to get back to Rachel's, and that right quick.

The taxi sliced through the ice of night like a hot blade through black butter. I decided that since speed and protection were paramount concerns, I'd hire a cab and swing by the office for my revolver. I found it in the third drawer I tried, under a stack of *Watchtower* and *Detective Fashion* magazines. I cleaned jam off of the cylinder with my tongue as I raced through Gino's sparsely populated public room. "Hey, Nick!" Gino called. "Why are you licking your g—no wait, don't want to know."

I ignored him and swung into the cab. "Punch it," I said to the driver. In minutes he roared to a stop in front of Rachel's flat. I threw him a fiver and looked up at the windows. There were shadows of several figures participating in some twisted pantomime behind the blinds. Hoping I wasn't too late, I swung up onto the fire escape and edged my way along the short outjutting of stone that separated her kitchen window from the front room window. The kitchen window moved silently up in its sash with ease, and in seconds, I had snaked to the floor. I drew my pistol, checked to see if my one bullet was in the right chamber, and pushed open the kitchen door a crack to survey the scene.

A slight figure in a trenchcoat and hat stood with his back to me. He was holding a pistol, which was pointed at the small mob of occultists on the far side of the room. Lazaris was stammering, sweating, trying to talk his way out of something. A couple of others I didn't recognize were obviously those lodge members I couldn't get hold of. Rachel was passed out on the couch—was she hurt? dead? I willed myself to focus and waited until the menacing stranger came within my reach before springing my surprise.

Jacob Luria's alien eye caught the glimmer of my own and narrowed in comprehension. The old man suddenly lurched, clutched at his chest and began crying for his glycerin tablets. I used the diversion to my best advantage. I slipped through the door, and whacked the intruder's gun hand with my own weapon. The menacing .44 clattered to the floor. I put my foot on the fallen weapon and raised my own for another strike when I saw...her. The intruder was a woman. A slight blond with thick luxurious curls that hung down her back like garlands.

I faltered with my hand raised above my head. "Mr. Chambers, I presume?" The woman asked, taking advantage of her own surprise. She only caused me to hesitate a beat, however, because in the next moment I brought the weapon down hard on the side of her head and the mysterious beauty crumpled to the floor like a whore's discarded kimono.

"Mr. Chambers, we are in your debt," said Lazaris with relief, walking towards me with his hand outstretched.

"Not so fast. Stay right where you are. You might be magicians, but I've just about had enough of your trickiness. Sit down and stay put." I kept my gun trained on all of them and herded them towards the couch. They didn't need to know that I only had enough bullets to wound one of them. "Check her pulse," I said to Lazaris. David put his hand to Rachel's neck and nodded at me.

"She's fine. Balzaar cuffed her, same as you did Balzaar. She should awaken soon."

"That's Balzaar?" I asked with surprise.

"Yes. Christine Balzaar, the only black magician in our midst, I'm sorry to say. She was...."

"Quiet. I've got the firepower here, and I'll call the shots. The way I see it, this black magician thing is just a cover. You're all in cahoots." Balzaar was starting to come to, so I slapped one cuff on her and the other to a heavy end table.

"The hatchet through the window was a diversion, to get me out of the apartment, so you guys could overpower Rachel and take the diaries."

"Hatchet?" asked Jacob, looking uncertainly at Lazaris.

"Then, while I was out, you sicced your Jew goons on me to keep me busy while you were here."

Balzaar was rubbing the side of her head where I had hit her. "Jew goons?" she asked. "What in hell are you talking about? And what are you trying to pull? You're all in cahoots!"

"Shaddup, and don't get tricky on me."

"No...." a low, pained voice moaned. Rachel stirred. "No, Nick. Listen to them. Listen...."

"Mr. Chambers, I don't believe we've met. I'm Rutger Bowers, and this is Jeffrey Stolte. Allow me to explain, if I may." The speaker was a stocky, balding man in a raincoat, with a moustache festering on his lip. Stolte was an elderly gentleman-type, clutching a bowler in both hands and looking so nervous he appeared to be in danger of losing bladder control.

"OK, talk," I spat.

"We don't know anything about a hatchet...."

"Do you think I'm an idiot? Do you think that's ornamental?" I gestured to where the hatchet was still sticking out of the wall above the couch.

"Well, Mr. Chambers, I don't know what to say. There definitely does appear to be a hatchet stuck in the wall, and odd as it seems, we are not responsible for it's being there."

"I am." I looked into Balzaar's eyes and saw an insatiable lust for power that had swallowed her soul, and if I hadn't looked away, may very well have devoured my own.

"You're right about the gang of thugs that waylaid you, however," Luria offered. "They were in our employ, and yes, they were intended to detain you...."

"While you roughed up Miss Leicester and stole her father's diaries."

"No, Nick, No." Rachel sat up, but looked like she could flop down again like a rag doll at any moment. "They came to talk."

"We came offering money," said Lazaris, "which of course, she doesn't need. So we also came bearing reason. We offered her our friendship, tutelage, and an honored place amongst us." Lazaris smiled. "She had just turned us down and bid us depart when Balzaar burst in and accosted her. She didn't expect us to be here, of course, and she was just considering how best to dispose of us, when you overtook her. We are very grateful, because there is no telling what that woman is capable of."

"Is that right, Rachel?" She nodded slowly, then slumped back down to the couch. I surveyed them, and wondered what to do next. I had to trust someone. I decided it would be David. "All right, here's what we're going to do. Lazaris, I want you to run down to the nearest five and dime. There's one open late on Columbus. I want you to buy a box of pens and about thirty composition books. Got it? I'm holding the rest of your friends—and the journals—hostage, so no tricky stuff." David gave a sharp nod and left quickly. "You," I indicated Stolte, "call an ambulance for Miss Leicester. Tell them to step on it."

"What about me?" whined Balzaar.

"You'll take your chances."

Lazaris arrived shortly after the ambulance had screamed away. I locked the door after him and slipped the skeleton key into my pocket, trapping them all in. "All right, boys and girls, here's what we're going to do. Each of you grab a stack of journals, a pen, and some composition books. I have every right to call my old friend Lt. Manicelli and have him arrest the lot of you. Let the courts sort out exactly what happened. But I'm not going to. I believe I owe my life to the man who wrote these journals, and though I don't understand exactly how any of this stuff works, I don't want his efforts to have been in vain. But Miss Leicester is entitled to her father's belongings. So we're going to sit right here until you have finished copying every last letter and punctuation mark. Any complaints?" They all shook their heads slowly.

"You have been granted the wisdom of Solomon," said the Eye.

"Yeah, or the stupidity of..." I grasped for the name of some mythological goof, but came up blank, "...some...stupid guy. Shut up and get to work!" I brandished the pistol again for effect and watched as they found places around the kitchen table and got down to it.

"What about me, Chambers?" Balzaar asked. "Let me out of this cuff and I can help."

"You've been enough help already, honey." I'd never hit a woman before, and I wasn't particularly conscious of enjoying it as I did it again. She slumped to the floor, out cold.

"Mr. Chambers, was that really necessary?" asked Bowers, with concern.

"No, it sure wasn't," I said.

Bowers frowned at me. "It's enough. Balzaar is our concern, and we will deal appropriately with her once the content of the journals is safely with us."

I shrugged and walked out onto the balcony where I could see both them and the lights of the city. I lit a cigarette and sucked on it, watching the smoke drift over the city, merging with the fog. I felt something poking me through my coat, and in a moment my fingers found the little Star of David. I felt its slight heft in my fist and held it up to shine in the light from the apartment. "Nick Chambers," I said quietly, "wandering fucking Jew." I laughed and pitched the star long into the smoky San Francisco night, to be swallowed up in fog. And although I was listening for it, I never heard it hit the street.

MIRAGE OFF MARKET

Dale West

Nick heard the groan of fatigued springs as he leaned back in his chair, elevating his feet onto the phone book laid across an open drawer. The chair, like everything in the office, should have been tossed long ago. Even the ribbon in his old Royal printed faded gray instead of black. Everything he owned was old, tattered, and scarred from age. Everything except the desk.

Although very old, the desk radiated class. It was made from the finest oak by gifted craftsmen. Nick used a lot of his spare time (which he had far too much of) keeping it clean and polished. He'd won the desk in a poker game, downstairs at Gino's.

Nick chuckled to himself. He'd been at the table for hours, winning some, losing some. Gino, the venerable Chinese bar owner, stayed ahead by virtue of the table percentage he raked off after every hand. That night the cards had been cold for everyone. There had been few good hands, and not many worthwhile pots.

Nick tossed in a fin as ante and lit a smoke while the dealer finished dealing the cards. He peeked at his hand. He held seven, eight, ten, jack of hearts, and the three of clubs. Knowing it was a stupid risk, he called the sawbuck bet and tossed away the trey.

Samuel Peterson, a real estate agent, who had drawn three cards, opened the betting with a ten-dollar bill. Thankful he hadn't given himself away, Nick saw the bet and rose twenty.

Intimidated by the stakes, everyone but Peterson folded. "Looks like it's down to you and me, Nick."

Nick just smiled. He dug into his wallet for the fifty-dollar bill he kept stashed for emergencies and threw it on the table.

Peterson's eyes went wild. "You're bluffing."

Nick leaned back in his chair. "Only one way to find out."

Peterson pulled out his billfold and turned it upside down on the table, disgorging a mere three dollars. "Crap, I'm tapped," he muttered, frustrated. "Gino, can you spot me fifty until I take this two-bit gumshoe down a peg?"

Gino laughed. "You think I'm a bank? And what if you lose?"

"I *won't* lose. I *know* he's bluffing. He's just trying to buy the pot."

"Maybe. But you know the rules. You can't pay, you can't play."

It looked like Peterson might chew the end clean off of his cigar. "Damn it, Nick, I gotta see your cards. How about I put something else on the table?"

"Like what?"

"My desk."

Nick caught a glimmer of something in Gino's eye, something that made him curious. "I've already got a desk."

"Not like mine, you don't. It's solid oak with walnut inlays. It's worth thousands of dollars. You only have to let me put it up to match your fifty."

Gino was shaking his head, amused. "You seen this desk, Gino?" Nick asked.

"I have seen it. It's beautiful. Too big and too classy for your office, though."

Peterson laughed. "That's for damned sure."

Nick narrowed his eyes at him. "OK, it's a deal. Let's see what you got."

Beaming like a proud parent, Peterson fanned his cards out on the table. "Full House."

Nick laid his cards down and finally released the grin he'd been swallowing since he drew the nine. "Straight flush."

Peterson's jaw dropped. "That...that's not possible! I...But...."

Shrugging with mock sympathy, Nick said, "So. When can I expect delivery?"

"You can't be serious! That desk is worth thousands...."

"So you said when you put it on the table." Nick collected all the cash on the table.

"Gino, reason with this hack, will you?"

Gino stood up. "Mr. Peterson, betting the desk was your idea, and you lost." His smile grew less happy, more threatening. "If you play cards in my house, you play fair and you pay your debts."

The room went quiet. Even a blowhard like Peterson knew better than to cross Gino. His face was red, but he nodded, retrieved his hat and hurried out of the bar.

The desk was delivered bright and early the next morning. Two beefy men maneuvered the massive desk up the narrow stairs. They suffered several busted knuckles before they got it through two narrow doorways, and into position. Nick had to rearrange his office to make room for the monster. He shoved his metal filing cabinet into the closet, and the small table were he kept his coffeepot into the bathroom. The damn thing filled his office like a size twelve girl in a size six sweater.

Nick ran the palm of his hand across the sleek desk top, appreciating the rich feel of it. But as the days passed, Nick began to realize that the new desk did nothing to change his existence. His phone still didn't ring, and no one came beating at his office door. His winnings shrank quickly and the rent came due in several days.

He slid open the top left drawer, fished out a well-used bottle of gin and a dirty highball glass. The bottle felt light. He lifted it, and inspected its contents with the sliver of sunshine sneaking through the blackout paint that covered the window. He emptied the bottle with a single swig, tossed the empty into the wastebasket, and rose reluctantly to his feet.

Nick made his way down the dark, narrow stairway that led to the street. On the sidewalk he paused long enough to light a smoke while he scanned the street for trouble. Satisfied his world was safe; he entered Gino's.

Wai, the eldest of Gino's two sons, greeted him. "Hey Nick. The usual?"

"Make it a double," Nick answered, squirming onto a stool. He put his feet up on the brass rail and slouched forward, supporting his chin in both hands, elbows on the bar.

"You don't look so good." Wai poured the gin and sat the glass in front of Nick. "Rough night?"

"Not feeling so good. Might be coming down with somethin'. Where's Gino?"

Wai answered with a shrug that could indicate *I don't know* or *none of your damn business.* "You're killing yourself sitting all day upstairs in that dark office. You need to get some sun. Why don't you go to the beach?"

Nick returned the shrug, with the same two possible meanings.

Wai shrugged and went back to washing glasses. Nick sat alone in silent thought until he gulped down the last of his gin. As he stood up to leave, he remembered the bottle he had just emptied. "Wai, can I put a bottle on my tab?"

Wai didn't say a word. He took a bottle from the shelf and put it into a brown paper bag.

When Nick reached the sidewalk he noticed a long black Cadillac sitting at the curb halfway down the block. Gino stood on the curb, bent over, talking through the window to someone in the back seat. A very large Chinese man waited nearby, obviously packing heat.

Nick had heard that Gino had Chinese Mafia connections, but it wasn't like Gino to broadcast his connections openly. Nick's curiosity flared. He pulled out his Lucky Strikes, shook one loose, fumbled in his pocket for his lighter, and lit it. He found a window where he could see the action in the reflections.

Gino flung his arms back and forth in front of him in denial. Then Gino gave a quick nod and stepped away from the car. He had set a bargain with the person in the car, but from the expression in his eyes, not the one he hoped for. Nick watched him as he spun around and walked straight into his bar. The goon waited on the sidewalk until Gino vanished, then he hopped into the front seat of the Caddie, and it sped away.

Nick instinctively took a glance at the license plate, then jotted it down in his notepad. When he couldn't see it anymore, he trudged up the dimly lit stairs to his office.

Later that evening, Nick sat at his desk plunking on his typewriter. The shrill buzz of the telephone startled him. He let it ring twice before he picked up the receiver. "Chambers' Detective Service."

"I'd like to speak to Nick Chambers." A man's voice, deep, strong and decisive.

"That's me."

"Mr. Chambers, my name is Anthony Gamboni."

The name sounded familiar, but he couldn't put his finger on anything specific. "How can I help you, Mr. Gamboni?"

"I need assistance with a very sensitive matter, Mr. Chambers, and it must be handled with utmost discretion."

"Mr. Gamboni, I run a first-rate service. I'm fast, methodical, and no one knows my business but me. Good enough?"

"Fair enough." Mr. Gamboni's voice became tense. "I suspect my wife is cheating on me. I want to know with whom, where, and how often—and I'd like this as quickly as possible. When can you start?"

"Just as soon as you take care of my fee and discuss the particulars."

"Will two thousand dollars be sufficient?"

Nick nearly dropped the phone. He'd been prepared to ask for five hundred plus expenses. "Yes, but I'll need half up front."

"Very well. I will send a man around at ten o'clock tomorrow morning. He will have your retainer and a dossier containing all the information you'll need. If you still have questions after reading it, you can call me here at my office."

"Perfect."

"Good. Until then." Mr. Gamboni broke the connection.

It seemed like an occasion to celebrate. He twisted off the cap on the new bottle of gin, poured a double shot, lit a smoke, and leaned back in his chair to contemplate how he was going to spend that much cash.

Nick dashed downstairs to Gino's. He couldn't recall where he had heard of Anthony Gamboni, but if anybody could help him, Gino could. The old Chinaman knew everybody and everything that mattered in the city.

Two regular customers sat at different ends of the bar, both hopelessly lost in their own loneliness. Gino sat behind the bar between them, reading the *Chronicle*. He looked up at Nick over the top of his reading glasses and laid the paper aside. "I wondered when you'd be in." He poured a stiff shot of gin in a glass and set it in front of Nick.

"Gino, you ever hear of a guy named Anthony Gamboni?"

Gino gave Nick a peculiar look, then closed his eyes tightly. "Big money. *Old* money. One of the Mayor's cronies." Gino held up his hand with two crossed fingers to emphasize the point.

"What's he do?"

"He's a businessman."

"What kind of business?"

"The kind you don't ask about."

Nick raised his eyebrows. "The mob?"

Gino nodded. "You should be very careful about crossing him."

"Check. What about his wife?"

"She's a show girl or actress, or something. If you believe Herb Caen, their marriage really set the snobs back on their asses. They didn't like him marrying below his status."

Gino picked up his paper and began to scan the headlines. "So if you're working, does this mean you are going to pay your tab?"

"You betcha." Nick finished his drink and pushed the empty glass in range of a refill. "Assuming I live to get paid." It didn't come out sounding as funny as he'd hoped.

The following morning Nick rolled off his couch, dressed, and moved insecurely to his chair. He sat down in his chair to put on his shoes, but his head hurt too bad to bend over. Someone knocked on the door.

"It's open," Nick answered, shoving his feet under the desk. Wouldn't do to show one shoe on, one off. He tugged at the knot of his tie attempting to smooth it out enough to look presentable.

A tall man in an expensive black pin-striped suit strode in. He obviously found this dingy little office distasteful. "Are you Nick Chambers?" He asked, trying to avoid touching anything.

"That's me."

"Do you have identification?" The man insisted.

"My name's on the door. You came to me. What do you want?"

"I work for Mr. Gamboni. He asked me to deliver this packet to Nick Chambers and no one else."

Nick pulled out his wallet and showed the man his driver's license. It had expired several years ago. "Now how about you?"

"I beg your pardon?"

"I showed you my I.D. Let's see yours."

Outrage flooded the man's face. "Why?"

"Because I like to know who I'm dealing with." Nick grinned with satisfaction as the man sneered, reached into his jacket, and opened his wallet. "Bradley J. Pitts," Nick read aloud. "Well, Brad, now that we're all chummy, have a seat. Something to drink?"

The man eyeballed the dusty chair with disdain. "No, thank you." Pitts opened his briefcase, withdrew a large manila envelope, and set it on the desk. He then reached into his jacket and produced a stack of hundred dollar bills held together by a silver money clip and put it down on top of the envelope. Nick felt a little giddy. It had been a long time since he had held this much cash.

"I'll need you to sign this." He handed Nick a receipt book and a pen. Nick signed and handed it back.

"Mr. Gamboni will expect to hear from you by the end of the week."

Nick nodded, pocketing the money. "I'll call him the moment I've got something to report."

After Mr. Pitts left, Nick dumped the envelope out on his desk and began to scan through the contents. In addition to some type-written notes on Thelma Gamboni's daily routine, there were several photos of the woman in question. One of them was some kind of publicity portrait of Mrs. Gamboni wearing a slinky satin evening gown and sitting provocatively on the arm of a chair. The dame was a looker. She was blonde, voluptuous, had great gams and hard eyes that sparkled for the camera. He could easily understand how a man married to her would have reason to worry. But Nick saw something else as well. She wore the apparel of her position well, but somehow she didn't look truly comfortable in them, a commoner in an opulent masquerade.

He picked up his phone, dialed the *Chronicle* and waited until the familiar voice answered.

"Harold Oates, here."

"Hey Harry, It's Nick."

"Nick! God damn! I haven't heard from you in a coon's age! How are you?"

"To be honest, I need your help. I'm on a job, and I need some dirt."

"Who's the patsy?"

"No patsy, a client, Anthony Gamboni. More to the point, I need to know about his wife, Thelma."

"That kind of info don't come free."

Of course not. "What's your price?"

Harry chuckled. "Well for starters, if there's a story in it, I want it."

"You write a story about my clients and me and I'd never get a job again. Come on, all I want is a little dope."

"All right, all right, it'll cost you lunch then. Not in some greasy spoon either, it's got to be a nice place."

"Sounds fair enough. Where? When?"

"John's Grill. Noon, today. Don't be late." Harry hung up.

"Wait!" Nick barked at the dead phone, then checked his watch. It was already after eleven. "That crazy bastard," he screamed as he slammed the headset into its cradle.

As Nick dashed out of the building he noticed the same Cadillac he had seen the previous day sitting a half block up the street. The same goon stood waiting next to the back door. Nick ducked back into the shadows of the doorway, lit a cigarette and waited.

Gino came out of the bar and hurried to the Caddie. The goon opened the door, let Gino get inside, then slammed it closed. Then he climbed into the front, and the Caddie sped off.

"What the hell is Gino into now?" Nick muttered. Not able to find an answer, he flipped the butt toward the curb, glanced down at his watch, and hailed a cab.

Harry glanced at his watch as Nick got out of the cab in front of John's Grill. "Hey, you're only ten minutes late! I'm impressed!" Nick just smiled at the sarcasm and opened the door for his friend.

John's was packed, but the headwaiter seemed to know Harry.

"Your table is this way, Mr. Oates." He seated them at a choice table near the front window, and walked away.

"Hey," protested Nick, "don't we get any menus?"

"Nope. I don't have a lot of time so I already ordered for us."

"Oh yeah? How do you know what I want?"

Harry smiled. "I just ordered what you had the last time we were here."

Nick raised his eyebrows. "You remember what I had? That was almost a year ago!"

Harry tapped a finger against his temple. "I never forget anything. It's what makes me so good."

As if on cue, a waiter appeared with salads and a gin and tonic.

Nick eyed the salad suspiciously. "I guess you aren't so good after all. I hate bleu cheese dressing."

"Maybe. But I love it, and know you're not going to eat your salad."

Laughing, Nick pushed the salad across the table. "Ok, you win. So what can you tell me about Thelma Gamboni?"

"She was an exotic dancer at Belle's, a club in North Beach that catered to bald, lecherous businessmen with fat wallets. That's where Gamboni met her. He fell head over heels, and began romancing her." He paused to shovel some more salad into his mouth, and then continued. "Word has it that she wasn't caught easily or cheaply. She ran just hard enough to keep the poor enraptured Gamboni at arm's length, but not so hard as to cause him to give up. Eventually, he wore her down. They started dating and became an item of gossip."

The waiter returned with their entrees, and whisked away the salad plates. Nick couldn't remember if a steak was, in fact, what he ordered last time, but it certainly looked like something he'd eat. Harry waited until the waiter was gone before continuing.

"They sure as hell set a lot of lips wagging," he said with his mouth full. "Depending on who you heard it from, their romance was either a disgrace to his position in the city or a match made in heaven. Three months later, he asked her to marry him."

"So was she just in it for the money?" Nick asked.

"Depends on who you talk to. The people who hate her the most say it couldn't be anything else. Those that are closer to the family say she really seems to love him."

"What do you think?"

Harry shrugged. "The race is too close to call. How's your steak? You take it medium rare, right?"

"It's perfect." Nick grinned. "Showoff." Harry just winked and began enthusiastically attacking his dessert.

The cab ride to the Gamboni residence didn't take long. Nick found a bench across the street from the Gambonis' home that would protect him from the moist air. He plopped down on the bench, studying the Gambonis' luxurious brick walk up. Then he sat back, lit a cigarette, opened his paper, and waited. He had just finished reading the green sheet when Thelma Gamboni came out.

She stopped on the top stair and buttoned up her long black overcoat. She was much better looking in real life than in the photos. Her platinum blond hair had grown longer and now she let it hang down over one eye like Veronica Lake.

She pulled her fur collar up and came down the stairs slowly, her stiletto heels rapping sharply on the masonry. At the bottom of the stairs, she turned and came straight towards him. Terrified he'd been spotted already, Nick ducked behind his newspaper, but she walked past without even glancing in his direction.

She didn't just walk down the street, she *undulated*. Nick gave her a little distance, stuck his paper under his arm, and followed, watching her hips move. He crossed the street so that he could stay close without being spotted.

She kept a constant pace, block after block, her heels pecking out a meticulous cadence on the sidewalk. Ten minutes later she turned into a small diner. He gave her enough time to get situated, then followed her in. He paced casually up the line of booths searching for her face among the customers. She had taken off her coat and hat and had sat down in the first empty booth she came to. She sat with her back toward the entrance, reading a menu. He passed by without looking directly at her and took a booth near the back. He slid in facing her direction and ordered coffee from the waitress.

Nick was finishing his third cup of coffee when a well-dressed young man entered the diner. He stopped at the front desk, bought a pack of Pall Malls, then walked straight to Mrs. Gamboni. Thelma stood up on his arrival and gave him a vigorous squeeze, obviously very happy to see him.

Nick sat too far away to overhear what they were saying. One thing for sure, they were delighted to see each other. The man sat down, across from Thelma, and quickly glanced through the menu. After the waitress took their order they sat in animated conversation. He reached across the table and took the lady's hands in his own, rubbing them warmly.

Nick took his miniature camera from his pocket. Using his napkin to hide it, he took several snaps of the couple. Nick twisted the film advance to the next setting and slid it back into his pocket.

Suddenly, Thelma's companion's eyes widened with shock, riveted toward the door. He slouched low in the booth, leaning his body in such a way as to use Thelma as a shield. Nick followed his gaze and was shocked to see Gino entering the restaurant, accompanied by a young Chinese man. Nick had seen this guy's picture in the newspaper. He was Byron Yan, right-hand man to Jin Long, Chinatown's crime boss.

Gino walked passed Nick as if he didn't know him, but the stiffness of his back said otherwise. He sat down in the last booth, his back toward Nick. Byron slid in across from him. Seconds later a tall, older Chinese man in a very expensive-looking suit came in and sat down next to Gino. Jin Long, in the flesh. The big bodyguard that he had seen beside the Caddie was watching from just outside the front doors.

Gino placed a bundle bound in yellow wax paper on the table next to Jin Long, who inspected it quickly, stuffed it into a brief case, and handed the case to his aide. Nick saw the package for only a second, but he had no trouble recognizing it. Gino always wrapped his money from the bar in yellow wax paper. Gino had just paid for something, and from the size of the packet, something very expensive.

Nick glanced back to the other table just in time to see Mrs. Gamboni hand her companion a small stack of twenties. He quickly stuffed them into his jacket. Then she stood up and stepped forward as she put on her coat. She was clearly being as expansive as possible, using her coat as a curtain to help cover her companion's exit. It was a slick move, but Nick found it fairly obvious. It certainly did nothing to shield him from the goon standing outside, who glared at their backs as they hurried away.

Nick started to get up to follow them, but stayed put when Byron Yan slid out of the booth and helped Jin Long to his feet. Gino stood, bowed with respect to Jin Long, and they all walked away from the table. When they passed Nick's table, he made eye contact with Gino, but if Nick expected some sort of acknowledgement, he didn't get it. The party was met by the bodyguard, who helped them into the Caddie. Nick watched until the coast was clear, paid the bill, and hurried in the direction that Mrs. Gamboni had gone, hoping to pick up their trail.

Nick caught up with "Dapper Dan" just as he was crossing Market, but Mrs. Gamboni had already parted company with him. He followed as closely as he dared. The man walked down Mission Street a few blocks, then entered a seedy hotel. Nick followed him inside and watched from the lobby as he climbed the stairs.

As soon as the lobby was clear, Nick entered and approached the clerk. "Hey man, you know that guy?"

"What's it to ya?" The clerk's voice sounded sarcastic.

"I just thought I knew him. Maybe from the army."

"He ain't never been in no army. Too fucking young." The clerk eyed Nick suspiciously.

"I still think I know him from somewhere. Just can't put a name with the face."

"You a cop?" The clerk glared with uncertainty.

"Do I look like a cop?"

"If you ain't a cop, then he must owe you money."

"Why do you say that?"

"Jimmy owes everybody money."

"Jimmy who?" The clerk glared defiantly, but Nick pressed on. "He lives here?"

"Just the past six days. Son of a bitch is already stiffing me on his rent. I'm going to kick him out Friday if he don't come up with some dough."

"He got a last name?"

"Do I look like a snitch?"

Nick decided to play the cop angle to see if it would get him anywhere. "You can talk to me now, or I can call in a uniform and we can all go downtown. Your choice." Nick let that sink in for a moment, then added. "Maybe I'll have the city inspector pay you a visit."

The man cursed under his breath. "Come on man. I don't need this. What the fuck you want?"

"What's his name?"

"Jimmy Smirks." The clerk wilted in defeat. "At least that's what he put on the register. Look. I don't know him from Adam, I just rent him a room. I don't give a shit who he is, as long as he pays his rent, which he ain't. Daisy, one of the working girls, told me he likes to gamble. Swear to God, that's all I know."

"He got any friends?"

"Not that I know about. You might check with the bartender down at Sloppy Joe's. Seen them together a few times."

"Name?" Nick demanded.

"Curly. Curly something."

"Anybody else?"

"There's this Chinaman. He's been in here looking for Jimmy several times. I don't have a clue who he is."

"Young or old?"

"Young guy. Dressed to the nines. That's all I know."

Nick believed him. He sneered and said, "If you're lying, I'll be back."

"That's it, man." The clerk actually crossed his heart with his finger. "That's all I know."

Nick shuffled into Gino's, his feet throbbing. Gino's youngest son Yu was behind the bar, shaking his head.

"You sure you want to come in here?"

Nick took off his hat. "What do you mean?"

Yu gestured at the back door. "Pop wants to see you, and man is he steamed."

Nick nodded. "Yeah, I can imagine he is. Gimme something to make me strong."

Yu poured a shot of something brown, and Nick threw it back, ignoring the burn.

Nick rapped on the door to Gino's office before stepping in. The old man motioned to the chair without looking up. Nick sat down and waited.

When Gino spoke his voice was soft but precise. "Why are you following me?"

"I wasn't following you. I...."

"Jin's man saw you looking down on me from your office window. Next you were seen watching us on the street out front. Then came the diner. I can excuse one such occurrence. Not three."

"I was there following the dame. It's that Gambino job. Her old man wants to know if she's cheating. She went in the restaurant. I followed her. I never expected to see you there."

"You took pictures."

Nick's face must have shown his astonishment. He had been so careful.

"You were seen." Gino said matter-of-factly.

"How? By who?" Nick questioned.

"Jin is a very careful man. He had the restaurant watched long before we arrived."

That explained it. Jin had a man there all along. "I took some shots. Mostly of the guy my client's wife is getting fancy with. Also got a few of her."

"Not of me? Or my friend?" Gino's voice became insistent.

"I swear on my mother's grave."

"The last I heard, your mother is not dead."

"You know what I mean." Nick wanted badly for Gino to understand.

"Jin Long is a dangerous man. If he suspects that you are spying on him, he will make you vanish. Do you understand?

Nick nodded that he did indeed understand.

"At the very least he expects me to get your film."

He dug around in his coat pocket, pulled out the camera. "These pictures are all I have on this case so far. Will I get it back?"

"I will look at the film. If it is as innocent as you say, you'll get it back and you can consider the developing a gift."

Nick nodded, handed the camera over, and decided to pry a little. "You and Jin Long go back a long time?"

"I only do some business with the man."

"Be careful."

Gino's posture changed. He became the official Gino, the one who ran a bar and didn't have time to waste with riffraff. "It is not your concern." He returned to his paperwork as if Nick had already left the office.

Nick slammed the door to his own office a little baffled. He had never seen this side of his friend. He flopped into his chair and noticed the creak of rusty springs. *I've got to get a new chair,* he promised himself. *Once this job is done, I might even be able to afford one.*

He started to put his feet up on the desk, but decided he didn't want to mar the rich surface with his shoes, so he pulled out a drawer and propped his feet on that. Sitting this way, he could just barely reach the top left-hand drawer of the desk. He opened it, reached in and pulled out a bottle of gin and his dirty highball glass.

Nick held the bottle up and eyed the level of its contents. *I drink too much,* he thought, and to prove it, he poured out two fingers and chugged it down in a single swallow. The warmth of it rushed down his neck and splashed into his belly. He poured another of the same size and decided to take this one a little slower.

Suddenly, the glass panels of his door shattered into thousands of tiny shards that sprayed the room with lethal shrapnel. Thunder and lightning erupted in the small office. Instinctively, Nick covered his head with his arms and dove for cover. He crashed to the floor face first, bounced hard, and scampered into the knee space under the desk.

The wood on the top of his cherished desk fragmented into thousands of splinters, buzzing past his head like angry hornets. Overhead, what had been solid oak, was rapidly being reduced to pulp. Through it all he clearly heard the unmistakable sound of glass bursting. Some small, detached part of his brain thought, *Not my bottle.*

He fumbled under his coat, drawing his own gun. His thumb tangled in the shoulder holster, and he dropped the gun. It hit the floor, and skidded out of reach.

"Damn it! Damn it! Damn it!" Nick cursed under his breath as he scrambled to retrieve the gun. This time he made doubly sure to do it right, took a firm grip, clicked off the safety, and came out from behind the desk.

He could see the shadowy shape of the shooter, an obscure outline seen through smoke and the shattered glass panels. He aimed, and he suddenly realized that it had been so long since the last time he used the gun he just couldn't remember if it was loaded.

He pulled the trigger and the dark office exploded with new thunder, but this was closer, and slammed his ear like a fist. He fired again. The first shot went high and left. The second wider and even higher.

He forced himself to re-aim and fire again, and again, his world becoming one of deadly intent. The assailant screamed as if hit, bolted, and ran down the stairs. Nick aimed his gun at the fleeing shadow and kept pulling the trigger, but the gun quit bucking. Nick slumped back to the floor. He knew there were more bullets in his desk drawer, but...

...but the desk had been reduced to a pile of kindling. Dazed, Nick slumped to the floor.

Yu came running up the stairs carrying the shotgun usually hidden behind the bar. "Nick! What the fuck is going on?" he yelled, peering into the office.

Nick recognized Yu, he could see his lips moving, but all he could hear was a loud persistent roar. He had never been so glad to see anybody in his life. He let his gun slide out of his hand.

Gino pushed past his son and knelt beside the detective. "Are you hit?"

Nick allowed himself to relax until he was leaning on the leg of his chair. "Someone tried to kill me."

"Luckily, he did not." Gino looked closely at Nick.

Nick shook his head, and pointed toward his ears. "I can't hear so good."

"Yu, call an ambulance."

Everyone in the room except Nick heard the scream of approaching sirens.

Nick's hearing had improved by the time they got him to the hospital. First the ringing subsided to a dull buzz, then he became aware of an annoying bell tone trying to get some doctor's attention. Apparently the doctor wasn't listening.

Eventually, a young doctor, still wet behind the ears, probed and poked at him. He stuck a strange-looking flashlight in one ear and then the other. "Well," the kid doctor said as he finished the examination, "the ear drum isn't broken, just stunned. You're going to experience some ringing, but with care, you should be OK in several days. Mind telling me how this happened?"

"Some crazy fuck tried to erase him." Tony Manicelli said, flashing his badge at the doctor as he entered the room. He pretended to shoot a finger gun at Nick's heart. "Somehow, he missed."

"Nice to see you too, Tony.

"When the Doc's finished with you, I got some questions."

Nick dressed and met Tony in the waiting room.

"Who did this, Nick?"

"Fuck if I know. Never got a look at him," Nick answered. He dug his fingers into his ears, trying to ease the constant buzz.

"There's gotta be someone who wants to kill you."

Nick smiled. "You know me, Tony, loved by all. You got something?"

"Not much," Tony admitted. "The shooter was serious about it. He used a Thompson, and we counted almost a hundred casings. He's gotta be the world's worst shot, or you would be one dead Dick. Unless maybe he was just trying to send you a message. You on a job?"

Nick nodded. "Yeah, but nothing that would make someone want to kill me."

"Care to tell me about it?"

"You know I can't."

"Come on Nick, someone just turned your office into a cheese grater. You gotta give me something to go on here."

Nick just shrugged.

Tony shook his head sadly. "OK, Nick. Here's what I'll do. I'm going to give you one night to think about it. I'll come by what's left of your office tomorrow morning, and if you ain't ready to cough up what you know, I'm going to arrest you for interfering with a police investigation. You got that? By the way, I'm keeping your gun. Maybe that will make you a little less brave and a little more cooperative." Tony snorted and stomped out of the room.

By the time Nick reached his office the ringing in his ears was nearly gone, replaced by a throbbing headache. The landlady already had someone board up the broken glass in his office door. He let himself in and inspected the devastation. The floor was covered in wood splinters and broken glass. He looked at the chewed-up remnant of the front of the desk. If it had been cheaper wood, or a quarter inch thinner, he'd be dead now.

He collapsed into his chair and pulled open the top drawer to pour himself a drink, but it contained only broken glass and gin-soaked papers. "Damn!" he muttered, feeling deeply depressed. "Someone is going to pay for this." He said the words aloud, as if it made them more believable.

So who wants me dead? he wondered. There was the dame, Thelma Gamboni. If she knew that her husband was having her tailed, she might want it stopped. Would she be willing to go that far? Then there was Jimmy Smirks, possible blackmailer. It would be in his best interest to keep Anthony Gamboni out of it. Lastly, there was Jin Long. That seemed to make the most sense, but Nick had been around long enough to know that sense didn't always have something to do with it.

Over the next few days Nick kept busy tailing Mrs. Gamboni. By the end of the week he had a handle on her normal routine. She was very active, working with several volunteer groups at City Hall. She did most of her own shopping and she paid a daily visit to the city library. Nick liked this library stop. He liked watching her while she got lost in her book while nibbling at her food.

Since the meeting with Jimmy Smirks, she did nothing that could be considered shady. The week had almost reached an end. If she didn't do something soon, Nick wasn't going to have anything to report. Unless Gino returned the photos he'd taken at the diner, he'd be completely empty-handed.

Then on Friday, Thelma broke her routine. Nick sat on his bench waiting, burrowing down deep into his coat collar to keep from freezing. The famous San Francisco fog had rolled in from the ocean at sunset. His hands were numb from the cold, and nothing he did seemed to help.

A cab stopped in front of the house and tooted its horn. Thelma came rushing out, jumped in, and the cab sped away. Luckily another cab came around the corner before hers got out of sight. Nick flagged it down, and jumped in. "Follow that taxi."

"What is this, a movie?" the cabby quipped sarcastically.

"Just go," Nick ordered. "Don't lose him, and there's an extra fin in it for you."

"Wow. A big spender." The driver smirked, but gunned the engine.

"Look out, they're turning right."

"Keep your shorts on, Mac. I got 'um."

The ride turned into a race across town. The other cab made a lot of strange turns, but Nick's driver was good, and managed to keep the other cab in sight despite the thick fog.

Thelma's cab rolled to a stop in front of a restaurant called Chase's. She exited her cab and walked toward the entrance. She paused outside, taking a long hard look up and down Larkin Street, then went inside.

Nick waited a few moments, paid his driver and followed her into the restaurant. He let his eyes adjust to the dim lighting, and looked around. He spotted Thelma across the room. She was being led to a table where Jimmy Smirks stood up to greet her.

The two hugged each other, then sat down. After they were seated he reached across the table and took her hand into his own.

"Can I help you?" Nick had been so intent on observing the couple that he was surprised when the hostess approached him.

"Dinner for one," he managed to sputter.

The hostess led Nick to a table, but he couldn't see Thelma's table from here. "Could I have a different table?" He asked. "Maybe one a little closer to the window? I like to look out."

"Certainly," the lady agreed. "Any one in particular?"

He pointed. "How about that one?"

"That will be fine." The hostess laid a menu down in front of him. "Can I get you a cocktail?"

"A martini. Skip the vermouth and olive."

She raised her eyebrow, but only said, "Of course. I'll be back in a moment," and walked away.

His view of Thelma's table proved more than adequate. If he listened hard, he could even hear some of what they were saying. He picked up the menu and scanned it, and cringed when he saw the prices.

When his waitress returned, he ordered the cheapest entree on the menu; a barbecued beef plate with a baked potato, no veggies, no salad, for a buck eighty-five. He sipped at his drink, lit a Lucky, and settled back to observe.

Thelma and Jimmy talked and she shook her head in disagreement. Whatever he wanted, she was having none of it. Nick silently cursed Gino for taking his camera.

His dinner arrived, and Nick tucked into it with gusto, hungrier than he'd realized. It was good, too. The beef was tasty and tender. He decided the price was worth it.

Jimmy's voice brought Nick's attention back to the other table. "This is my one chance. Maybe the only one I'll ever have. You have to help me."

"I'm sorry Jimmy, I just don't have that kind of money."

"You can get it from your husband." He got louder and more insistent.

"I will not bring him into this."

Jimmy took both of her hands into his, dropped his voice to a whisper, and continued to press his point. But apparently she had had all she was going to take and stood up to leave.

"Damn it! This is my one big chance," Jimmy said, pleading with her. "I can't let it get away. I'm not asking that much."

"I don't have it, Jimmy," she snapped while putting on her coat. "Anthony isn't going to go for any of it. He is generous, but not a fool."

"Come on, Thelma. I have to have all of it by tomorrow morning or I'm toast," Jimmy whined.

Thelma picked up her purse and stuck it under her arm. "I will try one more time, but I can't promise you anything." She walked away.

So, Jimmy was definitely trying to get money from Thelma, but it didn't sound like blackmail, more like a get-rich-quick scheme. After moping for a while, Jimmy picked up the cash that Thelma had left on the table and waved to the waitress for the check.

Nick chugged down the last if his drink and followed Jimmy to the front. He paid for his meal, left a generous tip, and walked into the street. He watched Jimmy hail a cab, and overheard him give the cab driver the address of the seedy hotel where he was staying.

Nick took another cab and followed. Jimmy had climbed half way up the stairs when Nick entered the lobby. He was tired and decided to sit in the lobby a minute and have a smoke. None of this made any sense. He was just about to give up for the night when, much to his surprise, Byron Yan entered the lobby. He went straight to the desk. Nick picked up a newspaper and hid behind it.

"Would you tell Room 219 that they have a guest?" he barked. The manager snarled, but picked up the phone and dialed. In a few moments Jimmy Smirks came charging down the stairs. Byron led him outside.

Nick could see them through the window, but couldn't hear what they were saying. He could read their faces, however, and whatever they were discussing, Byron seemed threatening, and Jimmy was frightened.

As Jimmy started through the hotel doors, Nick could hear Byron snarl, "One way or the other, this thing comes down tomorrow morning." He spun on his heel and stomped away. Jimmy rushed through the lobby and vanished up the stairs.

Nick returned to his office, carrying a bottle of gin he'd picked up downstairs, his head still spinning from the implications of what he'd just seen. Jimmy Smirks in cahoots with Byron Yan? He sure as hell hadn't expected that kind of wrinkle. He sat down behind his shattered desk. "What a fucking waste," he said to no one. The desk depressed him so badly that he couldn't stand to be in the same room with it.

He went down to Gino's, ordered a double gin from Wai, got a rack of balls from behind the bar and took them to the pool table.

He lit a cigarette, racked the balls, and broke.

He went over what little he knew while he played. Jimmy was trying to beg, borrow, or steal money from Thelma, but only they knew what for. If they were involved amorously, he sure couldn't prove it. With the exception of hugging every time they met, and holding hands at every opportunity, they seemed to be no more than good friends. Nick aimed at the four ball like a sniper and dropped it.

Gino, on the other hand, was in some kind of business with Jin Long, and they'd warned Nick to stay far clear of it. It wasn't unthinkable that Long had someone shoot up his office to drive the point home, but he had no proof there was a connection. Nick absentmindedly banked the seven ball into the corner.

And now there was this business between Smirks and Yan. Nick had told Gino that his case didn't involve Jin Long, but now he wasn't so sure. He had to know what the connection was if he was going to survive to collect his fee from Gamboni. *Nothing like being caught between the Mafia and the Tong*, he thought, and laughed.

There was only one ball left on the table, a long shot that would take a very gentle touch to keep the cue ball from following it in. He shot and watched indifferently as the ball dropped into the side pocket. Nick jabbed his cigarette out in an ashtray that had somehow grown full of butts. He fished in his pocket for his pack and found it empty. He crumpled the empty pack and went to the vending machine to buy a fresh one.

Gino, Wai, Yu, and several regulars were all huddled at the end of the bar playing "Liar's Dice." They slammed their dice cups on the bar, shouted at each other frantically, then groaned as they revealed their throws. Pleased, Gino picked the stack of bills up, stuffed them into his pocket, and walked away from the game.

Nick beckoned him over. "Gino. Could we talk?"

"What is it?"

"Better take this in the office."

Gino nodded and led the way inside. He closed the door.

"It's this Jin Long thing." Gino's face turned sour. "I know what you're doing with Jin is none of my business, but something strange has happened."

"Things I need to know about?" Nick had Gino's interest.

"Maybe. You know I've been following Gamboni's wife. She's been hooking up with this guy named Jimmy Smirks."

"The guy in these pictures?"

Gino reached into his desk and retrieved Nick's camera and an envelope of photos. Nick peeked at them. They were the shots he took in the diner. Nick smiled. "Yeah, that's the guy. Today I tailed him to a hotel lobby downtown where he had a heated conversation with your pal, Byron Yan."

Gino's eyes widened. "Are you absolutely sure?"

"I'm sure." Nick leaned closer to Gino, wanting to read his friend's face. "I didn't hear much, but whatever it is they're doing will happen tomorrow morning. I don't know what you've got going with Jin, but I don't want to see you get hurt."

Gino thought over what Nick had just told him and came to a determination. "It is good that you have shared this with me. My business with Jin is to arrange a wife for Wai. She comes from China, and will arrive tomorrow morning at Pier 45."

Nick's jaw dropped. "Really? A wife?"

"Good wives are difficult to find in the States. Western culture corrupts so quickly."

"What does Wai think about this?"

"Wai is a good son. He will recognize this wisdom and accept the responsibility."

Nick shook his head, trying to make sense of it all. "So what can any of that have to do with Jimmy Smirks?

Gino gave it some thought. "Nothing, as far as I know. I must talk with Jin Long at once."

"Are you sure that's the thing to do? If Jin is in on this, talking to him might get us in deeper trouble."

"I don't think Jin would abuse my trust in such a way." Gino insisted. "We've been friends far too long. Byron Yan, on the other hand, I do not trust at all. He is a sneaky little bastard with dreams of power. If anyone has violated our deal, it would be him."

"OK. You have your little chat with Jin. In the meantime, what should I do?"

"What you do so well, Nick. Put your nose where it does not belong and find out what we are dealing with."

Nick awoke the following morning feeling very bad. It wasn't bad enough that his ears still ached, but he also had a doozy of a hangover. He folded the blanket, straightened the couch, dressed, and made a pot of coffee. He was pouring the first cup when someone knocked on his door.

"Just a sec," he yelled. He unlocked the door and opened it wide enough to see Tony. "Come on in."

"Morning," the cop said going straight to the extra chair and falling into it.

"Morning," Nick said, relaxing into his chair. "What's up?"

"I wanted to return this to you." He pulled Nick's gun from his pocket and tossed it to him. "We don't need it anymore."

"No?"

"We got the shooter."

Nick couldn't believe his ears. Cops never got anything done that fast. "Who?" was all he could sputter.

"We got lucky on this one. You're not going to believe it. Daly City police stopped a guy for speeding last night. The dumb fuck had a tommy gun laying in plain sight in the back seat. Didn't take an expert to tell that it had been fired recently. We ran ballistics, and he's our guy, alright."

"Who was it?"

"The guy's name is Samuel Peterson. He says that you and Gino cheated him at cards awhile back. You took a fancy oak desk from him. Seems he really loved that desk, couldn't stand to part with it. He decided that if he couldn't have it, nobody would. So he buys a tommy gun and blows the damn thing into scrap wood. Isn't that the stupidest thing you've ever heard?"

"Well, fuck me running." Nick fell back into his chair, stunned. "So what happens to him now?

"Tomorrow we'll ship him off to the nut house in Napa. His wife says he ain't been right since he came home from the war."

"I'll be damned." Nick shook it off, trying to focus on his case. "Listen, Tony. What can you tell me about Jimmy Smirks?"

"He's a two-bit punk," Tony answered, "trying to make a quick buck anyway he can. Has some kind of connection with a major fencing operation here in town. He's also been suspected of smuggling. "

"Dope?" Nick was surprised to hear that.

"No," Tony answered. "At least not that we've heard of. He's more into jewelry and stolen artwork, small stuff out of Asia. Illegal artifacts from Egypt. Shit like that. He's been on our watch blotter for the past several months. Someone downtown got a tip that he's got something happening soon. You know anything about that?"

Nick nodded. "I think he's got something coming in soon. Maybe today. Now what about Byron Yan?"

Tony's face flushed with surprise. "Now there's a name. Works for Jin Long. Some say that he's next in line and that he's not the type to wait for things to happen naturally. What's he got to do with Jimmy?"

"I'm not sure. I've seen 'em together. They've got some kind of deal going. I may be wrong but I think it has something to do with a ship coming in at Pier 45 today."

"Be careful, Nick. Jin is not someone you want to fuck with. Neither is Byron. Both of them would kill you just for the fun of it."

"I don't think Jin is in on it. I think Byron is trying to slip something past the boss man."

Tony read the hesitation in Nick's face. "What aren't you telling me?"

Nick shrugged. "That's all I got. For now."

"I can't help if I don't know what's going on, Nick. Just be careful, buddy. This is a dangerous game."

Nick scanned the shattered office door, the bullet-pocked walls, and agreed with all of his heart.

Nick was beginning to reclaim his office and pondering the strange turn of events when someone knocked on his door. Feeling like his office had turned into Grand Central Station, he barked, "It's open."

A tall, distinguished gentleman wearing a full-length, white mohair overcoat entered, followed by Bradley Pitts. "Mr. Chambers?" the tall man asked. He stopped dead in his tracks staring at the damaged desk.

"Don't ask." Nick stood up to greet the man. "You must be Mr. Gamboni."

"Correct." He took Nick's offered hand halfheartedly, looking around the office, astonished. "Must have been one hell of a party. May I sit?"

Pitts quickly dusted off the chair with his hanky, and Gamboni sat without waiting for an answer. "What have you found out about my wife?"

"She's a hard dame to keep up with," Nick began. "I don't have a lot to report, but I can confirm that she has been meeting with someone." He handed over the photos he'd taken in the diner. "His name is Jimmy Smirks. She met with him twice this past week, both times in restaurants. Both times she gave him money, but I couldn't tell you what it was for. I never saw them do anything that would indicate that they are having an affair, but I'm sure that with more time I can find out more."

Gamboni was smiling. "No need, Mr. Chambers. I have everything I need from you. You have done an outstanding job in a short time."

"That's it?" Nick said, flabbergasted. "But I've only started!"

"You've given me more than I hoped for. Here is the remainder of your fee." He placed a stack of hundred dollar bills onto the devastated desktop.

"I don't understand." He left the money untouched. "I haven't found what you were looking for."

"But you have, Mr. Chambers. You see, the man that you know as Jimmy Smirks is Thelma's younger brother. He's a no-good bastard, and he has been trying to get me to support him since he came to San Francisco late last year. I refused. I thought that he went home long ago. If my wife hadn't hidden the fact he was still around, if I had known that the man she was meeting with was indeed her brother, I wouldn't have needed you in the first place." He stood up. Bradley quickly opened the door for him. "Thank you, Mr. Chambers. You have eased the apprehension of my heart. For that I am greatly appreciative." He took another long look at the desk, and left, shaking his head sadly.

Gino met Nick on the sidewalk in front of the bar. "You busy?" he asked in greeting.

"Not at the moment." Nick chuckled at the irony.

"Good," Gino said with solemn voice. "Jin is on his way here. Will you come with us?"

"If that's what you want. Where we going?"

"To meet the ship."

"Are you sure you want me there?"

"It is Jin's wish." Gino's voice held little room for options. "You accuse Byron Yan of cheating Jin. He wants you to be there when it is proven. If it is so, Jin would like to show his gratitude."

Or deal with me firsthand if I'm wrong. Nick felt the tingle of fear eating at his guts.

Gino read his face. "You were warned."

Nick nodded solemnly as the Cadillac pulled up to the curb.

Throngs of people maneuvered their way along the docks. Nick felt a little paranoid. Too many people in too small a space. Everyone appeared happy and primed to greet friends and relatives arriving on the ship, competing for better positions along the railings.

The passenger ship had nosed into the pier and the stevedores were winching in the stern and laying the gangway into place. The passengers waved at relatives from the handrails, and Nick found the noise level surrounding them a little befuddling.

The passengers started making their way off the ship one at a time with assistance from the crewmembers. The Chinese group that they were waiting for was one of the first to disembark. Nick spotted a young girl that had to be Wai's bride, flanked by two companions, one male and one female.

Once on the dock they were escorted out of sight into the Customs facility. It didn't take the party as long as Nick thought it might to reappear, this time on the free side of the barrier.

Jin's thugs politely forced their way through the crowd until they reached the girl. They greeted each other in Chinese. Nick, feeling awkward and out of place, stood back and kept an eye open for anything unusual.

They had almost reached the car when Nick saw Byron bump into the bride's handmaiden. It was an innocent maneuver, just a little accidental nudge that might have gone unnoticed if he hadn't been looking for it. In that moment, Byron's hand met hers, and a small package passed between them. Nick coughed as if clearing his throat, a signal he had prearranged with Gino and Jin.

At the same time, Jimmy Smirks, forcing his way through the crowd, ran into Byron. "Sorry," Jimmy muttered. Again the package changed hands.

Very smooth, Nick thought. *Son of a bitch has the hands of a pick pocket.*

As Jimmy made his way past, Nick reached out and took a firm hold on his arm.

"What the fuck?" Jimmy protested, trying to yank away from Nick's grip.

"If you want to live, you'll come with us." Nick advised, as two of Jin's goons took positions at Jimmy's sides, grabbing his arms.

Byron looked terrified. "What's going on?" He gurgled.

"Where is it?" Jin asked.

"Jimmy's left coat pocket." Nick answered, meeting Byron's gaze.

Jin eyed Byron pointedly. "So, my good friend," Jin began, "what is it you sneak into this country behind my back? I hope for your sake that it is worth the risk."

The goon removed a brown paper package about the size of a cigarette lighter from Jimmy's pocket and handed it over to Jin. Carefully, Jin removed the twine and unwrapped the paper. He held in his hand a small lump of painted clay. It looked to be poorly made and inexpensive, like something that had been made in a child's pottery class.

"Do you wish to explain?" Jin asked, holding the clay piece for Byron to see.

Byron stared defiantly. "It's a child's toy. It belonged to my niece. Give it back." Byron reached out to take back the prize. Jin looked accusingly at Nick.

"Not so fast," Nick barked. "Byron wanted us to think he passed the package to Jimmy. I'm betting he still has the real one. When he was handed the package, he accepted it with his left hand, but passed it to Jimmy with his right. The real package is still in his left-hand coat pocket."

"You son of a bitch!" Byron screamed. He struck the goon nearest him in the chest, wrestled away the goon's gun and aimed it toward Nick. "So, smart ass. You got things all figured out, huh? See if you can tell what pocket I am going to shoot you in."

The room exploded with gunshots.

Nick tried to leap away. He felt no pain, but couldn't believe that Byron had missed from such short range. He cringed, expecting a second shot. It didn't come.

An expression of bewilderment crossed Byron's face. He looked down at his gun, then at his shirt, where blood was blooming over his heart. Then he fell to the floor and lay still.

"Freeze," someone shouted. The crowd scattered, revealing Tony Manicelli standing with a smoking gun in hand. "Everybody stay put."

Several uniformed cops rushed through the chaos and surrounded everyone. "Get a medic in here," Tony ordered. "Search everyone for weapons." He kicked Byron's gun away and knelt by his side. He touched Byron's neck. A moment later he said sadly, "He's gone. Too fucking bad." He reached into Byron's coat pocket and pulled out the real package. He opened, it revealing a small envelope full of diamonds.

He stood up pushing the diamond into his pocket. "Alright, Sergeant, cuff 'em all and take 'em downtown."

Tony came over to Nick. "You OK?"

"Never better."

Tony smiled arrogantly. "Thought I'd keep my eye on you and see what might happen"

Nick nodded. "I thought you might. What's gonna happen now?"

Tony knew what Nick wanted. "We'll take everyone downtown and get their statements. From where I stand, we got our crook." He nodded at Byron's body. "Of course Jimmy is going down; so will the courier. We got nothing on Jin or Gino. They should be back on the streets in a couple of hours."

"How about the girl?"

Tony smiled. "I don't see any reason to drag her into this."

Gino smiled at Nick. "Well done, my friend, well done. My son will have his wife. Jin is not angry with you, nor am I." Nick had never seen anyone smile so broadly as they were led away.

Nick walked past Gino's, and for the first time in a long time, didn't try to go in. Gino was throwing a wedding celebration and Nick didn't want to crash a private party. He was nearly to the door of the building when someone shouted his name.

"Nick! Come over here!" Gino waved him over. Nick had never seen him so happy. "Come over and meet some people," he insisted. Nick reluctantly joined the party.

Gino dragged him through the crowded bar, introducing him to a blur of unfamiliar faces, most of whom seemed to be Gino's extremely extended family.

They finally reached the back of the bar, where Wai and his beautiful bride were holding court. Wai beamed and stood as they approached. "Nick Chambers, I would like to introduce you to Loo Yun Chin."

The girl bowed deeply.

"Loo Yun cannot speak English as yet," Gino said. "She has asked me to thank you for your assistance today."

"You're welcome," Nick said, bowing. He turned to Wai. "When is the wedding?"

Wai grinned like a school kid. "Next week. You're invited, of course."

Nick shook his hand, "Thanks." Then he faded back, making room for others to greet the couple.

What a strange world we live in, Nick thought as he bellied up to the bar for a stiff drink. *Nothing is ever what it seems to be.* He shook his head, enjoying the first drink he'd ever had in Gino's that was on the house.

THE KNOCKOUT IN THE LEOPARD COAT

Claudia West

"Listen, you rat bastard," Mrs. Lazarino shrieked, "it's already the 25th. Unless you cough up the rent in five days, you're gonna be *three* months behind."

Nick rubbed his eyes. He'd have loved to get his shrewish landlady off his back, but he hadn't had a job in ages. "Mrs. Lazarino, I promise I'll have it before the end of the month."

"See to it that you do, otherwise I swear I'll lock you out!" She hung up before he could reply.

There was a soft knock on the door. "Come in, it's open." He motioned for the woman to sit down, while he continued to talk into the dead phone. "Well, Mr. Danforth, I'm booked pretty solid, but I think I can squeeze you in. How about Tuesday morning about ten? All right. See you then." Nick stubbed out a butt in the ashtray as he hung up the phone.

"Mr. Chambers," the woman purred in a southern accent. "I'm sorry I came without an appointment, but I'm in desperate need of your help."

Nick looked up to see the woman with the sexy voice. He slowly surveyed her, starting with the black stilettos, up her long shapely legs, past the fake leopard skin coat pulled tight around her, up to her raven-black hair, hanging in loose curls cascading down her back. *What a knockout,* Nick thought to himself. He took out his pack of Luckies and offered her one. He feigned looking at his appointment book. "You're in luck, that was my last piece of business for today."

She reached out to accept the cigarette. Her hand was trembling so hard she could hardly take hold of it.

"I didn't catch your name, Miss...?" Nick stated as he lit their cigarettes.

She took a deep drag. "I'm Kathleen Sullivan, but most folks call me Kat." Her voice was a mere whisper. "Sadie sent me."

"You know Sadie?"

"She's a good friend of mine. She told me you helped her out of a mess a few years ago. She said you were there for her, when she really needed help." She took a deep breath.

Nick nodded. "So what brings you in today?"

"My ex-boyfriend ran off with our little boy." Just saying the words out loud brought renewed reality to her plight, and she broke down in sobs.

Nick handed her his handkerchief. "What do ya say we smooth the edges a bit?" He took a bottle of brandy from his desk drawer and poured some into his coffee. "Would you like yours straight, or in coffee? It's fresh."

Kat folded the handkerchief and dabbed at her mascara-smeared eyes, then blew her nose. "Coffee sounds great, thanks. I'm cold and scared to death."

"Your boyfriend?" Nick said, getting back to business. "When was the last time you saw him?"

"Ex-boyfriend," Kat corrected him. "His name is Joey...ah...Joseph Taglia. I saw him yesterday mornin', when he came to get Mikey for his weekly visit, about 9:30."

"How old is your son?"

"He's six," Kat stammered, her lips quivering.

"Where do they usually go for their visit?"

"They usually hop on a bus and go to the beach. Depending on the weather, they might go to Playland or the zoo. Joey is a no-good pool shark, but he's crazy about our kid. He says Mikey is the only good thing in his life. I wasn't worried when they were together. He takes real good care of him." Kat started sobbing again. "I just never thought he would do this."

She was quiet for a few minutes drinking coffee and smoking.

"Yesterday he borrowed a friend's car. He said he didn't have much time, because he had to leave town for a while. He told me he was in a fight, and he hurt the other guy really bad. He's already out on bail from a battery charge. If he gets picked up again, it'll mean prison. I never dreamed he was planning on taking Mikey with him." Kat was sobbing again. "Please Mr. Chambers, will you help me?"

"Call me Nick. Yeah, sure, I'll give it my best shot. But it means a lot more questions. Are you up to that?"

"Yes, Mr. Chambers...Nick. I'll be all right. I need to get my son back. I'll tell you everything I can."

Nick picked up the phone and dialed the deli down the street. "Hey, Louis, Nick Chambers here. What's the soup today? Could you send someone up here with a couple of bowls? Oh, and some crackers? Just put it on my tab, OK? Thanks." Nick hung up the phone.

"OK, Kat, before we get started, we need to take care of my retainer. It'll make me legally bound to your case."

" I...I only have 20 dollars right now," Kat drawled. She leaned across the desk, "But maybe we can work somethin' out? I can do anythin' you want." Then she sat back down in the chair and slowly crossed her long legs. Her fake leopard coat parted above her knees, just enough to allow Nick to get a peek of her black hose and garter belt—just enough to let him know that she wasn't wearing a dress.

He had to force his eyes back to her face. "I, uh, think 20 dollars should be enough," he stammered, trying to sound all business. He'd have liked nothing better than to accept her offer, but he couldn't take advantage of someone so obviously vulnerable.

Kat thought his embarrassment was cute. There was a knock on the door. Thankful for the intrusion, Nick called out, "It's open."

A very large Italian man entered the office carrying two covered bowls and placed them on the desk. Nick tipped him, and he left without a word.

Nick took the covers off the bowls, revealing steaming minestrone soup as thick as mud. It smelled delicious, but Nick seemed more concerned with the case. "Do you have any pictures of Joey and Mikey?"

Kat rummaged around in her purse and produced a strip of photos, the kind that comes from a photo booth. "Will this do?"

Nick took the strip and examined the various shots of a thick-necked goon and a mop-headed kid mugging for the camera. "That's perfect," Nick said, trying to reassure her. "How are you holding up? We still have a long way to go."

"I'm feelin' a lot better. Thanks for the soup. I'm not used to anyone takin' care of me. Now, I understand why Sadie likes you so much.

Nick never thought he made a good impression on women, but Kat was flustering him. He re-focused himself. "Did you get a good look at the car he was driving yesterday?"

"Yes, it was tan, a Chevy. Pretty new. '45 or '46, I think."

"Give me the best description of Joey you can, every birthmark and scar."

"He's Italian, six feet two inches tall, medium build, black hair, slicked back, and dark brown eyes. Forty years old. He has a tattoo on his upper left arm of a bulldog dressed in army fatigues. He has lots of scars on his face. One here," she traced a line diagonally across her right eyebrow, "and a deep one here," she touched the crease just below her full lower lip. "Lots of smaller ones on his cheeks. He's a snappy dresser. He usually wears a brown leather bomber jacket. That's all I can think of."

"What can you tell me about his friends and family? Where has he been living?"

"His family lives in San Jose, but I don't know the address. I never met any friends really, just other bums playing pool in bars. He's got a room in a flop house called the Regent Hotel on 6th Street." She took a deep breath, her bosom heaving. "What do you think, Nick? Can you find them? Can you get my boy back?"

"Well, it's just been a little over twenty-four hours. If we're lucky they might still be in town. I've got some ideas on where to start." Nick tried to sound reassuring. "You go on home and leave it to me. I need to get on it while the trail is hot. I'll call you if I have any more questions. Oh yeah, what's your number?"

"I don't have a phone, but you could call my sister's house. Her number is Webster 564. I'll keep in touch through her, OK?" Kat threw her arms around Nick. "Thank you so much, Nick. I'll forever be in your debt." Then she gave him a kiss and skittered out of the office.

Gino spotted Nick before he was through the door. "Hey Nick! How's my favorite deadbeat?" He had a gin and tonic poured before Nick had even reached the bar.

"Hey!" Nick did his best to look wounded. "I'll have you know I'm here on business."

"You going to settle your tab?"

"Not yet, but I do have a case. When I get paid, you get paid." He downed the drink before Gino could take it back, then showed Gino the photo strip. "You know this guy?"

The old Chinese man squinted at the pictures. "Sure, that's Joey the Shark! I heard he was in a bad fight at the Red Owl last night. What's Joey got to do with your case?"

"My client has a son with him. He ran and took his kid with him. I've got to catch up with this guy before the cops do. They'd probably put the kid in protective custody, if they get their hands on him."

"The cops aren't the worst news for Joey. The kid he put in the hospital is the son of Big Knuckles Carvalho, hit man for the mob."

"Oh, shit."

"You be careful, Nick. Don't get in the middle of a mob hit. They don't care who else gets killed as long as they get their mark."

"Yeah. Thanks for the heads up." Gino nodded as Nick waved and headed to the street.

For once, Lady Luck smiled on Nick. He not only got a cab quickly, but he knew the driver. "Hiya Max. Man, am I glad it's you. Can you stay with me for a few stops? I'll make it worth your while."

"For you, Nick, anything. Where to?"

"First stop is the Regent Hotel."

"The Regent? You packing heat?"

"Got it covered, Max."

The neighborhood was in real bad shape. Most of the buildings had long forgotten their colors. The sidewalks were strewn with discarded tires, old bedsprings, worn out furniture, and garbage. No one lived in this area but the very bottom of the heap, wounded vets so broken mentally or physically that they couldn't hold a job and the drug addicts who didn't even try.

The sign over the door read: $7.00 a week, shared bath. Clean sheets once a month. The man who answered the bell could have been a poster child for the neighborhood. He wore a filthy undershirt under limp suspenders that held up ancient slacks with the top button missing. His hair looked like it was slicked back with axle grease. He had a four-day growth of beard, open sores by his mouth, and a cigarette dangling from his lips, bobbing up and down as he talked.

He eyed Nick distastefully as he approached the counter. "What do you want? You aren't here for a room."

"I'm looking for Joey Taglia."

"I'm not his keeper." Ashes fell onto his chest as he spoke.

Nick slipped him a fin. "I need to take a look at his room."

"Join the crowd, big spender," he slurred sarcastically. "The slime ball skipped out yesterday morning early, owing me two weeks' rent. Two goons came last night and trashed the place. The cops were here poking around before that. There won't be anything left worth looking at, but knock yourself out. It's 2B and it's unlocked."

Nick had spent a lot of time in low rent districts, but this place was more than he could stomach. The stairs were carpeted with vomit, garbage, rats, and roaches, and perfumed with urine. Yelling and screaming echoed from the other rooms. The door to 2B had been left ajar. Nick pushed the door all the way open to insure there wasn't anyone hiding behind it.

The room was totally destroyed; the bed had been slashed, clothes shredded, every drawer pulled out and dumped on the floor. Nick sifted through it anyway. Nick was about to give up when he found a matchbook pinned between the mattress and the wall. He opened it and found a phone number scribbled in it. It was a long shot, but it was all he had to go on.

Disgusted and discouraged, Nick went back to the cab. "Max, stop at the first phone booth you see, willya?"

Max pulled away, only to stop after two blocks. "One pay phone, no guarantees it works."

Nick hopped out. "I'll let you know when I get back. Hey, you got a dime?"

Max dug into his pocket. "I'll add it to the fare."

Nick smiled at the dial tone, dropped the dime in the slot and dialed zero.

"Operator...."

"Hi. Can I please speak to operator number 229?"

The operator sighed. "One moment please." The line clicked several times, then a perky voice answered. "Operator two-two-nine, can I help you?"

"Sally, it's me, Nick."

The perkiness evaporated. "What do you want? You're gonna get me in trouble."

"Sorry, doll, tell them it was a family emergency. I just need a name and address for a phone number."

"Why else would you be calling me? What's the number?

He recited the digits from the matchbook then waited while she did whatever magic she always did.

"The name is Angelo Taglio, 1421 Rubio Street, in San Jose." Nick wrote it down in the same matchbook.

"Thanks a lot, Sal. I owe you dinner. I'll get back to you when this case is over."

"That's what you always say. A girl could starve to death waiting for you, Nick." She hung up before he could even defend himself.

Nick wandered back to the cab, his mind racing. Angelo had to be the family that Kat had mentioned, which made the odds good he was hiding there with the kid. Normally, when a case took him out of the city, he'd rent a car and add it to the client's expenses. There was no way Kat would be able to afford that, and he certainly didn't have the scratch for it himself.

So how do I get to San Jose on the cheap? Then it hit him. "I'll hop a freight!"

"You'll what now?" Max asked. Nick scowled at having said it aloud.

"Take me to the produce mart, and step on it." A few minutes later they were weaving through the narrow streets of the warehouse district.

"Any place specific?"

Nick scanned the area for a likely place. "There. Pull around to the back of that warehouse. That's good. How much do I owe you?

"Forget it, Nick, it's on me. I still owe you for getting my sister out of that mess last year. See you on the flip side."

The cab had barely pulled away when the train started blowing its whistle as it pulled slowly away from the produce mart. Nick looked around to make sure no one was looking as he ran alongside it and jumped up into an open boxcar. He rearranged some of the empty apple crates to make a reasonable place to sit for the two-hour ride, and was surprised to find one still full of apples. He opened it, expecting to find rotten fruit, but instead found glowing red, fresh apples.

"Someone must have missed a box when they were unloading," Nick muttered. He bit into one, testing it, then devoured the rest of it quickly and tossed the core back into the box. He suddenly realized how hungry he was, and started devouring the rest. "Look at me, Ma," he joked sardonically between bites, "I'm eating *fruit!*"

As the train started to slow down, Nick peered through the crack between the doors to see where they were. He could see San Jose coming up, and started watching for likely places to jump off. The train was still moving pretty fast, but he felt that if he rode the train into the station he'd be more likely to get caught. He spied a long break in the fence between the tracks and a field, and jumped.

He landed with a thump and rolled in the surprisingly rocky field. When he tried to get up, his ankle buckled. "Damn, just what I needed," Nick muttered. He hobbled to the road looking up and down. "Not a hack in sight when you need one," he thought to himself. Nick leaned up against a fence to ponder his fate.

"You look lost, city boy. You need some help?"

Nick looked up to see an old Mexican farmer. His weathered face looked like it was made of leather. He had shaggy gray hair topped by a tattered straw hat. He was leaning out of the window of an old flatbed truck with wooden slat side rails and more rust than paint.

"Yes, I do need help, thanks." Nick hobbled to the truck, hand extended to greet the old man. His hand felt like elephant skin to Nick. "My name is Nick Chambers. I could sure use a ride into town."

"Glad to meet you. I'm Lupi Garcia."

"I enjoyed watching you redlight from that freight train over there. I haven't done that in fifty years," the old man said, suppressing a laugh. "You think you broke anything?"

"I just turned my ankle. I don't mean to be rude but I'm in a big hurry. I need to get to Rubio Street yesterday. It's a matter of life and death."

"Life and death? You running from the law?"

"No, nothing like that. I'm trying to save a kidnapped boy."

"Shouldn't you call the police?"

Nick shook his head. "It's complicated. I will call the cops, but only after I try to get the boy back myself."

"Alright. Ain't none of my business, anyway."

They bounced along on farm roads past miles of orchards, cow lots, and barns of every description.

Nick finally spotted a sign for Rubio Street. "You can just drop me off here."

"Nothin doin'. If you have an address, I'll deliver you to the door."

"Thanks, Mr. Garcia. You're a life saver. I wish I could offer you something for your trouble...."

"Don't even think about it. You wouldn't be ridin' the rails if you had any dough. The way I see it, what goes around comes around, young man. Many people helped me when I needed it. I don't have much, but I share what I can, when I can."

Mr. Garcia pulled the truck over in front of 1421 Rubio Street. "I'll wait here."

"Look, you really don't have to...." Nick protested.

"You'll need a ride back to the train, when you're finished with your business."

Nick knew that there was a good chance he'd be leaving in a hurry, hopefully with the kid in tow, so he had no room to argue. "Alright. Thanks again, Mr. Garcia."

Nick limped down the sidewalk and knocked on the door. There was no answer. Nick was going around the side of the house to look in the back windows when he heard a young voice screaming for help. A little boy came running around the corner.

"Help me, help me! Come quick! My daddy needs help!" The little boy was hysterical. "Please mister, come help my daddy." The little boy tugged on Nick's coattail.

"Mikey, what happened?"

"My daddy was shot by some bad men, he's hurt really bad. Hurry! Hurry! Help my daddy, please!"

Nick limped as fast as he could to the backyard, Garcia following close behind. Joey was lying on his back in a puddle of his own blood. Mikey huddled close to his father's body.

"Mr. Garcia, would you take Mikey out front while I see to his daddy?"

Garcia moved close to Nick and whispered, "You aren't wrapped up in killing this man, are you?"

Nick shook his head. "Nope. I'm on the level. I just came for the kid."

The old farmer nodded gravely, then smiled at the boy "Why don't we go sit in my old truck?"

Nick looked the body over. It was a typical mob hit, one shot in the forehead and two to the chest. Knuckles' boys had beaten him there.

He quickly slipped Joey's wallet out of his pocket, removed the money, then put the wallet back. "Your boy needs this more than you do." Nick whispered under his breath.

"They killed him! They killed my daddy, didn't they?" Mikey ran over as Nick came around the house. He looked up at Nick, his eyes full of fear, brimming with tears. "Hey mister, how do you know my name?"

"Your mommy sent me to find you and bring you home to her. My name is Nick." He looked around at the nearby houses. "We should go. If any of the neighbors heard the shots, they've called the cops by now."

Nick took Mikey by the hand and led him to the truck, lifted him onto the seat, and climbed in beside him. "Mikey, this wonderful man is Mr. Garcia." Mikey didn't respond. He just slumped in the seat, sobbing. "Don't be scared anymore, everything will be alright now. I'll have you home to your mommy before bed time."

Garcia drove the old truck as fast as it could go. "I haven't floored her since back in 1924, when I outran the border patrol getting my family across the border. Where are we going, anyway?"

"How about a bus station?"

"Can do. You got money for tickets?"

Nick nodded. "Yeah. Mikey's daddy is picking up the tab."

After one of the bumpiest rides that Nick had ever had to endure, Mr. Garcia flogged the truck into the parking lot of the bus station. "Well, I guess this is it. I'd offer to drive you all the way to the city if I thought this old rust bucket could make it."

"You've already done enough. You've been a life-saver." He patted Mikey on the head. "Can I give you something for gas?" He reached into his jacket for his wallet, but Garcia just held up his hand.

"This was the biggest adventure I've had in years, you don't owe me anything. Just get the boy home to his mother." Nick shook his hand and helped Mikey out of the truck.

The door of the bus opened with a loud double bang startling Mikey awake, a look of terror on his face. He grabbed onto Nick's shirt, burying his face in it. "It's OK, Mikey. We're home."

Nick carried Mikey down the bus steps, and set him down on the platform.

"Mikey!" Kat was waiting at the gate, mascara running down her face. Mikey scrambled to his feet and ran toward his mother. Kat fell to her knees, arms outstretched. Mikey flew into her arms. Neither of them could speak. They stayed that way for a long time, then Kat mustered enough control of her emotions to speak. "When I came to your office this afternoon, I never dreamed I would be holding my little boy tonight. How will I ever be able to thank you?"

"You don't have to. In fact, I have something for you."

Nick dug into his wallet and retrieved the cash he got off the body. "Joey wanted you to have this. That much should let you stay home with Mikey for awhile."

"But what about your fee?"

"Joey took care of that too."

Kat smiled. "Nick, I'll never be able to thank you enough. Is there anythin' else I can do for you?"

Nick's first thought went back to the original offer she made in his office. But instead, he said, "Maybe you could have me over for dinner sometime. It's been a long time since I had a home-cooked meal."

QUEEN OF HEARTS, KING OF DIAMONDS

B.J. West

The phone rang like bells tolling the end of the world. The pounding it started in my temples made me briefly hope that it was. Then my stomach reminded me that whoever was calling might have a job for me, and I willed my hands to pick up the receiver. It was like holding ice against my ear.

"Chambers Detective Agency," I mustered.

"Hey Nick. It's Tony."

"Hey Tony. What can I do for San Francisco's finest today?"

"I gotta favor to ask you."

I knew that part already. For a cop, Tony wasn't too bad, and occasionally he slipped me a bone when I needed it most. He'd leak info to me if I was trying to find someone, or let me know if someone was in enough trouble to need a detective and couldn't afford one of the big names. Every now and then he'd ask me to do something for him in return, usually simple surveillance, or checking in with sources on the street that wouldn't take kindly to a cop asking questions.

"Natch. Lay it on me."

He cleared his throat and lowered his voice a notch. "We've got a girl down here that could use your services."

"She locked up?"

"I'm afraid so."

"What for?"

"Murder."

That woke me up the rest of the way. Murder was strictly police business, and it was a matter of pride that the force didn't use outside operatives for the big stuff. "OK," I said cautiously. "Where do I fit in?"

"She's a sweet girl, a real looker. She says she didn't do it."

"You think she's telling the truth?"

"Yeah, I do."

"So why don't you do something about it instead of calling me?"

Something in the way he paused made me imagine Tony looking around to see if anyone was listening to him. "The D.A. wants to put her away. As things stand, she'll be convicted, but the evidence is largely circumstantial."

"And you can't look into it yourself?"

"The Chief has pulled us off the case so Kelley can declare it closed on Friday."

I knew this drill all too well. Anyone in San Francisco did. District Attorney William Kelley had his eye on the Governor's office, and was building a campaign based on his "tough on crime" image. If putting someone innocent behind bars helped bolster that image, he didn't lose too much sleep over doing so. But there was still one more shoe that hadn't dropped.

"OK, so Goldilocks needs a helping hand. Why me?"

"She ain't got any money."

Thud. "Tony, this poor girl's situation is breaking my heart, really it is, but so is mine. My rent was due three days ago, and if I give up my troublesome food habit for a while, I might just be able to pay it."

"Yeah, but that's not the only outstanding bill you got. Remember our little card game a coupla weeks ago?" I closed my eyes. I'd been hoping if I put it off long enough he'd forget. I was kidding myself. "All I'm asking is that you come down and talk to her. Listen to her story, then poke around and see if you can find something that backs it up. Do that and you can forget about the fifty you owe me."

"It's forty."

"Plus the ten from the week before."

I cringed. "You should have been an accountant, Tony." I thought about the fifty bucks and all the ways I could have spent it if I'd won instead of drawing crap. But I knew I couldn't turn this down, I had relied on his privileged position far too often to haggle now. I sighed. "Give her my number."

"Stay by your phone." He hung up.

Tony had her call me less than five minutes after he'd hung up, which was pretty brazen. Maybe as long as it looked like the dame's idea, he'd be in the clear. Maybe the goons in charge of the lock-up had gone sweet on her, too.

She'd said her name was Marjory Bettencourt, and I couldn't get her voice out of my head. It had been shaped by many years of cigarettes and cheap whiskey, but now trembled with fear and loneliness. I tried to imagine her face, based on that voice and Tony's description of her. He'd called her a looker, but from the girls Tony liked, I always figured that was short for "looks like a hooker." He also said she was "sweet," which I was decoding as, "too young for me." The picture that was developing was Daddy's Little Princess, but already starting down the wrong path.

There's nothing worse than May in San Francisco. The rest of the world is relaxing into summer, but here on the peninsula it still felt like the middle of winter. I wrapped my coat around me as tight as I could and picked up my pace as I walked down Seventh Street toward the Hall of Justice.

I took the stairs in front of the jail two at a time and quickly pushed through the weathered doors. Warmth and the smell of sweat flooded over me. Gotta take the bad with the good, I guess. Sergeant Daugherty was at the front desk, his face dropping to a stern scowl the moment our eyes met.

"Why looky who's here," he sneered around his Midwestern drawl. "It's Sam Spade! I don't think I've ever seen you come through here under your own power before. Gino's closed today?"

"That's funny, Daugherty. Maybe Milton Berle needs a sidekick."

He wasn't amused. "What do you want, Chambers?"

"I'm here on business."

"What kind of business?"

"You've got a client of mine in the lockup. She wants to see me."

"Things so bad you gotta work for street walkers?" He smiled slightly.

"She's not a hooker, she's in for homicide. Name's Bettencourt."

The smile on the Sergeant's face fell like a rock. "*She called you?*" I nodded smugly.

Daugherty picked up the phone and dialed. "Hey Cliff, I got Nick Chambers out here, and he says the dish in 18 called for him. Would you check that for me? Thanks." He drummed his fingers for a moment, staring at me incredulously. His eyes shot to the side as his answer came. "No shit? OK, I'll send him your way."

He hung up the phone, equally confused and annoyed. "OK Chambers, go on down." I started to walk towards the elevator. Behind me, Daughtery laughed, "You sure oughta know the way by now!" He was still grinning meanly when the elevator doors squashed his head out of my sight.

Cliff was staring out the tiny reinforced window in the door to the visiting area, watching for me. He opened the door for me as I got close, and locked it immediately behind me.

"Nick," he said in an approximation of a greeting.

"Cliff." I thought back on all the times that ol' Cliffie's face was the first signpost I'd seen on the road back to consciousness. I associated it with a moment of relief that I was still breathing, followed by the sinking realization of where I was.

"Have a seat. I'll bring her out."

"Thanks." I sat down in a chair by the glass divider that separated prisoner from visitor. I'd sat on both sides of it in the past, somehow the chairs on this side seemed more comfortable. Then the door beyond the glass opened and an angel walked through.

No, not an angel. She was too scared, too vulnerable, and the thoughts she inspired in me weren't of God. But she did have a radiance, her spun gold hair shimmering, an ephemeral glow from her alabaster skin, a stab of pure presence from her ice-blue eyes. In another town, she'd have been a movie star, or at least a model. Here in San Francisco she was a murder suspect.

"You've got ten minutes," Cliff muttered, poking his head around the door into the small room. He seemed to be enjoying my reaction. I hoped I wasn't gaping openly.

She sat down on her side of the divider, perching on the edge of the chair, her hands folded in a tentative manner that implied the small purse that would normally rest on her knees.

"Miss Bettencourt, I'm Nick Chambers."

"Thank you for coming, Mr. Chambers." There it was, the voice from the phone. It was incongruous with her scared little girl face, but not with the stripper's figure that the ill-fitting jail clothes failed to conceal. "Officer Manicelli said you could help me. He said you're the best."

"Tony says a lot of things, Miss. Why don't you tell me what's going on and I'll see if there's anything I can do."

She paused, arranging her story in her head. "I've been accused of murder."

"Miss," I said, irritated, "we've got ten minutes, nine now, and you are in a lot of trouble. I suggest you condense this as much as possible." Fire flashed behind her eyes for a moment, she was used to being handled gently. She opened her full-lipped mouth to speak, most likely to protest, then surrendered to the fact that I was right.

"Alright," she said. "Last night, I went out dancing with my best friend, Gloria. We got back to her place pretty late, and I fell asleep on her couch. When I got home this morning, there were four horrid policemen waiting for me at my apartment. They told me that...."

Her lip quivered for a second, and then she cracked, sobbing heavily into her hands. "I still can't believe that Charles is...." She broke off into silence, her face still buried.

"Charles who, ma'am?" I prompted, trying not to let my irritation show.

She looked up, her face wet, her makeup smeared all over it. "Charles Rath, my boss." She dabbed her eyes with her sleeve as best she could. "And they think I killed him!"

"Why do they think that?"

"Officer Manicelli says that he was shot with my gun, but that's impossible."

"Why?"

"I keep it hidden in a drawer in my apartment."

"Hmm. Tell me more about your friend. Can't she verify that you were with her all night?"

"She could, but they said she hasn't been home. I don't know where she could have gone, so I'm afraid something might have happened to her, as well." She started crying again. "Mr. Chambers, I'm so scared. I don't know what I'm going to do."

"Is there anything else you can tell me?"

"I don't know anything else, I swear. I don't have much money, but I do have a little stashed away, so I can pay you something. Please help me, Mr. Chambers."

"On two conditions." She waited, expectantly. "First, quit calling me 'mister.' I'm not used to it and it bugs me. Call me Nick."

"OK, Nick it is. What's the second condition?"

"Can you make a pie?"

"What?"

"A peach pie. I haven't had one in years."

She laughed. With the mascara smeared all over her face, the smile made her look unsettlingly like a clown. "Yes, Mr.—Nick, I can bake you a peach pie. My momma has the best peach pie recipe you've ever tasted."

"Alright, then. I'll see what I can do."

The last second of our time ticked over, and like the damned bird on a Swiss clock, Cliff emerged from the door.

"Thank you, Nick."

I nodded as Cliff led her through the door. I stared at it a second, then headed out. Tony was waiting for me on the jail steps. He stepped forward to meet me. "How'd it go?"

"She's cute, but not the brightest bulb," I said. "She doesn't seem to have any idea what's going on. Care to fill in the blanks?"

"If we can go somewhere warmer."

He led me to his car, and we headed off to a small coffee shop in North Beach. I talked him into buying me a cappuccino—it was that or have me sit and stare at him while he drank his—and I covered it with my hands, trying to burn out the chill along with the last remnants of the hangover. He opened his briefcase and took out a manila folder. "This is her case file, so far."

I took it, looking at it skeptically. "It's awfully thin."

"Yeah," he said, the anger echoing in his voice. "Like I said, we've been discouraged from doing much about it."

"So what *has* been done?"

"The crime scene has been given the standard sweep, not that there was much left of it. Charles Rath was a diamond importer, one of the biggest on the West Coast. Last night somebody went to his office, struggled with him, popped him, emptied the safe, then torched the place. Miss Bettencourt was Rath's secretary. He was shot with her gun."

"Dust for prints?"

"Of course. They aren't being *that* stupid. Her prints are all over it, hers and nobody else's."

I pondered this for a moment. "OK, but she says she was somewhere else."

"Yeah, out dancing with one Gloria Jean Buckley. We've had someone at her house since this whole mess started. She's AWOL. Not much good for corroboration."

"It's a pretty damned weak case."

"Don't I know it. But unless something else drops in our lap, it's probably enough to get her sent to the chair."

"Got any ideas on where to start?"

"Yeah. Miss Bettencourt says that Rath has a business partner, a guy named Terrance Phillips. He's AWOL too."

"You gotta be fucking kidding me, Tony. The guy gets popped, his business partner flies the coop and you guys arrest the broad?!!"

"Look, I know how bad this is. I've never been so ashamed of the force before. But that's why I called you. I can't just stand by and let this girl go down because our Chief has no balls and our DA has lost his mind. I need you, Nick. So does the girl."

I thought about it a minute, throwing back the last of the coffee. It seemed easy, and it seemed like the right thing to do. Of course, that's usually the setup for my most spectacular failures. "So all I gotta do is find you something that clears the girl."

"Or give me some shred of solid proof she did it so I can let it go and still sleep at night."

"You know, there's a good chance that a jury will let her go."

"There's a chance they won't. You willing to bet a girl's life that a jury has any sense?"

I laughed and shook my head. I'd been at the wrong end of a jury of my so-called peers before. "OK," I said. "I'll take a quick pass at it. But you let me out of the fifty even if I don't find anything."

"Deal." We shook hands. Tony finished his cappuccino and stood up. He headed out onto the street. I sat a while longer, soaking up as much of the heat as I could while I read the file and thought about where to start.

I figured that the quickest and easiest way to deal with this case was to locate the two missing participants. Since the police were watching the Buckley girl's house, I decided to hunt down Phillips. He was listed in the phone book, but nobody was answering his phone.

The police had saved me the trouble of pulling his DMV records, so I knew he had bought a used '48 Ford just last month. It seemed like a low rent car for someone supposedly in the diamond business. Maybe he hadn't planned on staying in town very long. Whatever the reason, there was no sign of the jalopy outside his Van Ness address as I got off the bus.

The building was no palace, either. I mean, it was nicer than where I lived, but I was still imagining this guy as a big wheeler-dealer. I checked the directory, found his name, and rang the bell. Sometimes the direct approach pays off. Not this time. Next I pushed the manager's buzzer. The door was answered by a hefty woman in an overcoat, her hair in curlers. "Yeah?" she demanded.

"Ma'am, I'm trying to find one of your tenants, Mr. Terrance Phillips."

"I'm not his secretary. Are you a cop?"

"No ma'am, I'm not. I'm a private investigator."

She reappraised me, but it didn't seem to change her opinion much. "Is he in trouble?"

"No ma'am, but one of his employees is. I'm hoping he can help get her out of a jam. Do you have any idea how I might reach him?"

She frowned. "No, but I wish I did. He's late with his rent."

"When was the last time you saw him?"

"When he first moved in six months ago."

I scratched my head. "What about when he pays his rent?

"He leaves it in my mailbox overnight."

"Do you have keys to his apartment?"

"I'm not letting you in, so don't even ask."

"That's fine. I'm just concerned that Mr. Phillips may be, well, deceased in there." Her face blanched and her ample mouth opened wide. "Do you think you could go in and check for me?"

"Oh my God," she stammered, "do you really think he's...."

I shrugged. "I hope not, but it's possible. If you could just poke your head in...."

"Oh no!" she barked. "I can't do that....I mean, if he's....well, in there...." Her eyes glazed over with fear, and she juggled her key ring out of her coat pocket. She fumbled with it, separating the key to his apartment from the rest and thrusting it towards me. I nodded solemnly as I took the keys, as if they came with some grave responsibility that I was willing to shoulder for her. She stepped aside to let me into the building, then waited for me to lead the way up the stairs.

We walked in silence to his door on the third floor. She watched me intently as I turned the key in the lock and held her breath as I opened the door and let myself in. I glanced back and Mrs. Manager was peeking around the door jamb as though something might fly out of the room. I swallowed the smug grin and took a look around.

To say the apartment was spartan would be a massive understatement. It had been a nice place once, but that was a long, long time ago. A threadbare carpet the color of spat tobacco encrusted the floor like moss. A sway-backed bed squatted in one corner, a scratched-up dresser in the other. No sign of Phillips, or even that he'd ever been there.

Mrs. Manager had taken a tentative step into the room, sniffing cautiously for death, like it would have made it that much worse. The closet door was ajar, so I slowly opened it the rest of the way with my toe. It was empty except for a handful of naked wire hangers.

"He's not here?"

I looked around again. "Doesn't look like he's been here for quite a while."

Her face went from trepidation to anger. "Bastard. God damn it. He could at least have told me he was leaving so I could rent the room to someone else." I wondered if she planned on cleaning it first. She held her hand out for her keys, and I gave them to her.

I hoofed it back down Van Ness looking for a pay phone that actually worked, but by the time I found one I was nearly back to Market Street. I dropped a dime in and dialed the tow yard.

"City Tow," said the gorilla who answered.

"Yeah, I think you guys might have towed my car."

"What's the license plate number."

I read from Phillips' DMV file: "CGH932."

"Just a moment." I heard the phone hit the desktop, then the squawk of an old filing cabinet. Then the ape was back. "Yeah, we got it."

"Why? Was I parked illegally?!"

His voice dropped into reflexive numbness, a formality masking the fact that he was probably imagining busting my chops the moment I showed up. "Sir, the white zone is strictly for the loading and unloading of passengers."

"At the airport."

He huffed, "Yes sir."

"But I was only in there for a minute! What time did you tow me?"

"The manifest shows you were towed at six o'clock yesterday morning."

"At which terminal?"

He paused, confused. "You don't know where you left your car?"

"I got lost. That airport is so big...."

"Sir, the manifest just says that it was at the international terminal."

"OK, thanks. I'll be in as soon as I can."

"All right, sir. We'll be ready for you." Again, the tone of his voice implied the length of pipe he wished he could be holding when I arrived.

I didn't have another dime, so I headed for home, by which I mean my office. I had been sleeping on the sofa ever since I got kicked out of my last apartment. I was only up to the second notice on my phone bill, so I could do the rest of my calling from there.

But first I stopped in at Gino's. Gino himself was behind the bar playing "Chinese dice" with Manny Dunning, as usual. Manny bellowed in protest as Lady Luck smacked him in the chops again. I knew better than to play dice with Gino. The rules to his games were convoluted and changed often. Gino picked up the dollar and forced it into the crowded mug where he kept his winnings.

"Hey Gino," I said, my eyes adjusting to the dark.

"Hey, Nick. Mrs. Lazarino came down looking for you. She say your rent is due. She look pretty happy." Gino was one of those old Chinese men whose eyes disappeared completely when he smiled.

"Damn, Chambers," laughed Manny, "I've heard of expensive places, but that's steep."

I flipped them both the bird. One time a couple of years ago I had a long spell with no clients. I missed rent for three months, and was about to go for four. Mrs. Lazarino, my lonely widowed landlady, made it clear in no uncertain terms that cash wasn't the only currency she was willing to accept. When threatened with eviction, I had paid that price once. Much to her continual disappointment, I found a way to pay her from then on, no matter what it took. But to make matters worse, during a bender I had apparently shared that tidbit with a couple of the guys, and they had shared it with the whole damned bar. I wondered if I was ever going to live it down.

"I've got cash," I spat.

"I bet you do!" Manny laughed.

"You got cash for me, Nick?" rasped Gino. "I not make you same deal as Mrs. Lazarino."

"You're all heart, Gino. I'll have something for you next week."

"That's what you said last week."

"I know. But I'm working on a case right now, and when I get paid, you get paid."

"Is that why a cop came here looking for you? You know I don't like cops poking their business around my place."

"Was his name Tony?"

"Yeah. Tony. He say you call him."

I nodded. "Thanks, Gino. Hey, is it alright if I go up the back stairs?"

Gino and Manny laughed uproariously as Gino waved me through the bar.

"Detective Manicelli." The phone line crackled, which meant that it had started raining outside.

"Tony, it's Nick. I know where you can find Phillips."

"Great. I'll have him picked up right away."

"Not gonna be easy. He's in Barcelona."

"As in Spain?"

"Yup. One ticket confirmed for Terrance Phillips on Transworld Flight 314, with a stopover in New York. The agent seemed to think he was traveling alone."

"Damn it. Pretty cocky to go under his real name."

"Seems like he had cause to be. Any chance he could have known that Kelley would come down hard on a dame?"

"It's possible, if he pays attention to politics." I could almost hear Tony fuming.

"You guys check Miss Bettencourt's apartment for forced entry?"

"I don't think so."

"You might want to have someone do that. I'm betting you'll find something."

"OK, I'll go over myself right now."

"Let me know what you find."

"Will do. And Nick?" I heard Tony's desk chair squeak as he fidgeted uncomfortably.

"Yeah?"

"Thanks. I'm really sorry about all this."

"Don't mention it."

I sat at a table in the back corner at Gino's going over the Bettencourt file over and over again. Something about it didn't seem right, besides the obvious piss poor police work. Then it hit me. There wasn't an autopsy report. They'd probably been chopping up the poor boy about the time Tony gave me the file in the first place.

I felt pretty sure I was almost done with this one, and part of me was screaming to leave it alone while the fifty bucks was still a bargain, but I figured if I hung out too long at Gino's, it was a matter of time before old lady Lazarino came sniffing around again. That thought got me up on my feet and out the door towards the coroner's office.

Karl Gottlieb was almost as wide as he was tall and was as casual with a scalpel as only a coroner can be. He'd seen it all, and nothing could break his Germanic smirk anymore.

"Hello, Nick," he said as he came out of the cutting room. "Haven't seen you in a while. How's tricks?"

"Not too bad. Keeping busy."

"Which is why you are here, no doubt?"

"No doubt. I'm looking for a guy named Charles Rath."

"I'm sorry to hear that."

"Not here?"

"No, he's here all right, or at least, what's left of him is."

"Bad one, eh?"

The smirk never quivered. "Burned to a crisp. Had to identify him by his engraved Rolex."

"So asking him questions is pointless?"

Karl laughed. "You'd think so, wouldn't you? But he still talks to me."

I smiled. "And what's he got to say?"

"He says that he was approaching forty when he died, and that somebody didn't like him very much. His wrist was broken, and then he was shot twice in the face at very close range."

"Ouch."

"Oh no, he probably wasn't feeling much pain. He had a point eight blood alcohol level."

I whistled. "No wonder he burned so good. I guess he couldn't have put up much of a struggle if he was that blotto. Somebody must have gotten him drunk to soften him up."

"Oh, I doubt that," Karl said. "Judging from his liver, he was quite accustomed to it."

"Alcoholic?"

204 | FOG CITY NOCTURNE

"And a real pro at it. Some of the most advanced sclerosis I've seen in a long time."

I pondered this for a moment. "Was there anything else out of the ordinary?"

"Not really. There wasn't much left of his mouth, but what remained suggests that he was unfamiliar with the caress of a tooth-brush. Not surprising, really. That often comes with the alcoholism."

"Hmm. Any chance I can get a copy of the report?"

"For you, my friend, of course." He lumbered across the room and picked up a folder from his desk. Just as ponderously, he came back, handing it to me with a smile.

"Thanks, Karl. I owe you one."

"You mean you owe me another. "

I shook his hand and started for the door. "You know, Nick, you surprise me every time I see you here."

"What, you think I haven't got the stomach to come to the morgue?"

"No, I just keep expecting you to show up as a *client*."

His booming laughter followed me out the door and halfway down the block.

I paced in the cold on the jail stairs. Waiting in the lobby would have meant suffering Sgt. Daugherty's acerbic wit. Luckily, I didn't have to wait too long. Tony was renowned for his punctuality. At eleven sharp he opened the jail door and held it. Somehow, as she strode across the threshold, it seemed more that the doors had part-ed for her, like a girl Moses stepping forth into the foggy morning. As with her jail clothes, her thick wool floor-length coat tried valiantly to conceal the landscape rolling beneath it, and failed utter-ly.

"Hey Nick," said Tony. "You were right. Miss Bettencourt's kitchen window had been forced open with a screwdriver. No prints, though. Combined with Phillips leaving the country, Kelly had to let Marjory here go."

"Mr. Manicelli, Mr. Chambers, I can't thank you enough." Miss Bettencourt said as she stopped on the stair above me, and that voice cut right through me, sending a chill up my spine. I squirmed uncomfortably in the cold and Tony's half embarrassed smirk.

"That's not necessary, Miss Bettencourt. I was happy to help, and I owed Tony a favor anyway. Isn't that right, Tony?"

He nodded. "All square and then some. There's talk of the D.A. being investigated by the Mayor's office—not that it'll hurt him any. But at least he'll keep his fingers out of the pie for a week or two. Thanks."

I nodded. "Shall we get you a cab, Miss Bettencourt? You must be freezing."

"It is cold," she said. "But please, call me Margie."

I smiled. Tony put his hand on my shoulder. "Thanks again, Nick. I owe you one."

"Who'da thunk it?"

He punched my shoulder, tipped his hat to the girl, and trotted back up the stairs. With Margie standing next to me, I pulled the next cab out off the street like I was fly fishing with magic bait. I opened the door for her. "Well, good luck, Margie. Take care of yourself."

She looked confused, maybe even a little hurt. "Aren't you coming with me?"

"Should I?"

"Of course. I believe I owe you one home-baked peach pie." Her full-lipped smile suggested something else.

"Oh."

She scooted across the seat like it was buttered, making room for me. I'm not stupid. I followed her into the cab.

The aroma of peaches and flour saturated the room, adding an almost cloying perfume to the already uncomfortably homey kitchen. A small bakelite timer whirred on top of the oven. We sat at the quaint table, sipping scalding coffee from very old-looking white china cups. Margie had changed directly from her overcoat into an almost comical blue apron, complete with lace around the edges. She wore it with the strings cinched tight around her tiny waist, emphasizing her wide Midwestern hips, mocking the sincere innocence of the apron.

"So what are you going to do now?"

She shot a glance at the timer, then settled back into her chair. "Well, I don't have a job anymore, and I don't know if I was cut out for the city anyway. I think I'll go back to my parents' house, at least for a while."

"Let me guess. Iowa?"

She laughed, and it sounded like an oddly melodic cement mixer. "No, Kansas City."

"Of course." I sipped my coffee. It seemed a bit anemic. "Say, have you got something I could put in this?"

"Cream?"

"I was thinking something stronger."

"Oh. I'm sorry. I don't drink. I could dash out to the corner store, though...."

I held a hand up. "No, that's OK. I just thought you might have some here for when your boss visited."

She narrowed her eyes slightly. "Charles...Mr. Rath...didn't drink either."

I couldn't hold back a sardonic laugh. "Oh, I'm afraid he did. He must have kept it hidden from you."

She looked away. "I suppose so. I think there must be quite a lot I didn't know about him."

"Did you know that he was married?"

She opened her mouth, closed it, then looked away. "I don't see how that would be any of my business."

"Left behind a wife and two kids."

"I'm sure Charles would have made arrangements to take care of them."

"Sure did. Big insurance policy. They're pretty shaken up, naturally, but they won't have to struggle."

She was knotting her apron in her hands, wringing it nervously. Then she jumped as the timer bell rang.

"Oh!" she stuttered. "The pie is ready."

She slipped her hands into potholders that matched her apron, and opened the oven. Peach-scented steam roiled out, fogging the kitchen window. She lifted the pie out, setting it on top of the stove to cool.

"Smells delicious." I wasn't lying.

"It's going to be a few minutes before it's cool enough to eat, and

I...." She trailed off, bowing her head. It took me a second to realize she was crying. I got to my feet.

"What's the matter?"

She spun around and threw her arms around me and began sobbing in earnest into my shoulder. "I'm so sorry, Mr. Chambers. Nobody knew about Charles and I. It wasn't supposed to happen, and we were going to stop, really. He loved his wife and kids, but you know how it is when you have a stressful job. It just happened. And now he's dead. I feel so lost, and so alone...."

And then her mouth was on mine, devouring any reply I might have had. She tasted of peppermint and coffee, and kissed me with a passion that told of a hunger long suppressed, a need long denied. Her hands went up to my throat and I almost cold cocked her reflexively, but she was only fumbling with my tie, pulling it off my neck and flinging it to the floor behind me. I reached around her waist, tugged her apron strings undone, and pulled it off over her head.

Like I said, I'm not stupid.

Margie had unwrapped like the Christmas present I was never good enough for Santa to bring. Every curve her clothing had hinted at had been there in spades, and it was plain she wasn't as innocent as she made out. It had been a while and even longer since I'd had a dish like Margie.

Afterwards, we sat once again at the kitchen table. I had my shirt off, she had put her floral summer dress back on with nothing underneath. Watching her move as she cut the pie made me feel like a bumblebee faced with an entire field of daisies.

She set the pie in front of me, then smiled expectantly, almost demurely. She was going to stand there and stare at me until I reached a verdict, so I balanced my cigarette on the rim of the plate and took a bite. Her eyebrows climbed her forehead, asking, "Well?"

"Oh my," I mumbled around peaches. "That's great."

She frowned. "Just great?"

I knew a cue when I heard one, and I knew my line. "That is without a doubt the best damned peach pie I have ever tasted."

She hugged me. "So I guess you are paid in full?"

I chuckled. "You got that right, sister!"

She looked puzzled for a second, then shocked and horrified. "Oh no! You don't think I...because you helped me...?"

"Honey, I'm used to having people thank me by taking shots at me. A guy could get used to clients like you."

Her face flushed with fury. "Mr. Chambers, I don't know what kind of girl you think I am, but I do not use my body for currency!" Naturally, the tears began rolling down her apple cheeks, trailing down her long neck and plunging into the depths of her décolletage. I stood up and grabbed her shoulders. She tried to shrug out of my grip, so I turned her around to face me. She looked down to avoid my gaze, and I curled my index finger under her chin and brought her eyes up to mine.

"Relax, Margie. I was kidding."

"No you weren't."

"I was. I know what kind of girl you really are."

"Do you, now?"

"Yes. You are a very sweet girl going through some rough times. Sometimes it helps to have someone to hold you, someone to make you feel safe. I'm glad it happened to be me."

She stopped crying. "Really?"

"Yes. Let me prove it to you. When are you going home to your folks?"

"I'm catching a bus on Friday."

"That leaves us tomorrow night. Let me take you out for dinner, give you something nice to remember San Francisco by."

She smiled a little, wiping mascara all over her face. "You mean it?"

"I mean it." I took out my handkerchief and wiped her eyes. She looked like a raccoon.

"I'd like that" she sniffed.

"OK, I'll make the reservations. Shall I pick you up here at six?"

"That would be perfect." She smiled again, and kissed me, long and slow.

"OK, now stop that, or I'll never get out of here. You aren't my only client, you know."

"Just the prettiest?"

I laughed. "By a long shot. Now do you know where I left my shirt?"

The pie in my belly and the fading echo of sex went a long way to keeping the cold at bay as I walked up Stockton Street towards Gino's. I could still smell Margie's perfume in my clothes, and taste peaches mingled with mint. As I crossed Sutter, I tried to shake her from my mind, rebuild my focus.

I ducked into the stairs at the mouth of the Stockton tunnel. They climbed up to Geary and practically served as my front porch. As usual, the stairwell reeked of urine, vomit and rancid food, and was carpeted with bums, winos, and other refuse. The ones that were lucid enough to see me waved or grunted a hello. I nodded back. I found it prudent to maintain a friendly relationship with my "brothers in the gutter." They were the eyes and ears of the back streets. Besides, I was usually two steps from looking for a place to bunk beside them.

I found Chuck on the second landing. Many of the homeless considered Chuck their ambassador to the lower echelons of the working world, which generally meant information brokering to P.I.s and cops. Usually one of the more functional ones, today Chuck was a whole Chinese laundry to the wind, and even more astonishing, was sobbing openly.

"Nicky," he muttered when he saw me. "Nicky, he's gone."

"Who's gone?" I asked. I was careful to stand a few paces away. I had learned the hard way that nothing was more unpredictable than a street drunk, even one that's supposedly on your side.

"Paddy. My bestest buddy, Paddy." He wiped his nose on his sleeve, then took another slug off of the bottle of Jack Daniel's, completely oblivious to the fact that he'd emptied it some time ago.

"Where'd he go, Chuck? Where did Paddy go?" I'd met Paddy once. He'd drifted into town about six months before. He was very Irish, very friendly, and always very drunk.

"They took him. Been gone for three days now."

"Who did...."

"They did. The ones from the hospital."

"Why did they take him to the hospital? Was he hurt?" Chuck shook his head, mostly from side to side. "Was he sick?"

"No, no, no. He was fine. Just fine."

I sighed. "Then why would they take him to the hospital?"

"So they could do 'speriments on him. He's dead by now. All cut up and his bits put in jars with little labels on 'em. They almost got me once."

"What makes you think he didn't just move on?"

"He kept sayin' he had a date with a beautiful woman. Said she was gonna pick him up, feed him, and set him up with a place to stay. You know as well as I do that beautiful women don't have nothin' to do with bums like Paddy and me. It was all a trap. Oh, Nicky, he was like a brother to me." He sucked on the neck of the empty bottle again, looked at it accusingly, then suddenly threw it against the far wall of the stairwell. I shielded my face from the broken glass that showered the whole landing.

"Jesus, Chuck!" muttered a man I hadn't noticed before, sleeping in the shadowed corner. He didn't otherwise move.

"Chuck, did you talk to the cops about it? Maybe they've seen him around."

"Yeah, like the cops give a rat's ass about us bums. They're in on it, you know. They get paid by the doctors to look th' other way."

I gambled and patted Chuck on his filthy shoulder. "Give him a couple of days. Maybe Paddy is sleeping it off somewhere. He'll turn up."

"All cut into bits in jars."

Chuck slumped back against the wall and started rummaging through his pile of garbage, presumably for another bottle. I shrugged and headed up the stairs to phone Tony. I figured that I knew exactly where he could find Paddy, and it wasn't the hospital.

"You're late." Marjory answered her door in a sleek black velvet dress that flowed over every curve of her body like an oil slick. I squirmed in the stiff wool suit I'd borrowed from Tony.

I whistled. "Baby, waves like those would make even the saltiest sailor seasick."

"Is that what passes for flattery in the city?" But she was smiling. "Where are you taking me?"

"I figured we'd go to Salamagundie's, if that's OK with you."

"Are you kidding? Can you afford that?"

I feigned insult. "I thought young ladies didn't ask questions like that." She smiled, clearly excited. "Now grab your coat, the cab's waiting."

Salamagundie's was one of the swankier restaurants in town, perched high atop Berkshire Plaza Hotel. Huge windows opened out into a panoramic vista of the bay on one side, the jewel-like lights of the city glittering out the other. We waited in the lounge sipping cocktails until we got our table. I was enjoying the anonymity a place like this afforded me, nobody who could afford to have dinner here would ever have been caught dead running in my circles.

"Oh, Nick! It's so beautiful."

"Yeah. The city always looks so clean from up here."

She took a sip from a glass of champagne, her third. "I love places like this. I've always thought I'd be good at being rich. You know what I mean? It's wasted on some people. It's all they've ever known, and they take it for granted. They have no idea how good they have it."

"But you'd know," I said, stirring the whipped cream into my Irish coffee.

"I would!" she said enthusiastically. "I grew up in a farm house. I know what it's like to be poor, to be cold and hungry. I came to California to try and get out of that, try and make a little money, put some away, maybe send some back to my folks."

"Sorry it didn't work out."

She laughed. "Oh, it wasn't so bad. I met you, didn't I?"

She raised her glass to toast. I half-heartedly ringed mine against hers. "You really are a sweet girl. Very pretty and very naive."

"I suppose I am. Can you believe that when I came out here, I thought I could be in movies?"

"He won't be there, you know."

She stopped like a deer in headlights, mouth agape. "What?"

"He's not waiting for you."

"Who? What are you talking about?"

"Rath. Wherever he said he'd meet you, he won't be there. He's taken the money and split, somewhere where no one will ever find him, not even you."

"Nick, Charles is dead."

"Might as well be. You'll never see him again, no matter what he promised you."

"What are you saying? That Charles is still alive?"

"Please, Margie, don't play coy with me anymore. You helped Charles Rath fake his death so he could clean out the company safe and leave the country, while making us think his so-called "partner" had done the deed so the police would be looking for him instead. Well, it worked, at least for him. Do you know how much he got away with?"

"I don't have to listen to this fairy tale."

"But you want to know, don't you? According to the bean counters, Mr. Rath's company had a total inventory of diamonds worth more than ten million dollars. On top of that, he'd used those diamonds as collateral to take out two million more in loans, which he used to buy even more diamonds."

"Mr. Phillips must have taken it all."

"Mr. Phillips never existed. Rath invented him, then laid a trail to make it look like he left the country. The cinder we were supposed to think was the dearly departed Charles Rath was actually named Paddy Donovan, a bum picked up off the street, probably because he looked a bit like Rath, or at least after a good toasting. It was all a bit of slight of hand to set the police looking for the wrong person in the wrong place. Looks like it worked, at least long enough for dear Charles to make his getaway.

"I'm not going to sit here and listen to this."

"Oh, don't worry, you aren't in any danger, either. There's no evidence that a jury would take seriously, just a lot of conjecture on my part. I just thought you might want to know that you shouldn't waste your time. You might as well really go back to Kansas City like you were saying instead of wherever it was you two arranged."

She picked up her purse and stood up. "I don't know where you got such a stupid idea. Charles Rath is dead, and I had nothing to do with that. Even so, he was a good and honorable man. You have to be a bitter and deranged man to say such things about him."

"Yeah? Ask Gloria Jean Buckley how honorable he is."

She stared at me, her teeth suddenly clenched. "What...what has Gloria got to do with this?"

"You seen her around lately? You seen her since that night you were out dancing with her while your boss was supposedly being murdered? Funny how she turned up missing just when you need-ed her most as an alibi. Think about it, Margie. If she'd been there for you, you'd never have spent the night in jail. You wouldn't have needed me or anyone else at all. Instead, she goes missing, leaving you as the most likely suspect. Awfully convenient for someone, just not for you."

"I don't know where Gloria is. She's probably just...."

"She's probably just sitting on a topless beach somewhere in France living the good life with Charles."

"No, Gloria wouldn't...I mean...."

"Come on, honey. Open your eyes. You've been had. Your so-called friends set you up to take the fall. If you didn't have the luck of being taken in by Tony Manicelli and his soft spot for a broad in trouble, you'd be six steps down death row by now."

That was all she could take. She covered her mouth and bolted for the door, crying her eyes out. I sat back and polished off the last of my Irish coffee.

The waiter came over, looking aghast at the scene I had caused in his restaurant. "Will sir be dining alone?"

"I'm afraid not, Jeeves," I said, my composure flawless. I tapped the rim of the empty glass. "But I will take one more of these for the road. It's going to be a long, cold night."

I strode into Tony's office just before noon. I had figured that most of the dust would have settled by then, but he was still surrounded by a swarm of cops, suits and reporters. I tried to walk through the open door but a cop built like a tank strong-armed me into the jamb.

"Where do you think you're going, sleazeball?"

"I'm here to see Tony."

"You and everyone else in town. Take a hike."

"*Tony!!*" I shouted. Officer Beefy grabbed me by the lapels and started to shove me back out into the hall.

Tony looked up like someone had spat in his food. When he saw my predicament, he covered the mouthpiece of his phone with his hand. "Hey, Jensen, you idiot, let him go. Nick's the guest of honor here!"

Stung, the huge man released me. I brushed off my lapels like somehow he could have made them dirtier and pushed past him without looking back.

Tony gestured for me to wait as I approached his desk. "Yes...un-huh...I see." He scribbled madly on a note pad. "Yes, I got it. Thanks."

He hung up the phone. The bustling in the room settled rapidly.

"Well Nicky, you were absolutely right. Miss Bettencourt went straight home and picked up the phone to call Big Daddy. We had a bit of delay with the warrant, so our boy was still up the pole splicing wires when she made the call."

"Where was he? I'm betting nowhere near Spain."

"You win. He was in a ritzy hotel in Florida."

"What? He hadn't even left the country?"

Tony shrugged. "Nope. The idiot really was waiting for her. The feds picked him up ten minutes ago."

"And the girl?"

"She's in the lockup. You want to talk to her?"

"What for? I've heard everything she has to say."

Tony looked a bit surprised. "I thought you'd at least want to tell her goodbye."

"Spare me the violins, Tony. She'd have been just as happy to set up you or me to get toasted in that fire as she was that wino. Whatever it took to cash in and check out."

"Didn't stop you from putting it to her."

"Wouldn't have been able to bring her in otherwise."

Tony smirked at my back as I headed back out into the cold afternoon.

Gino's was packed as I sifted through the crowd to the bar. Gino said something as I approached, but it was lost in the din. I squeezed in between two regulars and slipped him a small roll of bills.

"You get paid?" he shouted.

"Sorta." Tony had given me eighty dollars for the mousetrap dinner. He knew that we'd only had drinks, but it was already on the books as an expense, so as far as he was concerned, it was SFPD money already spent. It would be just enough to pay my rent and get square with Gino for a little while. "Gimme a Johnnie Walker, neat."

"Black or red?"

I scowled at Gino. He reached for the black label.

As the whisky burned its way to my heart and brain, I thought of Mrs. Rath. She was the one getting the worst of the deal. She still lost her husband, only this way the insurance wouldn't pay. She and her kids would have to face life on their own, possibly for the first time. When I'd realized that the night before, I briefly considered letting Margie go.

Fuck 'em. Nobody ever cut me any slack, and a little hard work would be better for the tykes than boarding school anyway.

THE USUAL SUSPECTS

About the Authors

KEONI CHAVEZ

Alias: The Pooka

Distinguishing marks: Short-cropped
black hair going white at the temples

Modus Operandi: Keoni Chavez is a contributing writer for MacDirectory magazine, and has published articles both online (happypuppy.com, elecplay.com) and in print (*Wired* magazine). He is also the "Voice of GeneEd," doing voiceover work for this e-learning educational company. While he currently lives in San Francisco, he calls Honolulu, Hawai'i his hometown. You can read samples of his past work, both fiction and non-fiction, at http://www.nodewarrior.org/~keoni.

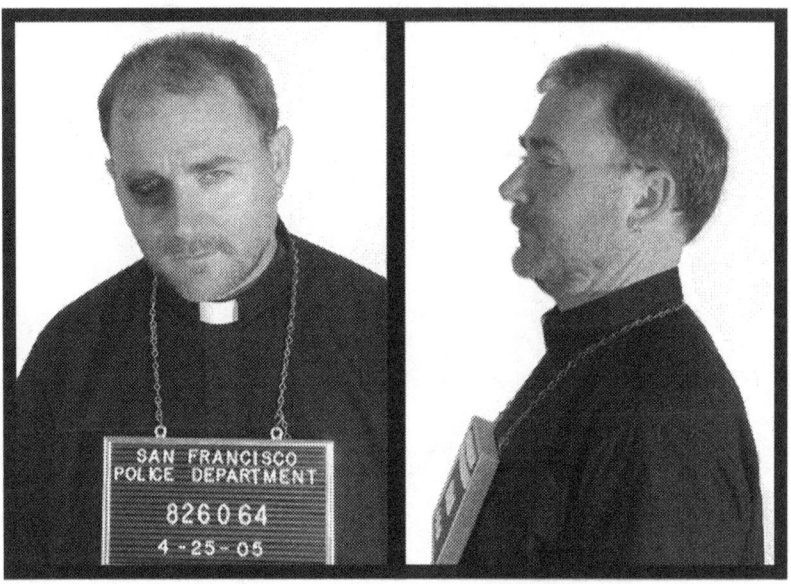

JOHN R. MABRY

Alias: Jack Russel

Distinguishing marks: A scar on the chest from the removal of a tertiary nipple, and a tattoo of the Tetragrammaton over the heart.

Modus Operandi: John R. Mabry is the author of many books, mostly heretical theology. He serves as co-pastor of Grace North Church (www.gracenorthchurch.org) in Berkeley, California—a parish that is liturgical in worship, interfaith in teaching, and consensus in leadership. He also teaches interfaith theology, world religions, homiletics, and spiritual direction at the Chaplaincy Institute for Arts and Interfaith Ministry (www.chaplaincyinstitute.org), also in Berkeley. He is a poet and musician, singing for two progressive rock bands, Metaphor (www.metaphor.org) and Mind Furniture (www.mindfurniture.com). Visit his website at www.apocryphile. org/jrm/.

BRYAN TOLIN

Alias: Pirate Bryan

Distinguishing marks: A hairline scar on
left wrist where a cat tried to assassinate him.

Modus Operandi: Bryan Tolin hates the physical labors of writing
and avoids them at all costs. He also despises with a passion everything he has ever written. Mr. Tolin prefers to live simply – eight
hours pulling weeds is far more attractive to him than eight hours in
front of a computer. He does not have a website—and would rather
surf the ocean. His memory has gotten so bad he can't remember if
he has 12 cats and one wife, or 12 wives and one cat.

B.J. WEST

Alias: The Spaceman

Distinguishing marks: A pierced left nipple and
a tattoo of circuitry in a band around his right bicep.

Modus Operandi: B.J. West is a digital artist and writer, most noted
for his contributions to the best-selling PC games of all time, "The
Sims" and its myriad sequels. He is the author of "The Writer's
Tarot," a deck of cards used to brainstorm stories and characters. He
is fascinated by space travel to the point of obsession, and can often
be found researching arcane minutia of NASA's Apollo program or
the 1960s incarnation of "Star Trek." You can find examples of his
work at http://www.strafe.com/bj/.

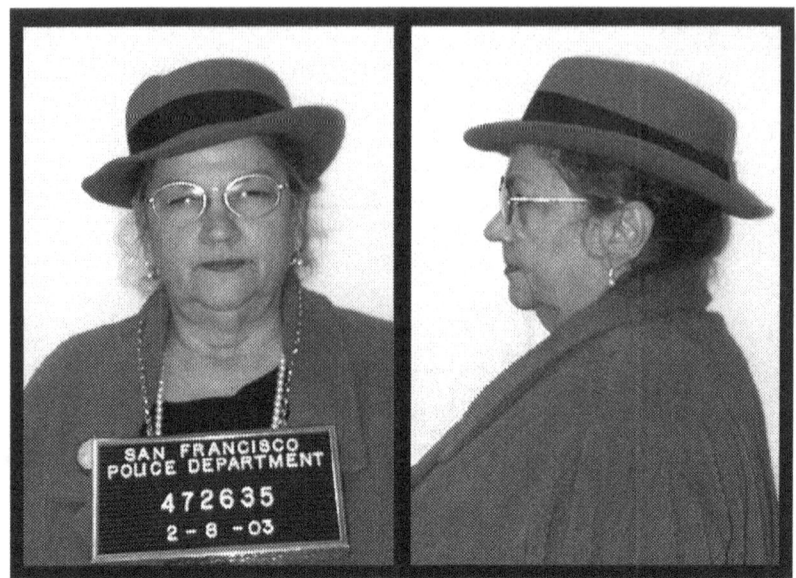

CLAUDIA WEST

Alias: Mama San

Distinguishing marks: Claudia has big brown eyes, dimples, and a ready smile, framed by her ever-present red lipstick.

Modus Operandi: A novice to writing, Claudia's rich imagination is more often put to use in the kitchen, with a large pot of homemade soup, or playing in the garden surrounded by fairies and listening to The Grateful Dead. Her clever disguise as a simple, sweet hippie mom successfully hides the devious mind of a heartless killer in a western, a down-and-out prostitute in a murder mystery, or in this case, the sharp mind of Nick Chambers, P.I.

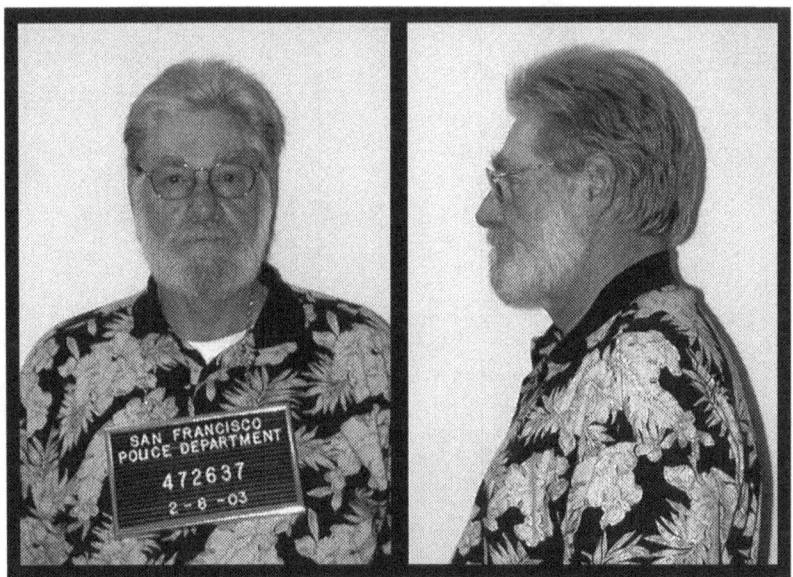

DALE WEST

Alias: Pop

Distinguishing marks: A full beard, once red, now white. He also has a tattoo of a parrot on his left shoulder.

Modus Operandi: Dale West is the oldest of the gang, husband of Claudia West, and father of B.J. West. He came late to writing, but brings great enthusiasm. He is often seen in the company of fairies and/or trolls. If missing, look first in the deep rough on the golf course.

www.ingramcontent.com/pod-product-compliance
Lightning Source LLC
Chambersburg PA
CBHW050523260626

47157CB00004B/1450